The Great Cricket Betting Scandal

Ted Corbett

The PARRS WOOD Press
<u>Manchester</u>

First Published 2000

THE PARRS WOOD PRESS
St Wilfrid's Enterprise Centre
Royce Road, Manchester, M15 5BJ

© Ted Corbett 2000

ISBN: 1 903158 03 6

This book was produced by Andrew Searle and Ruth Heritage of The Parrs Wood Press.

Front cover design by Glenn B Fleming

Printed in Great Britain by:
Fretwell Print and Design
Healey Works
Goulbourne Street
Keighley
West Yorkshire BD21 1 PZ

To Jo, the sunshine in my smile

PREFACE
1 August 2007

John Andrew Michael James Goode looked down at the mass of bodies in front of him and wondered why they didn't get a proper job. Perhaps there were no vacancies for binmen at the moment, he thought. He wondered if he ought to have such sardonic thoughts. Now of all times. Those same people would be calling this "the biggest moment in his life" by tomorrow morning.

Some of those cricket writers; they'd never make it as binmen, Goode thought. "Andrew," one began, "can you say just what you're feelings are at this moment?"

How does he think I bloody feel, Goode wondered. "Of course, I'm delighted," he said, glad to be on automatic pilot.

"You cannot go wrong being 'delighted' or 'disappointed'," his coach on the public relations course had told him. "It's a cop-out, but one you will find useful time and again. These are two natural emotions.

"If your side is bowled out for only a couple of runs and you want to wring their bloody necks, it might not be diplomatic to say so. You might need them to bat for their lives in the second innings, for instance. But no one expects you to be pleased and the good old 'disappointed' gets you out of a lot of trouble. You can express your wrath later in the privacy of your own dressing room.

"'Delighted' falls into the same category. You make a million runs yourself and people begin to watch for signs of a swollen head. So you're supposed to portray a suitable modesty.

"'How do you feel to make a triple century, take ten wickets and hear that your wife has given birth to triplets?' some radio man will ask you and the answer is easy. You make a joke of sorts. 'It doesn't happen every day,' you say and the whole world gets a laugh.

"But when you are asked, 'This is your fifth hundred in this series, how do you feel,' the listeners are already beginning to get a bit bored with you.

"So they are waiting for you to sound big-headed. A suit-

1

suitable 'delighted' at such moments will get you off the hook. And don't talk for too long. Remember, you're not addressing the guy asking the question. If you happen to hate him, forget it for a minute and a half. If you and he have been out on the town the night before, forget that too. Don't advertise your enemies; don't demonstrate your mateship. You're talking to a bigger, much more important audience than the man with the notebook or the mike. He's just the piece of wire between you and the people who can't all ask you the question themselves."

Goode talked on, suitably modest, suitably restrained until all the questions were done, most of them asked a dozen times in one form or another. He had wondered earlier in his career why two reporters would ask virtually the same question but as he got to know them better he realised giant egos were at work. Some simply sought further information, but just as many wanted to impress the new man with their own importance. They all knew they were likely to be caught by the television cameras.

Ted Leigh, chairman of the selectors, and therefore in charge of this Press conference, got up from his chair with the aid of his stick, a result of a knee operation which, as he realised, gave him the sort of old fogey look that labelled him as too woebegone in the eyes of some to pick England cricket teams. In his last great moment as chairman, he had just announced the captain of the side for the next few years, a popular choice. But you never knew how the baying hounds of the Press might react.

"Gentlemen, ladies," Leigh said. "I sense you have asked all the questions Andrew can possibly answer and so I thank you for your attendance here and I will conclude by wishing him all the best for what I am sure will be a long and successful reign."

One or two clapped, which Goode read as a good sign. He might not like every member of the Press corps, but he knew he needed the unpredictable bunch on his side and, like everyone else, he was grateful for approval no matter where it originated.

Leigh added: "Andrew is now going for lunch with one or two of us - to learn the secrets of the trade." There was a general laugh.

"Then he will be at Lord's at two o'clock for accredited photographers to take his picture against a more suitable background and then, as you will have no trouble in guessing, he will be will be off back to Birmingham where we will meet him on Saturday night so that we can pick the team for the Test against Australia beginning on Thursday.

"That team will be announced on Sunday morning through the usual channels, embargoed for 11 o'clock as usual, and he'll field questions for a few minutes before the start of play at Edgbaston on Sunday. All right?"

Goode took another glance down at the 70 or so reporters, cameramen, photographers, radio men and TV technicians in the Compton Room of the Regent's Park Hilton, which was still better known as the Westmoreland Hotel from the days when it was a haunt of cricketers and the watering hole of every Test team.

"I guess they will give me a honeymoon period, chairman," he said to Leigh, as the men and women of the media stood and began to shuffle out of the room or move round to get clarification on some minor point from the England and Wales Cricket Board press officers.

"Yes, but you had better begin to think what happens when the honeymoon is over," Leigh grinned. "You've got about 20 minutes, I'd say."

From some deep recess of his mind Goode remembered a joke. "It's the bride who gets screwed every night for a fortnight on the honeymoon and the poor bastard of a bridegroom who gets screwed every day for the rest of his life."

Goode smiled and said nothing. He knew that the English Press corps could be vicious when roused. There was a permanent fight for circulation, the writers had free rein to express their opinions no matter how ill-informed or hurtful, the ghosted former star players vied with one another to express wilder and more damning explanations of the tiniest incidents on-field; and if any player stepped out of line, on or off the pitch, the papers seemed to believe it was their right to demand resignations, fines, bans and censure. Somewhere in the background a mysterious "they" operated. "They wanted a strong piece." He had heard it a dozen times from writers whose strings seemed to be pulled by faceless men in the deep shadows. Andrew Goode wanted to meet one and tell him what he thought.

There was also competition from television, that free-ranging outlet the internet had produced its own media stars, and

3

radio stations seemed to spring up daily. What is more, all the electronic sources were interchangeable since the arrival of the digital systems, and the old certainties had died when BBC lost the rights to cricket broadcasting on both radio and television.

The papers still followed a traditional route but it was no use just blaming the tabloids. They might start the fire fight but when the first shock had exploded on to the front or back page everyone piled in. Broadsheets, with their space to pull in half a dozen pieces on the same subject; sports columnists, special writers, cricket correspondents with backgrounds in Tests, Oxbridge and Eton or Harrow; leader writers short of a subject to debate, disc jockeys with intelligence deficiency syndrome, archbishops with nothing better to do, headmasters on holiday, scout masters, generals, admirals and trade union leaders, all concerned, so it seemed, about the moral fibre of Britain.

They all shouted that what the England captain did today the whole nation might do tomorrow. At least one England captain had been hounded from office in the last few years, Goode thought. Would it be his fate too?

"It's the wrong day for such thoughts," Leigh observed, guessing what was in Goode's mind. "Better keep you busy. You've got a few people to meet and one or two surprises in the next few hours.

"But first an admonition and one I want you to listen to very carefully, Andrew. Have I got your full attention? This is serious, seriously serious to use a modern idiom."

"Yes, chairman, of course."

Leigh, towering above Goode who was still sitting, paused for effect. "Andrew, nothing, but absolutely nothing you see or hear in the next couple of hours is ever to be repeated. Do I make myself clear? There is a part to your new job that is secret. Very secret. Do you understand?"

"No, chairman, I'm afraid I don't."

"Good," said Leigh. "A 'yes' at this point would have worried me considerably because it might have indicated that what is about to follow had got into the grapevine that carries all cricket's secrets. In some mysterious way. Or that you were not really paying attention at all. Instead I see you are puzzled. Good. Now just follow me."

Goode got up and walked down the steps from the platform, and across the Compton Room. Instead of turning right to go up the stairs with the rest of the crowd leaving the Press conference, Leigh turned right through a door marked "Private - staff only."

Goode followed and found they were in a small office, empty of furniture. Leigh headed straight for a second door, produced a key and, after a struggle, wrenched it open impatiently. It led down a short passage which was brightly lit and smartly painted. They went through another door, and out onto a road so large that cars could have driven up and down it comfortably. "Where are we?" Goode asked. "Under the main road," Leigh said.

"This passageway follows St. John's Wood road exactly from here to Maida Vale. It's part of the escape route devised by a paranoid 19th century government convinced that revolution was about to overtake the nation. Every country in Europe was in revolt, but the good old placid British missed their chance to overthrow Queen and country by force. For reasons I will never understand.

"Anyway, one particular incident of black cloaks and a hooded man carrying a round black object with a fuse coming out of top - and no doubt marked "Bomb" - convinced authority that they could not possibly endure the sight of a King or Queen swinging from a lamp post so they put in an emergency escape route.

"In modern times, as you may see one day, a helicopter has been permanently and unostentatiously garaged underground near Lord's so that the Queen and retinue can hare down this road and fly out of the country at a moment's notice. It's not the only route, of course. They chopped trees down in The Mall a few years ago so she could get out by Harrier jump jet if necessary.

"There are roads like this all over London. Very useful to those in the know and if you have the right pass you can use them whenever you like. Stops a lot of nonsense about traffic jams. It's one of the reasons I ride a motor-cycle. You can go down this road at 40 miles an hour and never see another soul in the middle of the day."

"Do I get a pass?" Goode asked innocently. "I'd never be late for a match again." He was known in the game as The Late Andrew Goode and he was not the most punctual man in London

Andrew Goode and he was not the most punctual man in London or anywhere else.

"You will never be late again," said Leigh sternly, "but you'll have to rely on the adrenalin produced by your new status to make you keep an eye on the clock. You don't get a pass to this route, and it would take you too long to learn all the tricks. You've got enough on your plate at the moment with a new job in the middle of a series against Australia."

"What about that lot?" Goode asked. "Do any of the Press guys know about this route?"

"There is one man with connections who knows a great deal but you will realise who that may be in due course," said Leigh, and set Goode wondering again.

They crossed the underground road to the right hand side where a small gate - which needed Leigh's bunch of keys once again - led them into a smaller passage and then into an empty room just like the one in the hotel. Leigh unlocked a door and Goode found himself standing in the large toilet which lies in the cellars of the Lord's pavilion.

It was empty - no match was being played at Lord's that day - and Leigh again led him up the stairs and into the Long Room. "This place is full of hideaways, underground passages and quiet, not to say, secret rooms," he said. "You're now privy to all these secrets. You're remembering what I said, aren't you?"

"I am, but to be honest, I'm not able to take enough of what's happening on board to be a useful informant anyway," Goode answered.

"Good," said Leigh. "Now, look, I've brought you here to meet someone, but it's not my privilege to make the introductions. So we'll go first to see the secretary of MCC Thomas Lester who will then take you to meet two other people. Some pretty strange events are going to unfold in front of your eyes in the next few minutes, Andrew.

"It is a sign that we believe you are in this job for a long time ahead. You're 27, which is young to be England captain, but we want you to stay in place for a number of years.

"We feel you have the right background and education and temperament to be helpful in a number of ways that will now be made obvious to you. So I'll leave you here. Just as the chairman of selectors left me here 30 years ago when I was handed the captaincy. Go down the stairs there and say hello to Tom Lester. Afterwards he will walk you across the road to the hotel for lunch."

Leigh and Goode shook hands before Leigh turned and walked away with surprising speed despite his stick. Goode thought he had also been astonished by the clarity of the Leigh mind. Dressing room gossip said the old boy was ga-ga, hardly knew mid-off from stand-off and had to have one-day field settings explained to him with bits of paper, or knives and forks or whatever happened to be handy. Most of his brain still seemed to be functioning, Goode thought. The old man was not an old fart. Not yet at any rate.

He walked down the stairs and found he was facing a door marked "Secretary of MCC" but before he could knock Tom Lester had opened the door, thrust out his hand and begun to congratulate him on his new job.

"Come in my boy, there's a lot to talk about," Lester said. "Bring Andrew a coffee, Myra, the boy has just walked underground from the old Westmoreland, or the bloody Hilton on the Park or whatever it's called now and he'll need something to sustain him.

"Better give him one of your special biscuits too. No, he's lunching with the high and mighty, he doesn't need food. Now sit down, Andrew, because I guess this next few minutes will be a bit of a strain."

Tom Lester, a jolly man, had spent most of his life in the Army and expected whoever he met to be conventional enough to accept coffee at 11.30, wine with dinner, not swear in front of The Ladies and go to church on Sundays. He and conservative Lord's made a perfect match.

At that moment, the door behind Lester opened and the Prime Minister walked in.

"John, you tell me you've never been officially introduced to Andrew Goode," Lester said as they all shook hands.

"Andrew has, as you know, been appointed England captain for the remaining Tests of the summer. But it has been decided already - although not for public consumption yet - that he will also lead the side in the West Indies this winter and that he will probably - I will say almost certainly - be England captain for a number of years to come.

7

"We - that is to say those of us who have been consulted about his appointment - feel he may be a fixture, form and good behaviour allowing, of course."

Lester laughed politely as if to say that form and good behaviour were taken for granted in the case of such special people as Andrew Goode.

"That's why it has been decided that he should be considered in the special category of England captains and that this morning he should be introduced to all the right people, all those who will have to call on him in his many and varied duties."

Goode's head began to spin. He'd met the Prime Minister before but only casually, almost as an afterthought, in those dark days - was it a week or a month ago? - when his place in the England side was uncertain.

The Prime Minister didn't sit down. He stood behind Lester's desk, perfectly erect, seemingly perfectly at ease and made a short, formal speech.

He said: "First, Andrew, I offer my congratulations. I told Cabinet an hour ago and those of my colleagues who understand what cricket is all about send their best wishes.

"Some of them have an idea of what being England captain entails. I am bound to say that I did not myself until this morning when the Cabinet Secretary brought me a recommendation signed by some of the best known names in the game, saying they thought you and I should meet for an informal chat today. I gather there is a tradition going back many years.

"I'm sorry to say I don't have a lot of time but you will be handed a letter from me later today which will detail just how you are to behave if I call on you at any time. You can be of great service to this country in your new position, but I shall not explain any more to you except to say that I wish you luck and that if we meet when I next drop into a Test at Lord's no mention - I repeat no mention whatsoever - is to be made of this meeting. But I am sure that will be explained to you repeatedly this morning.

"Now that is out of the way, perhaps you could tell me how you plan to beat the shit out of the Australians. I'm sure the whole country will be behind you if you show the first signs of giving them a good hiding."

The PM made no secret of his love of cricket and for the

first time in the interview he seemed to shake off his formal mode of speech and become animated. He had also decided privately that in his second term of office - most unexpected after the 1997 election had appeared to send him into permanent retirement by way of the House of Lords - he was going to enjoy every second. And still contrive to spend as much time as possible at Lord's and the Oval.

"My God," Goode thought, "he's Prime Minister but when he talks about cricket he's an anorak. He thinks I'll just press a few buttons or something and everything will change. I bet he doesn't think that about the economy or the defence budget."

"I'm afraid I don't have a watertight, buttoned-down plan to offer, Prime Minister," he said aloud. "I have had a chat with Ted Leigh and with Graham Gooch, who very much wants to be involved, and with people I respect back at Warwickshire but I do believe that we are not too far off beating them anyway. Ted Leigh thinks I might have better communication with the younger players than. . ." and he let the rest of the sentence trail away.

"On the right lines, I'd say," the Prime Minister said and, barely pausing to shake hands with Tom Lester, walked across and put his arm round Goode's shoulder.

"There have been only half a dozen special category England captains in the history of the game and we feel you're one. You will learn great secrets and convey important messages - as old W.G. Grace did, as Gubby Allen did, as Peter May did - and you will be a valuable diplomat.

"Now, go to meet your government contact, the man who will act as your go-between with us. You and I will not speak about these matters again and you will accept instructions only from him. I have come here today to lend authenticity to his role - so that you might go forward in confidence.

"I will leave the rest; the history of the position, the nature of the work, the day-to-day working, to him. Good luck and, for the time being, good-bye."

They shook hands and John Major strode out through the door. It was only at that moment that Goode realised that beyond the door were two immaculately dressed men, presumably civil servants, and two men so taut and lean and obviously fit, even by the standards of the modern sportsman, that they could only be bodyguards.

They looked as if they might wrestle crocodiles for a hobby, and he found himself wondering if they really ate live children for breakfast or if that was just a moment of fantasy on his part.

He was awoken from his reverie by Tom Lester. "Finish your coffee in your own time," Lester said. "The Captain will see you at precisely noon. We must be on time. He is a stickler for punctuality, is The Captain."

Goode was impressed that he could identify the capital letters when Tom Lester spoke about The Captain.

At precisely five minutes before noon Colonel Tom Lester announced: "Well, it's five to midday and we'd better get moving." He swept Goode's coffee cup away in a single movement, handed it to his secretary and marched towards the door.

There was still no indication where they were headed, although as the minutes had ticked away Goode had come to the conclusion, given The Captain's apparent obsession with punctuality, that he must be going a shorter and shorter distance.

Not to the Palace to kiss hands with the Queen, he thought at 11.40; not even down one of Leigh's forbidden secret routes. No further than the pub round the corner, he concluded at 11.50 as the conversation with the Colonel began to drag. Now he could only think that he was being escorted to an office within the building.

He was glad he had found time while he was waiting to phone his parents on his new mobile phone, smaller than an old pocket watch, operated by voice command. Ever since the arrival of human body warmth batteries a few years ago mobiles had shrunk dramatically. Now it was possible to have a microphone planted in a tooth, an earpiece permanently in the lobe of the ear and all the software in a credit card with a microscopic battery in your diary, your wallet or your ballpoint.

His all-purpose bit of gear known as the Single Electronic Gadget which not only acted as a mobile phone but which could identify who you were talking to - on the phone or off - and record that in your diary along with all the conversation still resided in his inside pocket. No doubt it had all the big moments of this spectacular day. That would be useful in a few years time.

He began with Mum in Birmingham. "Yes, I know what

happened. I saw it on the screen of my mobile an hour ago. Glad to see you bought a new blazer - you looked really nice." Then there was Father in Brighton. "What tie was that you were wearing? Can you get me one? Oh, I see, only the England captain is entitled to wear one. Well, can you get me made the next England captain and then we can go to the dance together, both wearing our posh ties." He wished, not for the first time, that his Mum and Dad were still together.

Just as Goode glanced round the office and concluded that if he looked hard enough he might find an old-fashioned fax in these out-of-date MCC offices, Lester called and he had no choice anyway but to follow him out of the office, up the stairs and into another empty office.

"Our ancestors were a good deal wiser and thought a good deal further ahead than they are given credit for," Lester told him as he produced a key to unlock another door that led into a small passageway which gave little evidence of use. Spiders' webs were everywhere, dust had gathered where the draughts had blown it and there was a distinct smell of damp.

The Colonel marched on briskly. "When they built what was then thought of as the new pavilion, at the end of the last century roughly, they incorporated a number of passages which have been more than useful in times of, shall we say, stress.

"Mostly, of course, they have been used to smuggle people out of the ground when there were those here they did not wish to meet.

"Once again it was mostly our friends from the popular newspapers perhaps wishing to interview certain players who had behaved badly, or been censured by the disciplinary powers, or perhaps had an indiscretion in their private lives which might have come to the attention of the tabloids. I'm sure you know something of these matters.

"But there have been other occasions too, at least two or three of which - before my time, you understand, not particularly wishing to distance myself from these events, but just to give you an idea of the time span involved - might have had serious consequences.

"Royalty on one infamous occasion; VIPs of all sorts involved. Let's say no more. But we can conclude that these pas-

passages have been useful. Lets hope you never need to use one, Andrew, after today.

"You may also be interested to know that you are one of the few people aware of their existence. In other words, 'mum's the word.' You have heard that before this morning. What you are to hear in the next few minutes will make all this early stuff seem like child's play. And I say that without having any idea of the detail. All right?"

Goode was no wiser. Apart from the clue that he was to meet a mysterious man known as "The Captain" and the very briefest explanation over coffee from the Colonel.

He realised it was partly the embarrassment all cricket officials felt in discussing anyone's private affairs, partly a wish to cover up something he did not fully understand, and partly a feeling he should not be talking about his betters that produced Lester's torrent of words.

"The Captain is a very great man, played brilliantly at his school as a boy, a few times for a champion county, bad accident in the middle of a good war, commission of course, returned to this country and could not play at any sort of worthwhile level. Worked in the administration of the game briefly, now has a sort of roving commission. I have to tell you that many people think he is dead. Someone told me so - with proper regrets, of course - only the other day.

"Not dead at all. Rumours greatly exaggerated, as they say, but it suits his style. Very nice man, very kind, very diplomatic. One has the impression he carries a number of secrets, never talks out of school.

"Quite old, of course, but a great deal of wisdom, knowledge, experience, connections, and I might say, considerable power in high places. At school, no university unfortunately, cannot understand why. Should have had a Blue, but the Second World War got in the way. Fine batsman at school. Always been puzzled about his failure to attend university. Fine family background, going back generations, centuries rather.

"Insists on meeting you. Not every England captain. Selected few. Don't be nervous. You're about to meet a very nice man, very shrewd, very kind. He'll be a great deal of help to you as he has to me. Of course we were at the same school, thirty years apart, so naturally there's a connection. Owe him a great deal. Myself I mean. I'm biased, but he's a great man, great man."

At this point the passageway swung left and they found themselves in front of a small gate made of stumps. One of the stumps was shattered, Goode could see, but it had been loosely glued together. At the top of one of the stumps his keen eyesight made out the words 'Frances 1880-1906'. A small plaque said 'Crossland House 1850'.

"Some significance to this gate," said the Colonel, pushing it open and climbing half a dozen stone steps to a small door which swung open at his first touch without a sound.

They were in a small cellar, but the Colonel strode confidently ahead and Goode followed, up some more stairs through another door and into a very old-fashioned parlour.

Goode thought it must be Victorian in style and furniture but he had hardly time to ask when the door they had just used was pushed open and a tall, thin, elderly man walked in very slowly, very quietly and, despite his age, with the carriage of one not only trained as a soldier, but confident of his ability to lead.

There were no handshakes, no formal greeting, simply a "Thank you, Thomas" which caused Tom Lester to take his leave, remarking that he would see Goode back in his office when he had finished his conversation. The old man said: "Sit down, Andrew and I will find us a drink. Time for a celebration, I think.

"I have to talk to you about your additional duties as captain of the England cricket team. My name is John Walker - John Alfred King Walker in the old scorebooks - but I am known universally as The Captain and I invite you to address me in that way from now on."

He spoke very slowly and it seemed to be a great effort. Goode could tell he did not expect to be interrupted, that he was used to being in charge and that he would be intolerant of any foolish remark. He thought silence might be his best option.

The Captain had two champagne glasses to hand and a bottle of Roederer Cristal which he opened carefully and poured very slowly while Goode considered his own position in his new role. Appointed England captain with authority, so it seemed over ten of the best cricketers in the world, yet for the last two hours all he had done was to obey orders.

"Follow me" from Leigh, "serve Queen and Country and, by the way, beat the Australians" from the Prime Minister, "go to meet The Captain" from the Colonel and now "sit down until I'm ready" from a man who must be in his eighties and perhaps ten years older.

When do I get to issue a few orders? Goode wondered. When I'm as old as this chap? Or will I have to wait a really long time? He settled back into the oldest leather armchair he had ever seen and waited.

The Captain handed him a glass and Goode noticed the gnarled old hand was steady. The Captain said: "Good health, young man, and a successful captaincy. I hear you are just the man for the job, that you have a brain and keep it in good shape, that you read a lot and I've seen for myself you're a half decent batsman."

"My father and mother insisted I'd learn more by reading than playing," Goode replied, a little self-consciously since he was aware that every word he spoke might be held to judgement.

"And more still by listening," said the old man, quite sternly, placing his glass carefully to one side in a way that suggested he would forget it. "Which is what, I am afraid, you will have to do for the next little while since you have a lot to hear."

"I don't know what to expect," Goode heard himself say.

"I cannot explain everything at the one sitting but I will give you an outline of your extra duties although I guess you will have already absorbed one or two clues from John Major and Leigh and Lester. Lester in particular has no more than a brief idea about what is involved. Don't say too much to him, in other words.

"As for you, everyone speaks so highly of your capabilities that I have always assumed you would be both captain and the natural successor to those men who have had the capacity to be both captain of their country and servant of the Crown at the same time.

"Few people know it but this tradition of service by the best of the England captains goes back into the previous century. At that time we had a fight on our hands all over the world as we attempted to keep the more rebellious elements in the huge Empire under control.

"The captain of England - and sometimes I have to say the

14

"The captain of England - and sometimes I have to say the manager of the team - proved their worth in India, in the West Indies, in Australia and on the North-West Frontier, what is now Pakistan, as they sent back information, delivered quiet messages and listened to conversations.

"On rare occasions they had to perform tasks of much greater importance and even put themselves in danger as they sought to do the government's work. Let me emphasise this treading into murky waters did not happen often, although I have to tell you that one young captain died in 1888 - not of malaria as has often been supposed - but at the hands of a witch doctor in Central Africa.

"He must have been a very courageous man and the results of his work in the days of Queen Victoria helped to keep the union of nations together under Great Britain when it might have crumbled."

The old man paused dramatically. Goode could see he enjoyed telling the tale - if only because he had concentrated so hard on his yarn that his glass of champagne was still on one side untouched except for the first sip - and he did not interrupt.

"So you in your turn may be called on by your government to help out in times of crisis. How you perform the tasks given to you - whether it is talking to an ambassador at a High Commission party, or finding your way into the confidence of a Prime Minister, or perhaps in extreme circumstances being especially nice to his wife - will be left to you and you will never be required to forsake your first duties to the game in order to carry out this work.

"There will be a nice little sweetener - isn't that the modern term - whether you are asked to do the work or not. It will come in the form of a nest egg for your retirement at the end of what we are sure will be a long and distinguished career.

"If you need money or anything else to do your work you will find it is provided; and if at any time, for any reason, you find that your task is too distasteful, or too nerve-racking or too worrying for any reason, you have only to phone me and I will see that your duties are withdrawn.

"You are only the seventh England captain to be offered this work in 130 years. Two men ideally suited turned it down out of hand. Two more were written off as failures, one drank heavily, one was compromised by the advances of an obvious tart within a few hours of taking on the work.

"He always denied it but we knew it was true because we sent her to his room to ask for details of his new job and he told her about the interview he had had with me that morning!

"The man was a bloody fool and, I am pleased to be able to tell you, that he found life in the game rather difficult from that moment forward. There is still a line of communication around the counties which can ensure the right people get to the top and the wrong people are, shall we say, put to one side. As for the girl we sent, she is now high in the Civil Service, after proving repeatedly that she had a great deal more discretion, not to mention commonsense, than our friend the most stupid man ever to captain England. He did not last long I can tell you.

"One dropped out of the game after a single tour. So you will see we have made errors in our judgement of men and for that reason I have been more careful in my selections over the last 20 years than at any time in the past.

"I warn you too that there will be a test of your worth before you are sent on a mission but I am sure you will not let us down.

"Of course, you have a choice. We are confident in your ability to carry out the tasks; but you may not be sure of us, or your own ability, or feel you have too much on your plate at this time and simply find the idea unworthy.

"Here's my phone number. It is connected to an answer-phone and, such is the wonder of modern technology, it also tells me the number of the phone you are using. I make it a practice not to answer any phone but if you leave a message saying you need urgent help someone will reply immediately.

"There are a number of other tricks to this new trade but that is of no matter until you have decided if you want to take part or not. Ring that number and give me an answer any time before the end of the season. Your duties will not start until the tour of West Indies.

"Now I will let you get back to your lunch with the good Leigh and his co-selectors at table 36 in the buffet room at the hotel. They will already be seated when you arrive. I suggest you ask

Leigh if you can have his chair so that he has to sit with his back to the door."

The old man giggled to the surprise of Goode who had been listening for half an hour to this stern old man deliver his stern message. The ormolu clock on the mantelpiece seemed to tick louder and he noted that he should already have been back at the hotel.

The Captain was not finished. "For one thing your little jape will irritate Leigh who likes to sit watching the door. It's something in his mind although he always says it has to do with a threat from the Mafia ever since he told some Godfather figure to get lost or kissed his wife or some such nonsense. It's all a joke of course. He really just likes to see who comes in and out of the door. You'll do as I say, won't you?"

The Captain got up and walked over to his desk. "I want you to read something. It may influence you since it is one of the most dramatic stories about the special category captains. I do urge you to accept by the way. Yes, please do us the honour of saying yes. But first read this diary by one of the first captains of England to undertake tasks on behalf of the government.

"You will know the name. B L M Collinson, Bernard Lord Major Collinson, fine cricketer, good captain, popular man; should have had a far more impressive record than he did. Should have captained England for five years. Unfortunate end to his career. A bloody fool was appointed in his place. In a very special category indeed but not one to be given a secret.

"Now take this parcel with you. It's the original diary which he kept, unknown to the man in charge of this operation at the time. That man, also known as The Captain, added some notes of his own when the diary fell into his possession later. Read it carefully, Andrew.

"It outlines the job you are undertaking with great clarity. Both the captaincy and the additional tasks. Same principles of cricket and diplomacy, if that is the right word, apply today. Shows you something of the quality of Collinson too. Fine young batsman who was not allowed to fulfil his potential. Great shame. Shows the game in a poor light."

Goode did not understand what the old man was talking about so he did not answer but simply accepted the parcel and left through the front door. He was half way back to the pavilion when

17

through the front door. He was half way back to the pavilion when he realised that this apparently reclusive old-fashioned man had somehow learnt that he hated sitting facing the door when he was dining in public.

He continued to wonder all the way through lunch, mainly because contrary to The Captain's prediction Leigh made no fuss about moving to another place on the table. He was still thinking about his strange day as he was photographed at Lord's with his mysterious parcel at his feet. The following morning there were several pictures of him in the newspapers with a puzzled frown on his face, causing the caption writers to suggest he was worrying about beating the Australians. In fact he was wondering about The Captain and the diary.

He was unable to solve the mysteries in the taxi back to Euston, throughout his journey in the first-class compartment, which remained empty all the way to Birmingham, and during the drive to his home in the urban village of Allburton.

The meeting with The Captain worried him so much that he still had not opened the the parcel until he put it down in his hallway. "What the hell has he given me," he muttered as he pulled off the string and brown paper. "So old-fashioned," he thought.

Inside he found a thick leather folder and inside that 400 pages of handwritten foolscap neatly clipped together in chapters and several loose leaves. The first page had the words Report From The First England Captain to Aid His Majesty with Additional Notes by The Captain and Sundry Other Relevant Papers. "Christ, someone's put some work into this little lot," Goode muttered to himself. He carried the parcel into the room he thought of as his study, poured himself a glass of Perrier and settled down to read.

It did not take him long to realise he had been presented with a fascinating document. The remaining pages unfolded a tale of derring-do; "Just like Boy's Own Paper," he thought as he read the adventure story of a captain who had been dead almost 30 years before he was born. Like Goode, Bernard Collinson had received his first instructions in the same study in the little house just beyond Lord's. And been just as puzzled.

CHAPTER ONE
August 1st, 1906.
London

I received my commission today from the Prime Minister. Lord Harris said I should have an unusual task to go with the captaincy of England but I had no idea it would take this form. He said also that I must be silent about it. Yes and no, I thought when he spoke.

From the first indications that I might succeed to the captaincy I resolved to keep a diary. After all it might do me well when my batting and my bowling served no-one any longer. There is money to be made from a cricketer's book as Grace and Jessop and many others have shown. So even a few sketchy notes would suffice, I thought, and could be fleshed out at a later date. I had not imagined what an extra gift was to be dropped into my outstretched hands. Don't say a word to anyone, they all said. No-one said I should not write down my instructions in precise detail.

It seems I am to be a spy. Of sorts. They have done me the honour, and those are their words, of asking me to work for England and in particular to assist the Prime Minister, no less, if and when it is necessary. Cricket, it seems, comes first but from time to time someone will contact me and give me instructions that will help His Majesty's Government. They have promised me dull work, fetching and carrying, but I have an imagination and I feel as if I perhaps ought to ask Conan Doyle to write my story, and as if Sherlock Holmes stood at my shoulder. What else should a young man do?

I am excited by the idea of being captain of England, but so am I thrilled to bits to know that I can also sometimes go places and put myself at the disposal of His Majesty. So I am told.

Let me set out what happened right from the start and then there will be no forgetting the exact details because I know that other things will take their place and I will forget everything.

Right from the moment I made that 214 against the Australians for MCC several years ago now, and then took charge of the Gentlemen's side against the Players last summer, there has been talk that I might lead England to India this winter. None of the others - the great men MacLaren, Jackson and the like - wanted to go although I think Jackson fancied the tiger shooting. But then he is a traditional man and he said to me that he could not see himself in a hot climate for Christmas and gave me an old-fashioned stare. "I suppose you don't care," he said but he has not my height and he could not hold the stare in the face of my silence.

So I made some runs in the last three county matches, including 59 at Taunton when the pitch was poor, and 139 at the Oval on a batsman's wicket. Then at the end of the second day of our final match of the summer at the Oval, after I had made 78 in little more than an hour at the end of play and was still not out, Lord Harris came into the captain's room and said: "Bernard, a word, if you don't mind." I knew straight away what he was about.

Harris is a strange man but as honest as they come and you are never left long doubting what is in his mind. It's "Bernard" if he is on your side, or "Collinson" if he is about to tell you something difficult and even a coarse word if he is angry. He bears no grudges, he says what he thinks and he says it all loudly in front of everyone so that there are no secrets. Unless secrecy is essential as it was that day.

We sat down under the awning at the back of the pavilion and he said right away: "We - that is to say the MCC committee - want you to take the team to India. There will be 14 men and yourself, there is already an itinerary of sorts but it will be a difficult trip because their board will change things at the last minute and you will have your hands full with poor hotels, trains that may or may not run on time and they are, need I tell you, having a war at the moment."

"Yes, sir," I said by way of reply. I did not want to seem presumptuous.

"You won't turn us down if we make this offer in a formal fashion, will you?" He looked me in the eye and I thought he might be weighing up my character, perhaps looking for some last clue about me.

"No, sir. No-one in his right mind turns down a free trip to India and the chance to play cricket too and see all those sights," I said in one breath.

20

"Good man," he said. "I knew you would. We have a special regard for you and we think you will be our man for some time. Now listen carefully. Have I got your full attention?"

"Of course, chairman," I said.

He seemed momentarily distracted. "If you have plans for the evening I am afraid you will have to drop them," he said. "Are you dining with someone? A lady perhaps? The Kent captain?"

"I have no plans to dine at all, sir. I often refrain from too much food late when I am in the middle of an innings."

"Good. Go and sort out your kit or whatever you have to do and I will see you at eight at Lord's. In the Secretary's office."

I shall not forget the next three hours as long as I live. Lord Harris had the Secretary of MCC with him when we met in the office; the two led me back through the passage behind the pavilion, and down behind the grandstand and so into a hut where the printers were still busy with the scorecards, and through another door and into a garden beyond the walls of the ground. Down another passageway, across a small back lane and into the back garden of a house so overgrown with ivy that it was almost hidden.

"You are about to meet a man who you may recognise but who will be known to you as The Captain," said Lord Harris. "He is a great man, one of the finest minds in the country and he has a message for you. He and some other gentlemen will explain the honour that is being accorded to you; it is your place to listen. We will leave you now. Remember: listen, absorb, learn. If you have questions I will answer them later. This talk will not last long. We will be waiting for you in the Secretary's office."

As the two gentlemen turned on their heels and walked off I saw the door open and the unmistakable figure of W.G.Grace framed in the light from the hallway behind. "Come in, young man," he croaked. "There is someone here you must meet."

He turned down a narrow passage and I followed. You can imagine my confusion. Two hours or so ago I had been hitting out in an attempt to set up a declaration: now I was walking behind one of the legendary figures of our game, not knowing what came next. What is every other well-known cricketer doing at this moment, I wondered. I had not met Grace before and I was curious about what he might do or say.

W G turned left into a small room and I followed. There,

W G turned left into a small room and I followed. There, warming himself with his back to the fire, was a man I had no trouble recognising. The Prime Minister. Alongside him stood the former Viceroy of India, Lord Curzon. Sitting in a tall chair at one side was a man with an austere look. I sensed rather than guessed he might be a Cabinet Minister. It turned out to be the Foreign Secretary. As my eyes grew accustomed to the atmosphere and the light I realised there were at least two other men in the room. One stood mostly in the shadows. I could only note his athletic build, his steely eyes, his cruel mouth. He said nothing throughout my stay and I was left to guess he might be some sort of protector to the Prime Minister. He frightened me.

There was another man with what I can only describe as a noble brow. An athlete of some sort, he had the clear marks of aristocracy about his bearing but there was also the air of a man born to contemplate. He sat upright in a deep leather armchair and did not speak throughout the meeting but I had the feeling he missed nothing. An untouched glass of champagne rested on a small wine table beside him. Sometimes Grace looked at him as if seeking his approval but he received neither nod nor smile.

It was W G who spoke first. "Bernard, meet the Prime Minister, Sir H Campbell-Bannerman. On his right Sir Edward Grey, the Foreign Secretary and Lord Curzon, recently in India. Gentlemen, this is Bernard Collinson, the captain of England for the coming tour of India and for sometime afterwards, we think." Grace made no further introductions. The unpleasant looking man at the fireplace and the man in the armchair were ignored but I am sure this gesture was by agreement. Some of that night's doings seemed to have been rehearsed.

Grace went on. "Now Bernard, my dear chap, listen to what these gentlemen have to say. They have something important to tell you."

The Prime Minister stepped forward. "Bernard, I am told by my friend Lord Harris that you have been appointed captain for the tour to India this winter and that there is a belief, even before you begin your first tour, that you will keep the position of captain of England for some years. He describes you in glowing terms. He speaks of your cricket brain as being exceptional, says you have a first-class degree, and that for someone who, if I may say so, comes from a middle class background, a remarkable ability to mix with all classes. I gather too that you have a patron, a man who believes you are first-class, in the civil service sense of that word."

I interrupted. "My mother and father ran a shop, sir. In York. We are proud of our achievements. Serving in a shop - as I did in my school holidays from the moment I first went to grammar school - teaches you how to deal with everyone on an equal footing." I had the beginnings of a Socialist leaning and this talk of "class" - especially when it was pronounced as if the word contained a double-R - set my teeth on edge.

The Prime Minister laughed. "I meant no slight," he said. "Excuse my snobbish ways. I intended to praise you, not abuse your parents. I will know better in future. After all, I may need your vote one day." He and the Foreign Secretary both laughed and I joined them because I could see that they wanted me on their side more than I cared if they approved of me or not. I noticed that the nasty looking man's expression did not change. He looked as if he might enjoy a day-old baby for breakfast. Lord Curzon appeared to be bored by the conversation. The man in the armchair did not move. His long fingers rested easily on the arms of the chair and his breathing was steady. He said nothing but he was easily the most personable man in that room full of public figures.

"Let's leave your egalitarian views behind and return to your elevation to the captaincy," the PM went on. "The powers within your game say you are an exceptional talent. They need a new, long-serving captain because there is some doubt about the ability of MacLaren, that strange man Jackson is too independent and WG here is too young." WG grunted. I suspect that he had heard the joke before. After all he was born in 1848 and at Trent Bridge a few years ago he was laughed off the ground when he could not bend to pick up the ball because of his bulging stomach.

"So they see you as a long-term captain, they admire your batting and your spirit and the other players say you are the right man. But beyond that an England captain has many duties. As an ambassador, a social animal, an after-dinner speaker, a representative of his country in every sense. We have no doubt you will accomplish that as well as leading England to victory which should not be too difficult in India, unless they have a million more like Ranji, the young heathen."

I simply said: "He's a damned good bat, sir. If we are beaten by 11 like him I may return with my head held high."

The PM smiled. "He's also Johnny Foreigner, Bernard, meat and drink to an Englishman. We've shown it a dozen times in the Khyber Pass and most recently in South Africa against the Boers. Don't let's have any defeatist talk here. I know you can deal with any 11, indeed with any 22, Indian wallahs." They all had a good laugh at that; except Curzon. He looked as if he would rather be anywhere else in the world. The face of the man in the armchair did not flicker.

I wondered about their intelligence. As good cricketers came from South Africa and India and Australia as were ever born in this country, yet there is something about the Englishman that under-rates all foreigners. So we lose thousands of men in the Veld and think their small bands of raiders are slimy cheats. Hundreds die in the Khyber Pass and we call the Afghans cowards because they will not stand and fight us in red uniforms so that we may shoot them more easily. Up to this moment I have spent all my 30 years in England yet I guess that Indians, Eskimos, Malays and Australians are just as we are.

All these thoughts flashed through my mind in an instant, unbeknown to the great and good opposite me. "I expect to beat them, sir, because they are not as practised as we are, but they have English coaches now and they must be improving."

"I'm sure you will," the Prime Minister said, without as much condescension as he might have used. "Anyway to more important matters." He turned to Grace. "Tell the young man, WG, and then I will have another word."

Grace sat down and began to speak in that high-pitched voice of his. It was distracting but I listened as Lord Harris had advised. "I have to tell you that what you are hearing now is confidential. You are not to repeat this conversation to anyone. You will not tell your mother or father, you will not tell your fiancee now or in the future, you will certainly not tell the next floozie you meet. You will not repeat it to anyone, including your most trusted companions, team mates nor anyone else. What is about to be revealed to you is secret, young Bernard, and must remain so. Is that understood?"."

"Yes, sir."

"However if you wish to back out of this now you may do so."

"No, sir. I admit I am full of curiosity."

"If by the end of my short speech you wish to drop out you may do so. If at any time in the future you feel you have too much on your plate do not hesitate to plead overwork. But if you continue you will find there is a rich reward at the end, that you will be given all the support, advice and help you need and that you will have no financial worries for the rest of your days. You may never have to perform a single act, nor even think about this meeting again.

"All we are asking you is that if at any time the government of the day needs your services you will do as they ask. They in their part guarantee that they will not distract you from your first duty as captain of England but only call on you if they see a way you can help because of your position. Is that clear?"

I paused and the Prime Minister took the hesitation for doubt. "Come, Bernard, we are not asking much. Indeed we may not ask for anything. But if you are better placed to deliver a message to our friends or our enemies, if you can move in a place that will be unthinkable to send a High Commissioner, or if your fame as a cricketer makes some move easier for you than for one of our secret agents, then and only then, we may ask your help.

"Let there be no misunderstanding. We will not hand you a rifle and tell you to capture half the Boer Army with your team of young amateurs and gnarled old pros. We will not ask you to crawl into the stockade and steal the enemy's plans. But we see ways in which you could be the best man for certain difficult tasks. Don't forget, there are those who would lay their lives down for a cricketer half as famous as you. Don't you see it in their eyes, sometimes?"

"I will do everything I can for the good of my country," I said. I liked the idea and they seemed pleased I had agreed to help. I had always loved a mystery and an adventure. There were unanswered questions in the air, but I found that if I listened and let them give me explanations that suited their vanity they were happy. They could not shake off their belief that a young sportsman must be stupid even though they had been told I thought quickly. They obviously considered me a simpleton and I saw no reason to disil-

Shortly afterwards they gave me a brandy and, after some idle chit-chat which only proved they knew even less about cricket than most strangers to the game's inner circle, the politicians let me go. Lord Curzon followed me to the door. "Here's my card, young man. I know India as few Englishmen can. I ruled it for years. Too long really. Please make an appointment to see me on Monday. I can be helpful, even if I don't know as much about your game as these other gentlemen. Don't forget. Come and see me."

I walked down the path and so out into the street with my head in a whirl. I had learnt within a couple of hours that I was to be captain of England and a spy! Heavens above. They kept telling me how little a duty they were asking me to perform. They seemed to have no idea that it does not happen to men very often to be named captain of their country, but to be asked to carry on as a courier between governments as well is a very rare thing indeed.

In the Secretary's office Lord Harris was waiting on his own. He had a cab on call and we went off to take dinner in Baker Street. I toyed with some fish; and noted he too ate little. I warmed to him, mainly because he allowed me to take part in the conversation. The politicians had wanted to talk. Harris was prepared to listen too.

At the end of the meal, he ordered a brandy for himself. I declined his offer to join him. One was enough. Better a clear head for the morning.

"They will test you, you know," he said. "Beware of what Grace said. They must have a bigger plan than they have given you wind of. Watch how you go. They have seen how important our game has become in the colonies but they are using you to try their plans and, I have to warn you, these are not nice fellows. If their ideas fail they will look for a scapegoat and it may be you, young Collinson. So watch how you go. But I am not suggesting you put the idea aside. They will also make you wealthy."

We left the restaurant and walked down Baker Street towards Marylebone Road. There were cabs to be had but it was a warm night, we were in no hurry and I thought I might walk back to my flat.

Suddenly Lord Harris waved at the nearest cabbie. "I'll be off to my club. Can't take you, I'm afraid, and I guess you will need a little sleep," he snapped, unexpectedly flustered. "I will talk to you in the morning at the Oval. Take a long slow walk back to St. John's Wood and think what you have learned. Exercise and brain in unison, what." He leapt aboard the cab, and then reeled back. "Excuse me, madam, I do apologise," he said, even more flustered now. "I did not realise anyone else was aboard. Are you about to get out? May I take this cab. Allow me to cover my confusion by paying your fare. Thank you, ma'am; cabbie, take me to the St. James Club. You know the way? Then off we go." All this in the loud voice of an actor reaching the climax of a bad play. As his cabbie whipped up the horses I was already wondering what M'Lord was playing at.

I had been to the St. James Club, with Harris as it happens, so I was a little surprised when I saw the cab head right at the end of Baker Street rather than going straight on.

The passenger, a petite lady wrapped tight in a cloak, was looking at me. "Who was that impetuous soul?" she asked.

"Lord Harris, ma'am, we've just finished dinner and he was anxious to get off to his club."

"Then he'll be late for he has gone the wrong way for the St. James," she said.

"You know the St. James?"

"By a coincidence, I work in the catering department. One of the workers behind the scenes, not one of those who sees the likes of my lord every day," she answered. I saw now that she was pretty and smiling.

"That is strange," I said. "Where are you going now." She looked hard at me.

"I am going to Viceroy Court. It's a few hundred yards from here."

"Yes, I know it. I'm going that way if you care to walk with me."

Of course it was a little out of my way, although the back of Viceroy Court lay behind my apartment block but, as I said, she was pretty and I was in a state of excitement from the events of the evening and one does not often meet a pretty lady in such circumstances late at night.

"I know you," she said. "You're Bernard Collinson, the cricketer. My sister has a post like me in the catering department at Lord's. You may know her. She pointed you out to me once."

"Indeed," I said, slightly surprised at her familiar tone and the easy way she took my arm. "I know the lady you refer to by sight, but not to speak with."

"You are tall and not easily forgotten," she laughed. "Jane - that's my sister - said you had none of the appetite of the other players, that you were always a gentleman and that you made the others put money in for a tip at the last lunch of the three days."

"I guessed that waitresses, cooks and the like are not as well paid as the players," I said. "I was also making a point to the players."

"What point was that, pray?" she asked. I thought she was mocking me.

"That it was time they considered the plight of others instead of continually whining about their own station in life. They lead a privileged existence. They should think of those less fortunate."

She mocked me again. "Aren't we the big brave Socialist then?"

Even on a day like this it was difficult to get me off my hobby horse once I was mounted. "I come from a middle class background. I had to win my way to Cambridge. There I was lucky enough to meet a patron who treats me royally, gives me money, allows me to play as an amateur and who has been directly responsible for me being able to play cricket when others of my sort might have to earn a living in less pleasurable circumstances. I feel the need to help the less fortunate."

She was still giggling. "Then you may make me a drink when we return to your flat?" It was a question or more likely an order.

"No, I shall take you straight to my rooms so that there will be no waiting for the main event of the night," I said, guessing that boldness was needed at this juncture.

"I like a direct man," she said. "Yes, I will be just as straightforward. I will be pleased to drink a while in your room."

So we walked more quickly, in through the side door of the apartment block, behind the concierge's office lest any nosey flunkey delay us or question my right to take a lady upstairs, and so even more rapidly now to my flat. I rushed her to the bedroom and immediately grabbed hold of her and thrust her on to the bed.

She looked up at me with an unblinking stare. "There is

the time for hurry and the time to be slow," she said. "I am glad to be in your arms in such a rush, sir, but from this point forward I will take charge and I promise that a little less haste and a little more patience and we will have the greater enjoyment. For a start you must watch."

She pushed me to one side and plucked off her hat and, in a single movement much like Hobbs at cover point when there is a run-out in the offing, threw it to the hat stand in the corner. Then with a second movement she whipped off my hat and threw that too so that it landed on top of her own hat.

I was so impressed I laughed out loud. "You will see, Bernard Collinson, that the entertainment you have found by chance will be even better than your imagination produced," she said, bowing from the waist.

She pulled off her cloak and underneath she was wearing so little that I gasped in amazement. "It's a good job it's August," I said disturbed by the sight of her breasts bulging from their stays and my eyes drawn to a neat black triangle emphasised by a pair of white silk stockings held round her tiny waist by a wide vivid green sash.

"You won't find me cold," she said as the stockings came off in a flash. "Nor will you see more of me. I can put the stockings back on if that makes you randier but the sash stays in place. Just to maintain some mystery, you know. Now let's deal with you. But first turn off some of these lights."

The single light switch turned all on or left the room with a single light over the bed. I turned them all off and drew the curtains. Meanwhile she followed me round the room taking off my coat, my tie, my shirt and throwing them on the floor.

I sat on the bed and allowed her to pull off my trousers, my shoes, my socks and my pants. At the sight of my prick, now in full bloom, she gasped; an artifice I thought but by now I did not care. She handled it tenderly and the old familiar pleasure seeped through its full length.

"A two-hand prick. Lucky me," she sighed and knelt in front of me and began to run her tongue on the underside. Her own hands were busy about herself. "Let me help," I said hoarse by now. "I can do better for myself but by-the-by you may find your way around me," she said.

In a minute or two she drew me to the bed. "Come here, come inside and come," she said. I lay beside her and put my hand on her thigh. "If you draw your nice long fingernails down the inside on my thigh I will be most obliged," she said. I did. "Oblige me once again, very very slowly," she whispered. I obliged her and she bit my ear. "Again."

It needed only one more obligation, as she put it, and she was easing me inside a hot wet gaping hole that had to be felt to be appreciated. "Wait," she said. "Now, now, now, you can thrust as hard as you wish. Don't wait for me. Come on, come, come, come."

I do not know how much she enjoyed that brief passage. She sighed and talked and encouraged and finally screamed but, even though I was breathing fire and shooting stardust, or so it felt, I had this wondrous impression I was the victim of a confidence trick. Which was just as well.

In no time at all I finished and she timed her final yelp to perfection and held me prisoner inside her so that I was still hard as she began with her hands and found her own pleasure. "Just one little thrust to oblige a lady," she whispered and bucked and plunged and shrank into a ball and finally grasped me hard round the shoulders, like a child threatened with separation from its mother. She lay in my arms babbling like a child too and finally shed a few tears.

I lay beside her strong and male and wanting to sleep. But I dare not.

"Is it true you will lead England to India?" she asked. By this time I was back in charge of my brain at least and thought it the strangest post-coital question I had ever been asked. It took me by surprise since I was wondering if she was to be added to my list of conquests, or my other list of female cricket aficionados who have been so willing in the past, or my list of solos: those seen once and never seen again.

"I know no more than you," I said. "The newspapers say I will. I think they are not often wrong about such major matters whatever the public says about their accuracy. I expect an official announcement soon. Meanwhile no-one has said anything to me."

I wondered why I was talking so formally to this lady. After all had we not recently been on the most intimate terms. What was it about her that made me feel I was being interviewed?

Was she a Press woman, using feminine wiles to get her stories?

"You have been lucky tonight," she said. "But I bet this is often the way of things for the famous. A hapless female comes along and you sweep her into your bed. Don't tell me that I am the first. You will have a batting list as long as your dick. Do tell."

"I have never been as lucky as I have been tonight and I can tell you that if you wish to repeat this incident I will be happy to oblige you again," I said.

She wriggled. "I may," she said. "Who were you addressing - that rude man who invaded my cab - when we met. Heavens," she laughed, "it must have been nearly two hours ago. How quickly we have become, how shall I call it, lovers, fuckers, intimates?"

"Don't use that word," I said, suddenly proper, "it does not become a lady. Please don't say it again. It is improper in the conversation of a man in a man's environment, but even in bed it ill becomes a lady."

She went scarlet. "What is good for a man is good for a lady," she snapped. "I may take your prick in my mouth, but I may not say what we have done. If that is your definition of a lady you may excuse me now, sir. Fuck you, and your snooty ideas. You may have the understanding of the equality which the various classes should try to attain, but you cannot see the need for an equal place for men and women. Rethink your Socialism, Mr. Cricketer, you still have much to learn. About liberty, fraternity and equality."

At that she leapt out of bed and began to dress.

"I admit I have a prejudice," I said. "I apologise. I meant no harm. I was patronising. I want you to say you understand. I will not say such a thing again."

"You will not have the chance, sir," she muttered. Then, just as swiftly, she changed her mind and walked back towards me and kissed me on the lips. "I will stay a little while longer. Tell me what you have been at tonight. I admit I am curious since it was only a few hours earlier that my sister showed me you and Lord Harris walking at the back of Lord's. You had not been at dinner for four hours. No, you had an important meeting. Believe me I have guessed that you might have been at dinner with the Prime Minister. I saw him and Lord Curzon just before I saw you and Lord Harris."

31

"No," I said, suddenly understanding what was the cause of all this rush to bed. "I had dinner with Lord Harris but since you must know he indicated to me that I must hold myself in readiness for a call to be captain in India. There is to be an announcement soon. Perhaps it may be today. Lord Harris has a regard for the Saturday edition of the Morning Post it seems. He holds Pelham Warner in high esteem and he will give him the news first. He spent some time explaining that such items of news are important although I cannot understand why."

She had finished dressing and wrapped her cloak round her and waved from the door. "You'll do," she said. "Thanks for everything, sir. I expect we may meet again, but I will report to my superiors that you keep your secrets, that you can hold your drink and that you can think quickly. I do not know what you have been asked to do by this dextrous government but what I have observed tonight assures me you will do it well." I had no time to be surprised by this lady's admission, although the truth had begun to dawn on me in the last few minutes.

So she left, shutting the door quietly behind her, while I, feeling both exultant and no longer in the need of sleep, began this diary.

CHAPTER TWO
August 3rd, 1906.
London

My first duty the next morning was to get in touch with my stoutest pal, our wicket-keeper, Jake Johnson. We came out of the same street in York, his parents were customers at my parents' shop and so it was natural that we played together, and went through grammar school and university together. As every cricket man knows ,Jake's wicket-keeping put him in the highest category; safe and sure, but capable of the most astonishing takes on either side of the wicket and the holder of the University record for the number of catches. He said, modestly, that he had fine bowlers getting the batsmen to edge the ball to his hands but I used to stand at first slip when we played together and I can assure you that not all those catches fell directly into his gloves. He was also as cunning as a fox on the cricket field, a great friend and fit even at the end of the longest day. He loved a gamble too; just like every other sportsman.

Jake was also my ears in the dressing room where I rarely stepped now that I was captain. The players knew he was a conduit to me and used him to relay their dissatisfactions. They would have been better advised to ask that the captain had a place in the dressing room rather than being isolated but you can't change everything in a year. When I had been captain another couple of years I planned to move out of my little palace but I knew that there would be a to-do over such a decision and I was not ready for that yet.

There is a small door into the pavilion at the Oval where a man may slip into the dressing rooms when the crowds milling outside think he is on his way to the offices and the morning after my extraordinary meeting with the Prime Minister and his friends I chose to use this entrance to avoid notice and to creep into the place without attracting the attention of the clerical staff. I did not want to meet any of those busybodies on this particular morning.

All the way down the passage I could see Jake as he began his preparations for the day's play. He was out in our second innings already but he knew that I might declare immediately and that he must be ready to take his place on the field at any moment. Thus, even though there was an hour before play began, he was going through a series of stretching and bending motions that might have daunted a heavyweight champion. I also guess that he would have already run four miles to the ground, even though it meant taking the jeers of the passers-by. On a good day, perhaps after spending the night on his couch following one of his boisterous parties, I have allowed myself to be persuaded to run with him and kept up quite nicely. "You are not such a great athlete," I once teased him. "I am matching you stride for stride." He allowed himself a small smile. "But this is your first run of the day. It is my third," he declared and, as I discovered for myself, he was telling the truth. His first two consisted of 50 trips up and down the steps of a nearby bridge. A great man.

"Come here, Jake," I called to him as I approached the dressing room. "I have news for you." I could see the dressing room was empty but I beckoned him outside and up the stairs to the captain's room. I knew we would not be disturbed there. No club servant, no maid bearing morning tea, no committee man on some self-important mission and indeed no player dare enter without knocking. We were safe in this room of privilege and I could tell him everything. Well, almost everything. "Jake," I said excitedly, "I am to be captain of England. They even think I may be in charge not just for the tour to India but for several years afterwards. Lord Harris gave me the news last night. There will be an announcement any day now. What do you think?"

I knew the answer before I asked the question. "Great," said Jake, "I offer my congratulations." And he grasped my hand heartily. "But before we go any further - there is only one question to be settled. Who will you take for a wicket-keeper?" He grinned mightily.

"I will take you if there is a chance," I said. "I guess there will be other names but I shall ask for you to be wicket-keeper and vice-captain. There is no-one I would rather have to run this tour."

"Who will be manager? Will he have a deputy? Who picks the team? Surely you have a choice. Perhaps the major say. And who will come who is more famous than we are? Will they take young Hobbs? He is going to be a great batsman, mark my words. Rhodes? Hirst? Or will it be a chance to try out the younger players?

34

Woolley? - they say he'll skipper the side one day. Johnny Douglas? Yorkshire have a few promising lads. Most of them in the second team waiting for the old 'uns to die off. There's one there - I can't remember his name - that they say is as good as anyone who ever plays. He's been five seasons with the second team and never been out."

I had to fall for it, didn't I? "Never been out - he must be good." Jake grinned. "Yes, he's never out. Bowled - it was a no-ball! Caught - he missed it! LBW - he got a thick edge on the ball! The other players have a sweep every time he bats on his excuse. One time he comes in and gives the last batsman a terrible telling off. 'I know you tell me it's swinging, but you didn't say anything about what is happening off the pitch' he bellows. Still they do say he can bat. He might be there and then we can bet on his excuses too. Try to get him along, skipper. He'll make for a laugh whatever else."

"No, Jake, this is a serious business." Sadly, Jake never knows when to mix business and a laugh.

He's excited and he won't shut up. "They say that a tour of India is a tough one and that laughs can be few and far between. No man ever went there who did not catch a dose of Delhi belly or the squitters as they call it. Still, it's the shits, put it how you may. It can last the whole trip from the moment you're ten miles off shore until you get back to our green and pleasant land. I had the story of it from Ranji himself. Do you know even he gets stomach trouble whenever he visits the place - and he was born there."

"Right, Jake, but I'm sure it is all a tale invented by the locals to frighten the poor white men. I'll take you to dinner tonight and you can talk your way through the night but in the meantime there's a match to win. Have we got enough? Do I bat another half an hour?"

He stood up to go. "That's down to you, skipper. We're 285 ahead - I reckon we need a few more and if we are going to bowl spin all day that means a lot of overs and if they get going their middle men can do a lot of damage in an hour just before tea and maybe we won't be able to haul it back."

"What are they thinking, Jake?"

"Well, in the tavern last night they seemed to think we'd bat on because you would want a century which is yours for the asking at 78 not out and in some form."

"You sure, Jake?"

"Yes, skipper."

"Then we'll put 'em in when I get a few short of the hundred, just to upset them. See how that leaves them unbalanced."

Jake nods sagely and off he goes. When we get out there they put on their quick men and I just nudged them around on the leg side - the old bread and butter stroke off the legs - and their fielders don't rush after the ball and in 15 minutes I was 98 not out and thinking I might as well have the century and a few more runs so for the whole of one over I just stood in the crease and let fly. Six to 100, four, four, four and, just to upset them some more I declare in mid-over. Not a word to their skipper, just "Come on Sam" to our quick bowler who is batting at the other end and off I go. I decide I can apologise later for the rudeness and explain I just want to get them on the wrong foot.

It's funny, but when I passed the pro's dressing room I sensed an atmosphere. Not that anyone said anything. Quite the opposite. But I have the feeling that someone is upset. "Pads on Jake, it's time to win the cricket match" I shouted through the door without thinking much except that Jake looked a bit grumpy. I'd forgotten all about our earlier conversation and my promise to declare in the 90s and I took no notice until we were on the field. I told Ernie Caversham to bowl at the pavilion end as usual and he did not even bother to reply but just grabbed hold of the ball and stomped off as if he had a grievance.

"What's the matter with Ernie," I asked Jake as I settled down at first slip and he said: "I've said you'll declare short of your hundred and he has bet his match fee with one of the spectators and he is not too pleased."

"Damn! He's no right to be betting on matches he's playing in." I was very angry by this unexpected piece of intelligence. "Who's he laid this bet with?" Jake laughed. "Who do you expect? The Champagne Gent. George Ramsey. The committee man in the loud suits, the five pound notes sticking out of every pocket and a mouth louder than his clothes. Who else?"

Ramsey was always hanging around the dressing room. He had been told to keep out, that it was the players' private room but most of them liked him and they never objected to his presence, so why should I make a song and dance of the matter. But he was at the back of a lot of trouble. If a player had a hangover when he ought to have been at his fittest, he had always been out with Ramsey the previous evening. If a player had a grievance about pay, or his place in the side, or when he should bat, or how his field had been set, somehow Ramsey was always on the scene to add his twopennyworth. He was trouble and now he had won money off one of the young ones who had been warned before about betting on matches in which he was taking part.

What should I do? Take him off? He might just be annoyed enough to bowl them out for nothing. It would be a public humiliation and that's never very clever. Apologise? Not in any circumstances. My anger is over-riding my judgement.

The first ball came down quicker than an express train and left their opening batsman writhing as it struck him on the inside of his right thigh. I hoped I was right to leave Ernie Caversham bowling. His next ball was quicker if anything and raced an inch past the off stump. The third was wild and wide but the fourth was a yorker, as fast as you might wish, and the poor opener heard the stumps fairly explode behind him.

Now I know what to do. I walk down the pitch and find Caversham hands on knees fairly panting with his effort. "Listen," I say. "Find enough energy to bowl another three or four like that and I'll see you get the money back. The committee won't mind forking out a few shillings to see you right if you beat this lot. Come on, son, put your mind to it, use that bad temper of yours and you won't necessarily be in Carey Street tonight."

He grunted and walked back to his mark. You'll remember what happens in the next eight or ten overs. Our Ernie whips out five more batsmen before lunch and the rest was just a matter of plugging away to get rid of batsmen who know there was not a hope in hell of victory. They were eight down when I brought Ernie back and he whipped out No.9 and No.11 in his first over and we've won by 200 runs.

I led him in by the arm just to show the spectators who was the man of the day and I don't even have to ask the committee for a bonus. The chairman left his lunch to come down the steps to greet him and shake his hand and whisper "Come and see me afterwards, lad. I think this club owes you a few bob." I learnt later that the chairman heard the story about the bet and that his heart went out to the lad who is, after all, only 22. Besides the chairman is also a bookmaker and probably thinks he will get the cash back in no time.

When we have all had a chance to get our breath and sip some of the chairman's champagne and take a look at the championship table in the Evening News we realise that we have set the pace for the title. A few more glasses of bubbly and I take Ernie to the captain's room and say: "I don't want any excuses, or explanations, or anything else, Ernie. Just learn something from today even if it is only that decisions made before a day's play have to be revised in view of events on the field. Talk to one of the older players. Have a grumble about me, or what I did, or what was going through your mind and listen to what he has to say. That's all. No punishment, no complaints from me, no report to the committee. And by the way, thanks for those wickets. Now, bugger off and have another drink."

That night Jake and I dined at the Connaught, after a few drinks in the tavern, a few more in the bar and then a bottle of wine with dinner and a port or two afterwards. We were about to go when Lord Harris appeared. "Harump," he said, "Collinson and his best friend, the wicket-keeper." I realised he was also carrying a lot of drink. It made him extremely indiscreet. "I suppose you think this man will be your wicket-keeper in India," he said. He was swaying. "How much have you told him, damn you?"

"Good evening, my lord," I said, not wanting to get involved in what promised to be a difficult conversation. "Johnson and I are celebrating our famous victory over Kent today. We beat Kent, perhaps you know, sir, by nearly 200 runs." Lord Harris was a man of Kent, of course, and I thought a little gentle joshing might turn his mind back to cricket.

"I know all that," said Harris, taking a spare seat at the table. I could see his dining companions behind a pillar further down the room. "So you have every reason to feel pleased with yourselves, you brown hats." Surrey are the brown hatters, a phrase of insult within the game, as if we were brown noses, or worse.

"Caversham must have the credit," I said. "He bowled like the wind. I don't believe he has ever bowled better, eh Jake? You should send him to India, sir, if you wish to shake up those little

Indian batsmen. He is only 22 yet I believe. . ."

I am not allowed to finish the sentence. "Aye, and you want to choose half the rest of the Surrey team too I dare say," says Harris. "Well, let me tell you young Collinson, being captain of England does not entitle you to so much as an opinion about the composition of the touring party. You will be told who is to be in your party and you will make the best of it and be judged on your results on the field and how you handle the men we give you. I have had enough of this business of the captain being given a place at the table when the team is chosen. I have heard nothing else all day. Who do you think you are, sir, to demand a place on the selection committee? You will not have one so long as I am in charge, sir, I can tell you." With that he got up and walked off back to his own table.

Jake looked at me hard. "I reckon that ruins my hopes," he said. "Still I can't grumble. In my own imagination I was an England player for a few hours. Then some drunken lord gets himself into a bad temper and I will be lucky to keep a place with Surrey or Flintshire. As for you, he didn't mention that you had to step down but it sounds as if he and his MCC friends will unseat you as soon as they meet." He grinned happily at the thought of our impending misfortune.

"He is a man who says wild things in drink and forgets them when he is sober in the morning," I replied. "No problem. We will have nothing to do with the man once this party is chosen."

The next morning I made a telephone appointment to see Lord Curzon that afternoon and went to the Dominion Office at 3pm promptly with some misgivings. I could not make out whether by his silence at our meeting in the house behind Lord's he did not approve of the arrangement that the Prime Minister sanctioned; or whether by asking me to see him he had his own slant to put on the affair. I was not left in doubt for very long.

I went through the massive portals, inscribed on either side with Latin tags the precise meaning of which escaped me, and so up a marble staircase wide enough to be used for the passage of a herd of elephants and down corridors so long that I joked with my guide that I might need a map to find my way back and that if a No.22 omnibus passed that way I would leap on straight away. He was a junior messenger at the reception desk and I guess he was largely ignored by those he directed round this huge building for he responded immediately to my humour. "You're unlucky, sir," he said. "There's usually a bus every five minutes but they don't run on a Friday morning."

He then whipped out an autograph book and asked for my signature. "I'm a Surrey man from Brixton, sir, and I get there any time I can," he said. "I saw what Caversham did to Kent, sir, wonderful bowling, sir." I was happy to sign his book and saw that it contained the signatures of half the Cabinet. "We'll win the championship with any luck," I said, "although two matches away from the Oval before the end of the summer sets the odds against us."

"Is that because you don't like playing away, sir?"

"No, young man, it is because only the home captain writes a report on the umpires which may be why we feel that sometimes we get the worst of the rub when we travel. I hope I am not corrupting a young mind, but the umpires in this country are not always fair and honest, although they have an enormous knowledge of the game and its laws and its customs. But they have to look out for their own interests. There is such a thing as a captain's decision. If any appeal is on the margin it is usually given to the home captain. We have tried to change it so that both captains make a report on the umpires but without success so far. Some of us feel that if both captains made a report there would be a chance of fairness and balance by the end of the summer. Instead we have a system that encourages the umpire to weight his decisions in favour of the home side. If you want a confirmation, look at the number of games we win away. We are a good side and we don't win any proportion of our away games."

By now we had arrived at a door so large that I supposed Lord Curzon had been given it by some Maharajah but the lad opened it easily enough and announced: "Mr. Bernard Collinson to see you, my Lord." He backed out rapidly, only pausing to whisper, "follow the red carpet to the top of the stairs and go down three flights" before he disappeared.

"Sit down, Collinson," boomed Curzon, and I could not help noting that he glanced at his watch, presumably to see if I had had the temerity to be late for my appointment. I sensed he would not be an easy man to deal with on the previous evening and as the thought went through my head again I glanced up to see him scowl.

"I have asked you to see me so that I can offer you some advice on India," he began. Lord Curzon did not need to tell me he thought he was wasting his time, nor that he realised that I would forget everything he had said as soon as I left the room. His attitude from the beginning was one of a headmaster talking to a small boy.

"You will never have come across anywhere in the world, no matter where you have travelled, like India and it is so different, so much of a cultural opposite from the society in which you have been brought up that I will not even attempt to tell you how to cope. Initially, you will have to work it out for yourself. But you will need help from time to time - in matters of how you can approach certain people, how to deal with local officials, who you must believe and who will let you down - so that I have prepared a letter which my secretary is now typing, with the names and addresses of men you can trust. Two are native Indians - although naturally of the very highest class - and one is a native-born Englishman who has lived in India most of his adult life, who speaks several of their languages and who owes me and the Crown services. I trust he will be grateful enough to repay some of those debts to me through you.

"He is not a nice man. He has, as we say, gone native, but when he is sober, when he is not enchanted by yet another young boy, and when he is in the mood, he can put one on the right path. You will understand him and his ways because he is still at heart a European, although a degenerate one. I have written to him to say you are on your way and that he is to be helpful when he can. I know I shall not receive a reply but I also know that if you go into the great market behind the station in Karachi and ask for The Englishman you will be directed straight to his most recent abode.

"You may trust Dunne Sahib, as he is known; you will have to learn how much you can depend on the other two. I will not keep you a moment longer but I will finish my homily with a few words I heard from a tradesman in Karachi. 'We are an unscrupulous people in this country' he told me, 'We cheat our nearest rival and we are cheated by him and, what is worse, we expect to cheat and be cheated.' Bear that caution in mind and you will at least be aware of the difference between the two civilisations. One other word. Do not underestimate any of them because their

English is idiosyncratic or because they have a face darker than your own. They have a long history, they listen to the lessons of their past and they can be as tricky as any race on earth.

"Now, sir, go and think what I have said. Pick up your letter from my secretary on the little office on the left of the main door and, here let me shake you by the hand before you set out, have good fortune on this important trip."

With that he ushered me out. In the whole of the five minutes I had been in his presence he had not offered me a cup of tea, not asked how I felt about the forthcoming tour and, apart from gripping my hand as if he hoped to crush the life out of it before it bit him, not really acknowledged my arrival or departure.

I took my letter from his secretary and could not help noting that she had obviously been to his charm school. I thanked her, remarked on the weather and said I hoped I might see her soon. She said: "Very good" and went back to her typewriter. I followed the young messenger's directions down the corridor and descended the stairs but there was no sign of him when I left. I made one last attempt at conversation at the reception desk. "Good afternoon," I said to the uniformed man in the top hat. "Thank your young helpmate for showing me the way round this rabbit warren."

He did not look up and did not even nod in my direction. I began to wonder why since I had been made captain of England I seemed to have run into only men who gave me orders, women who wanted me to behave according to their pattern and servants without the courtesy to say good-bye.

You can imagine that by the time I reached my flat I was not in the mood to talk to anyone. "Manners maketh man," my father used to say and of course simple words of thanks and farewell are important if you offer a service in a small shop. I wondered what he and my mother would have made of the experiences of the last two days and I was muttering these thoughts as I walked up the stairs which may be why I took no notice of the man who ran past me as I reached the landing which contained my front door and those of two other flats. In fact it was not until afterwards that I realised he had existed.

I pushed my key into the lock and was surprised to find that the door gave way before I had turned the lock. I almost stumbled into the flat and immediately tripped over something bulky on the floor. All the doors into the rooms that led off the hallway were closed so there was only the light from the landing to show me what was under my feet.

I switched on the light and then it did not take me more than a few seconds to realise what had caused me to fall.

There was a body beneath me. The body of the young lady who had been so free with her favours on Friday night. And she was dead.

CHAPTER THREE
August 5th, 1906.
London

I remember as a child falling from the branches of a tree in my parents' garden and, even though the fall was probably no more than ten feet, I had several clear thoughts as I passed through the air. I must not cry when I hit the ground, even though I would be in pain, I must do nothing to upset my mother who was alone in the house, and I certainly must not cry out. I even began to make excuses for being in the tree. The tenth of a second it took me to fall to the ground is still clear in my mind. Something to do with the adrenalin produced in a moment of danger, perhaps.

The feeling I experienced as I looked down at that young lady's body was precisely the same. Time seemed to stand still. Each thought was clearer than the last, I seemed to have total control and I knew exactly what I must do.

I had read enough of Sherlock Holmes to know I must touch nothing. Instead I walked back from the body and so out into the hall where there was a telephone connected directly to the porters' lodge. Charlie, our brightest porter, took no time to answer.

"Charlie, there's a body in my hallway. It's a young lady. I'm pretty sure she has been murdered. Send for the police and then come straight up here as soon as you can. Do you follow me?"

There was a pause. You might have thought that Charlie did not know the correct procedure for dealing with bodies in second floor flats. But he soon got over his shock. With any other resident he might have been inclined to think they were pulling his leg. But I expect he knew me to be a serious man. "I'll phone, then I'll be right up, Mr. Collinson."

Meanwhile I took the opportunity to look again at the body in my hallway. Intimate as we had been I had no idea of her name since it was clear from the moment we met that she would allow no exchanges of a social nature for all the permissiveness of her behaviour. Her body was completely wrapped in the same cloak she had been wearing the other night and only her face and one arm was peeping out of its folds. I touched her hand and found it cold. My amateur knowledge of biology, vaguely remembered from school days, told me she must have been dead for some time.

Charlie arrived breathless. "The ambulance is on its way, sir, the police will be here shortly," he gasped. "Oh, that's her is it, sir? She's that young lady you. . ." and here he paused. He did not want to tell me that he had seen the two of us the other night as we sneaked in. But I knew he would tell the police. It simplified matters, actually. Otherwise I might have been tempted to lie with disastrous consequences although in the event what I said made no difference.

Poor Charlie did not look very happy to see a dead body. I guessed he was no more than 19 and he had never seen anyone dead before. In the end he turned his back on the girl. I stared, still unable to believe the circumstances in which we had met, and that I should find her dead after only meeting her the once. I do not wish to dwell on the subject but to meet a girl, to enjoy her in bed and then to see her again only when she is dead is a devastating experience. I suppose I had also realised just what a dangerous business I had entered. In my excitement at being made captain of England and being offered the chance to help my country I had not seen the inevitable consequences. No-one - and certainly not a man as shrewd as the Prime Minister - offers a pension for life without expecting a return for his money. I should have realised that at the time. Too late now. I was up to my neck in a most hazardous affair and the prime suspect in a murder case about to start.

While I mulled over my predicament and cursed myself for ever getting mixed up with these secret matters I followed Charlie's example and wandered out of my flat on to the second floor landing. There at least I was not confronted with the evidence of my folly.

Within a few minutes there was a hubbub downstairs as both police and ambulance arrived together. They all came clattering up the stairs and pushed us out of the way. The senior ambulanceman knelt by the body and pronounced "She's dead, gentlemen" and then gasped as he pulled aside her crumpled clothing. "My God," he said. "What a sight!" Now we could see what I had not cared to uncover before. The girl and her head had

45

almost parted company and the result was a ghastly, bloody mess. I am no expert in such matters but it looked as if her head might have been severed with one massive blow.

The senior policeman, a sergeant, got slowly to his feet. "I think you two chaps can remove the body to the morgue," he said. "Nothing we can do for her except guide her murderer to the gallows." He said the last seven words with relish. I could see he was not a kindly man as he ran those thoughts across his eyes.

"Now, sir," he said to me. "What is your part in this nasty business? But first," and he turned to his constable, "take this young porter downstairs and ask him what is going on here. It might help us if these two chaps were kept apart." Charlie was led away. He was white around the gills and I felt sorry for him. I was left alone with the police sergeant whose ambition, I already realised, was to handcuff me and lead me off to the station as soon as possible.

"Yes, sir," he said, possibly reading my thoughts. "You live here? Is that correct?"

"I do," I said. I thought I might just answer his questions but he must have seen my intentions. "I want you to fill in all the details if you don't mind," he said. I felt very lonely. Perhaps it was the remark about guiding the murderer to the gallows that gave me the dank feeling.

"I have this apartment from my benefactor since I had no lodging in London and need to be near the Oval where I am captain of Surrey," I said. I have often found that the sooner one lets authority people know who one is the better. I did not impress our friend the police sergeant one jot. He seemed to know who I was already.

"And you living almost on top of Lord's?" he said. There was a question in his voice but I didn't allow myself to be led along.

"Anyway, to business. Who is this young lady?" He had taken out a notebook and begun to write.

"I'm afraid I don't know her name. We met three days ago and I have not seen her since." He was not to be put off by a bland statement. "Where did you meet her, sir?"

"I was walking home from dinner and she left a cab which my friend took. We were going in the same direction so I walked along with her. I'm afraid I don't know her name or anything about her except that she said she was going to Viceroy Court."

"And I guess you were intimate with her?" He was shrewd and I wondered what sign I had given that betrayed the truth about my short friendship with this young woman. Luckily, since I still have no idea how I might have answered, I got no chance to say yes or no.

Suddenly there was a commotion downstairs and the sound of people arguing. "I am from New Scotland Yard and I am going up those stairs whether you say I can or not," bellowed one voice. "Sergeant Maynard! Tell your man to let me come up to see you. Sergeant Maynard! It's Bill Russell, Chief Detective Inspector Russell, here. I am to take charge of this investigation. It's too big for your potty little local organisation. Now tell your man to stop behaving like a complete prat and let me upstairs."

"All right, sir. If he's got a handlebar moustache and an unseasonal thick overcoat let him up here, Wilkinson. If he's short on any of those details throw him back down the stairs." Maynard was laughing now. I suspect he was relieved to have the case taken over by someone he knew.

Russell appeared at the top of the stairs panting. Charlie was right behind him, closely followed by the police constable.

The police officer wasted no time on introductions or handshakes. "Hello, Mr. Collinson. Nice to meet you, sir. I've had an urgent call from the Dominion Office about this case. It seems this young lady here was one of their people. Brave girl, they say. They are enormously upset at what's happened to her and they will have someone round here in no time. Nothing to do with you, Mr. Collinson, they said. They've had a word with my boss and explained something to him which makes him tell me that I am going to have my work cut out to solve this one. I get the idea that they will handle the investigation themselves and try to edge my people out of the way. That will be down to politics right at the top I dare say. But in the meantime we had better make a start."

He bustled about making notes all the time while Sergeant Maynard kept looking from me to Charlie like a dog who has just lost a favourite bone. He had thought he was going to be headline news for arresting a famous cricketer and, as he would no doubt put it, guiding him towards the gallows. Instead his few moments of fame were fast disappearing. Thirty years in the force completely wasted. You could almost see the words forming on his lips.

Russell stopped striding up and down. "Very efficient job. Leaving the body here I mean. Very professional. Three men if I guess correctly. Maybe four. Two to do the job. Two to make sure that not a trace was left. Cleaners up we call them. Common in these international murders." He seemed to know all about such matters.

He went over to Charlie. "How did they bring the body in here, young man?"

Charlie was very eager to tell the story. "Three darkie chaps came up to the desk about an hour before Mr. Collinson came home. Indians by the look of 'em. Said they had a carpet to deliver to this flat. Carpet over their shoulders. I showed them up. They left the carpet in the hall and I showed 'em out. I stayed with them all the time as Mr. Collinson had said nothing about having a carpet delivered. That's all I know."

"Where's the carpet," I asked. "Gone," said Russell. "I've seen it all before. It's just done to add confusion. Three men bring in the carpet at lunch time. Right?" he asked Charlie.

"Yes, sir, while me mate was on his break."

"So you were on your own?"

"That's right, sir, and the phone kept ringing and I didn't know whether I was on me head or me heels."

"Exactly," said Russell. "They or a companion were making the calls. Just to get you confused. Then after the three had gone upstairs with you, their mate comes in and hides somewhere. As soon as they have gone and you are distracted he sneaks upstairs - by the back stairs if I guess correctly. They have left the flat door half open, and he takes away the carpet and any other evidence the rest have left. Off he goes leaving us figuring out this and that as best we can which delays us. Even if we have any idea where they are headed. Typical of what I may call an international crime. Very typical of dago crime. They just throw confusion everywhere. Not that it makes any difference. I already know what the next move will be."

As he stops speaking, and right on cue, a tall willowy figure arrives at the top of the stairs. "Good afternoon, everyone, gentlemen, Mr. Collinson, good afternoon, I trust I find everyone well, despite this unfortunate little matter. I'm Davenport, Justin Davenport of the Dominion Office. Just here to clear up the nasty smells, let in a little light on a murky subject, glad to be of assistance, don't you know."

Davenport was in full uniform - that is to say immaculate morning dress, complete with silk handkerchief and silver grey tie with a huge knot and a pin with a gleaming jewel in the centre - and looking every inch the fop from Eton and Harrow, Oxford and Cambridge with a few years at Yale and Harvard and on the Grand Tour just to top up his education. Charlie was at his shoulder and looking relieved.

"You must be Mr. Collinson, glad to meet you, very honoured, soon to lead England I believe." He walked across and shook my hand. Very muscular shake too, to my surprise. Rough hands too. He looked at me hard. "We need time to talk, Mr. Collinson. Very urgent. Things you need to know. Please wait on me here, sir. I will talk to these policemen first. Come with me, gentlemen. Charlie, isn't it? Be good enough to find us a small private room and bring us some tea, Charlie. As quick as you like, man. Mr. Collinson, I will be with you in 15 minutes."

He certainly had an air of authority so that even the policemen fell in and did as he directed. They sped off down the staircase - lifts still had a poor safety record and were not yet widely used in London flats although one is to be installed by the time I return from India in the spring - and I was left alone to enter my rooms again. I found myself stepping round the place where the body had been.

The place was as I had left it. Jumble of cricket stuff in one corner which I intended to clear out at the end of the summer, laundry on the table which Charlie would collect the next morning, mail partly sorted and mostly dealt with on the sideboard.

And the note on the floor. It simply consisted of a sheet of quarto paper with the day's date at the top of the page. "Dearest Mr. Collinson, Please forgive our intrusion but we felt you might come to your senses if we showed you that we mean business. Do not cross us or you, who have the repute of being such a calm man, may also lose your head. May good luck attend you on your tour of India." There was no signature. I suppose you would not expect to find one in the circumstances. It was the odd note of good wishes at the end. First, this crowd murder someone and dump the body in a man's flat. Then they threaten him and wish him good fortune.

Very strange. A bit like winning a match and then wishing your opponent the best of luck in the remainder of the championship.

I put the note back where I had found it and set about making the flat comfortable for the return of Davenport. I did not forget to put the kettle on for tea, as this seemed to be a priority in his life.

Then I knelt down to take a second look at the note on the living room floor. I was so intent that I heard no knock at the door, which I was sure I had shut firmly, and no footstep in the hall when suddenly Davenport was beside me.

"Dear boy, don't get up. I see they have left you a note. Only to be expected. They are trying your resolve. I feel we owe you an explanation." He strode further into the room, picking up papers, magazines and whatever took his fancy as he made for the best chair. "I suppose a cup of tea is out of the question, what?"

"I've put the kettle on. It will be boiled directly. Wait here while I attend to this tea-making. A biscuit?"

"You wouldn't have a cream cracker, would you? I adore them. Especially with a cup of tea at, let's see, what's the time? Five thirty! Good heavens. Mrs. Davenport will wonder where I am. Still, duty first." You might never have thought he was married. Too smart. Too self-determined.

I went to make his tea and brought it through on a tray. When I came through the door I saw he had the note in his hand.

"I say, I am most frightfully sorry that you have been involved in all this nasty business. Very distressing. Very upsetting for you, outside our circle I mean, not least because you met Miss Crossland so recently. Let me explain a few matters, Mr. Collinson. Sit down, this may take a little time."

He rearranged the cup and saucer on the tray with great deliberation. Put the plate of biscuits on the other side of the tray. Even placed the spoon on the saucer so that it was precisely parallel to the handle of the cup. He did it very deliberately. I watched fascinated by this odd performance.

"Well, Mr. Collinson, as you will probably have guessed I am from a branch of His Majesty's government that deals with the nastier matters of state. In simple terms - as the newspapers might have it, so to speak - I am a spy, but spying on those who would spy on this nation or bring us to our knees. Our branch has no name, you will see no mention of us in the papers or hear about us in the House of Commons and we are paid out of secret funds from this nervous government. I can tell you that there are only a few of us, all highly-trained men and women. We lead normal lives most of the time but sometimes we find ourselves involved in matters too secret to discuss and too dangerous for the ordinary man to think about without shrinking.

"It can be unpleasant but I guess that someone has to do these nasty jobs. Work for patriots I always tell myself. I can tell you, since I have the word of everyone who knows you that you have the greatest discretion, that there is blood on my hands, and that I expect there will be more blood on my conscience before I leave the service. Sometimes our enemies are Englishmen, plotting to overthrow the government, sometimes they are foreigners, laying their masters' plans for war.

"At the moment we are dealing with a gang whose roots are in India which is why the government planned to use you. Indeed it is why the whole of this cricketing tour of India was sanctioned, so that we might infiltrate your party and, by making discreet use of your services as captain of the team, gain an advantage within India. That is where Miss Crossland came into the scheme of things. She was orphaned at an early age, but her parents lived in India all their lives. She was born there and spoke more than a smattering of Urdu, Hindi and Bengali before her parents died. An important man, an ex-Army man actually, adopted her and saw she got to university. Then she was recruited for the service by a great friend of our organisation. Her adoptive father, in fact.

"Her little test, carried out the other night, was not the first tried on you. Do you remember the pick-pocket who tried to steal your watch in Piccadilly a couple of months ago. He was in our employ. We wanted to see how you would react; how quickly you would change from a party mood to deal with a serious situation. It was your mental reaction which interested us. We already guessed you would be physically adept."

I said: "I was lucky enough to see the thief coming out of the corner of my eye. I am blessed with extraordinary vision." I recalled the incident vividly, mainly because at the height of the scuffle, the villain produced a knife. Luckily, as I saw it then, Jake was with me and between us we managed to grab the knife and the attacker and get the police. They promised to let me know when he would be in court so that I could give evidence. Later I received a message that he had absconded. I now saw the whole incident in a new light.

Davenport had nibbled his way through all the half dozen biscuits on his plate and was helping himself to a third cup of tea. Mrs. Davenport would not need to provide his supper, I thought.

"I think I had better make it clear that I know all about the meeting you had with the Prime Minister last week but that Miss Crossland acted on her own initiative, after learning she had to work with you. She had a report on my desk the next morning. Don't worry, Mr. Collinson, she left out much of the intimate detail.

"Charlie, however, has already told the police he thinks the murdered lady and the girl he saw you sneak into the flats the other night are one and the same. That fool of a police sergeant said - without so much as a wink, mind you - 'we are still looking for Jack the Ripper and we may have him in our grip upstairs.' I had to remind him that when Jack was murdering ladies of the night in Whitechapel you were about ten years of age." He smiled and added: "He then said 'Perhaps he is following in his father's footsteps.' I suppose you are sometimes subject to those sort of remarks?"

"From the coarse and ignorant who seem to think that because I have a most un-English face I may not be trustworthy," I said. He made no answer and I did not want to guess what he was thinking.

"So is it Indians who have committed this murder?" I asked.

"They have to be the obvious suspects and indeed it requires a vivid imagination to know who else might wish to be rid of Miss Crossland," Davenport replied. "The note suggests that it was a warning shot across your bows but I guess there is more to it than that. I have phoned to my office to ask that her apartment at Viceroy Court should be searched and then guarded. I hope I may have a letter from her in tomorrow morning's post but it may be that she was attacked before she could send me notes on any suspicion she may have had. The police surgeon says she had been dead since the early hours but until we discover her recent movements we cannot be sure what has happened. He adds that she was strangled and that her head was removed after her death. Strangulation is a specialist method of murder in India."

"Did you work with this lady - with Miss Crossland - for long?"

"Not for long enough," said Davenport, dropping his voice. "We expected her to reach the heights in this strange profession. I am very much distressed by the death of this attractive, hard-working and imaginative young lady and I have orders from my head of department to spare no expense nor effort to bring her murderers to justice."

He looked round but whether he was weighing up evidence or searching for another cup of tea I was unsure. "Have you anything to tell me which can help us take this situation a step further forward?" he asked.

"I fear not," I said. "I met Miss Crossland once only. She left this flat after no more than an hour. It cannot have been much after midnight. I have not seen her since although I hoped she might get in touch with me. Ships that pass in the night."

With that he ended the conversation and said farewell, leaving me with the feeling that he knew far more than he had told me. Why otherwise would he and whoever ran his secret bureau be so sure I was not responsible in some way for Miss Crossland's death.

His departure left me to spend the night alone in my flat. I admit that sleeping in a flat that had recently contained a corpse disturbed me, although as a logical adult I knew that its presence could not possibly harm me. I almost sent for Jake to come over and spend the night but the thought of telling him the story was too much to bear and in the end I had as good a night's sleep as might be expected.

Sergeant Maynard had a point, of course. The flat in St. John's Wood was far from ideal for a Surrey player, except that it was not too difficult to reach the Oval and, for a captain of England, with all those meetings at Lord's, it was brilliantly positioned. Down the stairs, two at a time, over the road, turn left at the cemetery, over the main road, and there you are. As I found out the next morning when the sun was shining brightly and the air was fresh. Unlike most August days in London when the atmosphere resembles a Turkish bath.

I saluted the gateman in much the same way I might greet the opposing captain and presented myself at the main door at the rear of the pavilion. Two old chaps I'd known all my cricketing life were on the door but they still contrived to regard me with suspicion.

"Hello, sir, you here on some sort of hofficial business?" said the elder, resplendent in a blazer he probably wore during the Crimean campaign. It had clearly not been cleaned since.

"'E's 'ere as part of that committee meeting. I've 'ad a note from Lord 'Arris," said his companion.

But the guns at Sebastapol had been too much for the older chap's hearing. "You're Surrey," he said. "You can't come in unless you've got hofficial business. If you don't mind me saying so, sir."

"'E is official. Mr. Collinson is the new captain of England. You can't be more official than that."

"Now, sir, if you was the new captain of England and going to help Lord 'arris and the other gentlemen select a suitable party for Hindia I'd be only too pleased to let you in."

I waited patiently for the two to sort out my status but eventually they came to the conclusion that Lord Harris was referring to me in his note and that I ought to be allowed up the stairs, through the Long Room and into the committee room. The younger of the ancient pair, whose blazer had obviously been freshly brushed that morning and whose shirt showed signs of recent washing, guided me although he might have known I'd made this journey a dozen times before. He stumbled along so slowly that I told him not to bother. He made reference to some ancient by-law that insisted that professionals - I had always been able to play as an amateur - should always be accompanied through the Long Room. I guess they thought the pros would steal the paintings. Yet they leave the portraits of the great, the old books and ancient bats lying around without any impediment to stop any Tom, Dick or Harry stealing off with them.

Lord Harris greeted me at the door. "It's the new captain of England, Mr. Collinson," said the old retainer. "Be quiet, damn you," snapped Harris. "We have not yet made Mr. Collinson's appointment official. I only told you as a matter of information, not so that you could blurt this news all round the world. Be more discreet, man. You never know who might be listening." The old chap, dismayed at being reprimanded for his courtesy, slid away. God knows why Harris has to treat lesser men so badly, but he always does.

Not all the committee were yet gathered - which meant that all of four people heard the old man's premature announcement which cannot have been news to any of them - so we sat in an awkward silence until another ten souls gathered and Harris set the meeting in motion.

"Gentlemen, you all know Bernard Collinson, the captain of Surrey, at the end of the table. The sub-committee of five you voted to pick the team for the trip to India this winter - lucky devils, warm instead of cold, servants to do their every bidding instead of arguing and beautiful Indian maidens to fulfil their every wish! - have named Mr. Collinson to lead the party. I am not going to elaborate on their reasons, although a number of men had earlier made their intentions not to take part known to MCC. So we decided it was a great opportunity to test out Mr. Collinson with the thought that he was young enough to be a captain for some years to come if that was the desire of the selectors.

"I will be happy to take a brief discussion but I am asking for your backing for this appointment."

There was a buzz round the table and I heard various other names mentioned before a tall man in a high hat said: "We gave you the responsibility Harris, must support your choice. No doubt thorough discussion in your sub-committee - I'll support your suggestion and, my guess is that Mr. White will support me." Another man shouted "Seconded" as if he might be appealing for lbw and the rest fell into line without any discussion at all. "Substantive motion" someone called and there was a growl of approval and Harris stood up and motioned me to join him at the top of the table.

"Mr. Collinson will now give us the benefit of his thoughts on the tour," he announced.

I have to tell you that Mr. Collinson felt as if he had been slapped with a wet lettuce, as my father used to say. I had not a thought in my head but I remembered what Harris had said when he interrupted our dinner a couple of nights earlier and picked up on that theme. "Great confidence in whichever team I was asked to lead. . . looking forward to the experience. . . hoping to find someone with previous experience of India to give me some guidance. . . already spoken to Lord Curzon."

There were a few grunts of approval, particularly at the mention of Lord Curzon's name, and I felt I made a good impression. They all stared as I strode back to my seat, but I had barely resumed my seat when Lord Harris said: "Thank you, Collinson, if you don't mind waiting outside while I get approval for the team. As I told you the other night, you are not required to sit in on this discussion. Not your concern, frankly. But don't go away. We may still need your expertise if a member of your own side is under discussion."

I got up once more and went to sit in the Long Room. There was a Middlesex match about to start but I made little of the proceedings. Like most players I am a poor watcher of a match that does not concern me. After 40 minutes or so Pelham Warner came back into the pavilion at the end of his innings and saw me.

"Well, Collinson, are you here to spy on our batting? No, sir, I think not. Awaiting that bloody committee and the high-handed Harris, I'll be bound. They've named you captain and now they are going to hand you a sheet of paper with the names of your team. I know. It's happened to me a number of times. Imperious, stupid old man. Out of his time, you know. How can a captain take a player he rejects either as a man or a competitor. Still I hope you are able to make the most of it. Blyth's a temperamental bugger - but all slow left arm bowlers are. Lovely to watch from 70 yards away but impossible to captain. Try to avoid him if you can."

I said: "I've always go on well with the man but he is difficult. We had a drink together during the match last week and he seemed fine but I heard him speak most outrageously to one of their committee men and I see he is left out of the side, no doubt for that reason."

"So I hear," said Warner. "I'd find it difficult to see whose side I was on in that argument as the Kent committee seems to consist of fools who have never played the game."

"I also heard him berate one of the cricket reporters, using language that only has a place in a house of ill-repute."

"That's another well-balanced argument," said Warner. "I sit among them in the Press Box sometimes, writing my match reports and wonder if I live in the same world. Which particular . . " but at that point Harris emerged from the committee room and shouted at the top of his voice: "Ar, Collinson, taking more advice, I see. Come back in here and listen to the men we propose."

I said farewell to Warner who headed up the stairs towards the dressing rooms and went back inside the committee room. Harris had let the door slam behind him so that I had to open it for myself and when I went inside I heard some laughter which made me suspect that Harris had made some sort of joke at my expense - or perhaps Warner's - when he returned.

"That's our 14 players, including yourself. A manager is to be appointed and you will be informed of the name in due course. The committee has approved the list so there will be no discussion but we invite your - moderately expressed - comments," Harris commented.

I looked down the list. I was glad to see Jake Johnson. "Morrison of Derbyshire will be senior pro. Long service, intelligent man, could be the foreman on any factory floor," said Harris. "You pick your own vice-captain." His voice almost had a jeer as he finished that sentence.

"I would like to name Jake Johnson," I said and the whole committee laughed out loud. "I offered those present the chance to bet against Johnson as your choice but there were no takers," Harris said. I have sworn he was giggling like a teenage lass. "Anyway, if he's your choice, so well and good. On your own head. He would not have been our choice."

"He's dedicated to his craft, he has a good cricket brain and, as a bonus, he and Morrison are friends," I said, defensively, for I felt exposed by this strange way of appointing key men. "He is also a good friend to me which may be important if I am to take a party of strangers to a country none of us have ever seen before. There is bound to be tension from time to time."

"You may come down from your high horse, Bernard," Harris said, soothingly. "We need not start with a quarrel. We wish you well on your journey which, as you have already discovered, may have its adventurous side. I will have a word with you in a moment or two, but first we have two more items to discuss. Please wait outside."

I had to wait no more than a quarter of an hour which was passed well enough in the company of John Littleboy, the slow left arm bowler from Nottinghamshire, who was named where Colin Blyth might have been and who was 12th man in the Notts team taking on Middlesex in this key championship match. He was just 23, the descendent of coal miners going back beyond his grandfather's time and, not only strong in body, but well able to look after himself in an argument.

"I thought all Nottinghamshire miners were fast bowlers like Tom Wass," I said.

"Strong int' back, weak int' head, me mum used to say, isn't that what you mean, Mr. Collinson," he said. "Well, I didn't waste my time at Oxford or Cambridge, but we're far from daft in our family. You'll not find many men can add up in their heads as quick as I can, nor calculate odds faster. Mum was the daughter of the colliery bookmaker so I get it from him. She taught me how to back count, how to memorise figures and all that stuff." I liked him.

Finally, Harris emerged and took me to one side. "I have heard about your troubles. Some report of it may appear in the Press to coincide with our announcement about your appointment but that cannot be helped. I have had to deal with one or two hotheads who wanted another name in your place but in view of all the arrangements - and the fact that it would appear to kow tow to the murderers and their threats - I could not allow that to happen.

"I'm afraid there are a few unpleasant days ahead but the Press will not dare to report all the facts and you will escape lightly. At least I hope so."

And with that we parted: he to play more political games with his friends in the government, I to prepare for the great Indian adventure.

CHAPTER FOUR
September 30th, 1906.
London

The next few weeks have rushed past as I tried to fit a thousand private and public acts into my life.

There was the whole matter of Miss Crossland's death. The police wanted statements, the Dominion Office insisted that I went to their office and both read the notes on the case prepared by Justin Davenport and - most embarrassingly - Miss Crossland's own report on her meeting with me just to be sure, by cross-checking the facts as she presented them with my own memories, that she had written it and not her murderer. The police also had a book of photographs of criminals to be looked through lest I had seen someone hanging round my flat who proved to be one of the gang. Charlie had to go through the same business and insisted on discussing the incident endlessly with me.

The newspapers let me off lightly. Miss Crossland's body, they all said, was "found in an apartment block not far from Lord's" and, happily, I was given no attention whatsoever. Lucky to escape without my presence at the scene being revealed but I was too busy to notice much anyway.

There was also the small question of the last few games of the summer. Surrey were still engaged in a desperate fight to win the title which eventually went to Kent even though we had that astonishing victory at the Oval. I made two hundreds in the last two games, with little effort. The newspapers all agreed that I was showing the selectors that I was the right man for the job and that the new responsibility - far from weighing me down - might bring out the best in me. What rubbish they write. The truth, although they could not know it, was that when I got into the middle no-one could sneak up on me and demand that I answer another dozen questions about a murder. It was a relief to be out of the way of the main problem in my life.

Sadly, my captaincy was exposed in both matches since I

59

lost the toss twice. On the first occasion we were invited to bat first and caught on a green pitch at Chesterfield and bowled out in our first innings for 95. So my first hundred took six hours to make a draw. You know how it is at Chesterfield. The ball rears off a length and raps one on the knuckles, or hits one in the lower stomach or the inside of the thigh. Derbyshire have a gang of fast-medium bowlers who know every inch of the pitch and how to exploit it. You can see them in the annual averages; all with more than 50 wickets and conceding so few runs that if they had anyone who could bat at all they must win the championship every year.

My effort was wasted for we had nine wickets down when the rain fell at tea on the third day. The following morning, after a bad journey to Southampton on trains that seemed determined to ignore the timetable, I won the toss and put Hampshire in. They made close on 600 runs and so my second hundred in four days was again in search of a draw.

I was glad Jack Hobbs, still learning his trade in those days, was batting with me for a while because I felt we might have to bat together often in India and told him so. "I hope so, sir," he said in that careful way of his. We all knew even in those days that he was a great player in the making and of course he was given his county cap - by my predecessor - after his first county game. All the same I was never quite sure what to make of Hobbs. If I had been him - the greatest player of his generation and with a deep and intimate knowledge of the game - I would have wanted to lead Surrey and England but he seemed far too content to accept the belief that an amateur must be captain. Something to do with his upbringing in Cambridge and too much respect for tradition, I suppose.

I was also in attendance at Lord's many times in the six weeks between my appointment and our departure in the middle of October. I had asked for all the players who were not - like Hobbs and Jake, but not the unlucky Caversham, ruled too inexperienced, too raw - at Surrey or not in the teams we were playing to be at Lord's so that I could tell them exactly what I expected of them on the field and throughout our three months in India. Some were receptive to new ideas, others seemed to think they had wasted their time, and the rest treated their journey as an excuse to be away from home and have a good time in London. I suspect these talks had little value and I determined that if I led another tour party I would dispense with such nonsense and leave my talking for the long hours on board ship.

I was beginning to gain a fair knowledge of India thanks to a number of interviews I conducted with men who had been there previously. Lord Harris had been governor of Bombay and played cricket in the country, Lord Hawke had led two tour teams to India and I also had the good fortune to unearth a third man who had organised and played in a university trip to the place.

They all told me how to deal with matting wickets which I must see were stretched tight if we were to get a true and honest surface. They all said that since the Indian is cunning enough to avoid effort in the heat - and two of these gentlemen ascribed their behaviour to "native inborn idleness of the highest degree", a description I decided to test out before I believed it - most of the bowling was spin and that we might be unfortunate to find one fast bowler on the whole trip. The Indian fielder was far from enthusiastic they said and even in the heat we might run threes for any ball heading towards the boundary.

Hawke damned their cricketers in no uncertain terms. "Only half a dozen of first-class quality in the whole country," he told me. Harris was more generous although he told me time after time that he had to stop the batsman having drinks whenever a wicket fell. The most recent tour of India had been in 1902-3 when Oxford University Authentics contrived a joint venture with Calcutta Cricket Club. The Oxford secretary E. Britten Holmes was most helpful, although his tales of both the derring-do of his own players and the difficulties in travelling left me feeling some trepidation.

They all berated the standard of umpiring too. "Cheats" was an expression I heard so often I began to wonder if it might be true. "Are you sure," I asked Holmes. "Aren't they simply incompetent? After all we get mistakes in county games and in Tests, but no-one would dream of accusing our umpires of cheating. It's not on." But Holmes was sure and furthermore claimed it was no use trying to befriend the umpires as we learnt to do in this country. "They seem unmoved by charm, or inviting them to join one for tea," he said. He implied that, although he had not thought it necessary to try, that a pound note handed over at the right moment might win a decision or two. "But that's not what we want, old fellow, is it? We want a fair and square match and I don't see any way you will get that."

I told all the players we might have troubles. For one thing, bad umpiring unbalances a team. Paranoia runs round a dressing room. As soon as one or two top of the order batsmen get a wrong decision, the rest of the side begin to find excuses. No batsman comes into the pavilion without a story of how his lbw was going to miss the square leg umpire and the wicket-keeper taking the bails off without the ball in his hand and being bowled by a no-ball. The result is a very unsatisfactory game of cricket.

This tour was the most important ever undertaken by MCC to India by a strong mixture of professionals and amateurs, and at the end there was to be a match against an All India team in what was sure to be dubbed a Test match by the local Press. It would be regarded as such by the whole cricket community, whatever MCC said, and if they played out of their skins as a result we might be stretched. There was also the question of the crowd's reaction. We must be on our best behaviour. I reminded the players of this requirement time and again. One of the points made repeatedly by MCC was that they could see a big future for the game in India and they wanted me to be the head of a goodwill mission as well as a touring team. Captain, spy, ambassador, missionary. "What else?" I wondered. I felt that if I had been handed a broom and asked if I minded leaving India clean before I left that would be no more than I could expect.

Then there was the strange business of the 2,000 guineas deposited in my account. Not once but twice. The cashier at my branch in St. John's Wood pointed the first out to me. "MCC have lodged 2,000 guineas for you, sir," he said. I was shocked. I had the luck to be able to play as an amateur as a result of meeting the good man who sponsored me simply because he liked my style at university. Money never came into my calculations. He simply put a hundred guineas into my account whenever it ran down. I always had enough, since he also gave me one of his flats without charge. Surrey were generous with expenses too; I lived the life of Riley, whoever he may have been.

So why did MCC, who knew of my private income, show so much concern as to put money in my account? I asked Lord

Harris on my next trip to Lord's. "A mistake, dear boy," he said. Then he winked. "But we should like an account of its spending, just in case you are out of pocket. Give us some detail - enough to satisfy our auditors but you don't have to be too precise - of where the money has gone when you get back. If you are short we will make up the difference. If there is a surplus, no matter. And not a word to anyone. You are an amateur and must remain so. But a man deserves a reward for his efforts and, as you know, there are long-term plans for you in this game and in a wider field. We cannot send you on His Majesty's business as a bankrupt."

So I had another duty. A travel agent had been appointed to stay with the team and he would take care of hotel bills and train fares and the players would be given a small allowance but incidental expenses might have to come out of my 2,000 guineas which had to be accounted for. Oh dear, sonny Jim, as the maths master used to say to me at school, arithmetic is not your best subject, is it? He used to add: "If you don't improve I shall have to take my cane out of its cupboard." There was no cupboard and no cane but we liked the old boy and we gave him little trouble although I never became adept at mental arithmetic.

The other 2,000 guineas came from the Dominion Office, I was told on my next visit. "Just in case," said Justin Davenport, mysteriously. "In case of what?" I asked. "Shhhh," he said and giggled. "Just don't put it all on your fancy for the St. Leger." That giggle worried me, I am bound to say.

Our last match was at Headingley so it was an easy matter to slip to York to see my parents for a few days afterwards. I fancied I might not be able to spend any more time with them before I left for India and, such had been the rush, that I had only had time to send them a brief note giving them the news.

Whenever I walked from the station at York, over the railway bridge and right towards The Mount I felt that none of the problems that seemed so pressing in London mattered a twopenny damn. The city lies below sea level which is why the people there are so unwilling to move. The whole population seems content with its lot as its thousands head for their work in the rail yards or the great chocolate factories of Terry's and Rowntrees. Dad is a typical example. He brought Mum back from Japan - he'd been a sergeant shorthand writer posted to the British Embassy and she had been a waitress at the nearest coffee shop - after his discharge from the Army and because he had to spend the last few days of his service at Imphal Barracks he decided that rather than go home to Bristol he might restart life in York. "All right for a couple of years," he said to himself as he used his savings and his discharge money to buy a small shop just round the corner from the Theatre Royal.

Then I came along and it was a good place to bring up a young lad, especially as the Knavesmire was close by which made a wonderful playground for a boisterous lad. I got on well at my primary school. I made my way to Archbishop Holgate's Grammar School and my education prospered. I was able to go to Cambridge where I met the man who was so generous towards me. Dad was 60 and ready to retire. Even though I was at university I was far from a poor student and so between my money and his savings - "I'm a thrifty Yorkshireman since I came to live here," he'd say with a grin - Dad bought a lovely old house on The Mount where he and Mum could live out their lives.

I knew what to expect when I knocked on the door. Mum opened it straight away. She had to have been waiting for me. She had been nearly 40 when she left Japan and nothing Dad said or did, no amount of living in England and no amount of helpful advice from her friends, could wipe out the years on ingrained Japanese behaviour.

"Hello Mum," I said. "Otaerinasai. Welcome home, my son," she said and bowed deeply. In my turn I put my arms around her. "Come into the best room," she said and bowed again as I took my shoes off and she let me pass in front of her down the hall and into the room reserved for guests. A fire blazed even though it was still warm in September and a table was laid out with a feast that might have been designed for a son who had not been able to afford food since he was last in this house. Just Mum saying welcome home. She would have been far happier with half a dozen children but she had no trouble in lavishing her affection on her only son.

Dad came in and hugged me. I often wondered how this big affectionate man survived with a wife who was unable to display any form of warmth in public but I guess he knew she would walk through fire for him and that he would not have gone to all the trouble that comes to those who marry across the racial divide if he had not loved her very much indeed.

As for me, there was never any trouble in my life as a result of being from a mixed marriage. I got teased at school sometimes but I was a big lad and by the time I got to Archbishop's my reputation as a cricketer made me exempt from all forms of bullying. No-one mocks the school cricket captain, especially when he is 6ft 2in. At University there were more taunts than I had ever experienced before - and more behind my back I suspect - but gaining a Blue in my fresher year stopped the mockers in their tracks. I was captain for the next two years and playing for Surrey so that gave me an elevated status that put me beyond unpleasantness.

There was only one nasty incident although it changed the course of my life for the better. Going back to college late one night I met a bunch of drunks. They had finished their examinations and were letting off steam as one less tipsy than the rest tried to point out to me. They were just shouting and preventing me from going any further down the street and merely being silly when I heard a mutter of "Lets show this Chinky bastard how a true Englishman uses his fists."

Here comes trouble, I thought. I might have been nearly 13st but I could not take on six or eight drunks if they all thought the same way. At that moment I heard another voice which boomed down the street as if it might come from the town crier.

"Hello, sir, is there a fight brewing? Can I join in? If so I am very willing. Fighting is my business, or was, and I am still game for a scrap as our colonial friends put it."

I looked round and saw a man no bigger than my mother. Diminutive hardly began to describe the man. He was also slim as a twig, trim as a tiny guardsman, with a white beard that betrayed the fact that he could not be less than 60 years of age. He was wearing an immaculate evening suit which suggested he might be at least moderately well off. But the magnetic part of his make-up came from inside. He had a voice that could command attention anywhere on earth so that when he spoke you forgot size and age and deportment.

"Why, it's young Mr. Collinson. Are you troubled by these revellers? I do hope not. Now, gentlemen, you have had your fun. Please go about your business and allow Mr. Collinson and I to go about our duties too," said the stranger.

I did not recognise him but the others were suddenly sober. One or two said "Good evening, my Lord" in rather obsequious tones, the rest shuffled and in a minute or two they had all dispersed and I was left alone with my saviour.

"Good evening, young man," he said. He held out his hand. "I am Lord de Whittlesey. Some still call me Field Marshal de Whittlesey. I led troops into the Khyber Pass. You don't know? Well, you are wise to know nothing of war, it is a terrible business, but for a while it was the only business I knew and so I practised it with enthusiasm. Now I live in this town where I was brought up in poverty and went for a soldier to my profit.

"I have wanted to run into you for some time. I think we might have things to discuss. Have you the leisure to walk with me to my house which is a little way down this street and round to the right. Five minutes walk, no more."

I admit I was reluctant. Why would a rich and powerful man want to talk to a first year student? I followed him but determined I must keep my eye on this tiny, forceful man.

I need not have worried. His intentions were entirely honourable. We walked to the end of the street, turned right into a mews and so to what had obviously been a stables. Through a gate, up a stone staircase of the most ordinary type and so to an oak door studded with nails as it might have been in the Middle Ages. Lord de Whittlesey produced no key but appeared to touch one of the studs and the door swung open immediately. There was no sign of a footman or butler as we entered the hallway, which was fairly ordinary, but when we walked through into the passageway that led to the living quarters I gasped.

Here was every indication of luxury as it became obvious that the dwelling extended from one end of the mews to the other. The passageway led to a balcony that ran round three sides of an open hall that might have come straight from a Medieval castle, except that the hangings, and carpets and decorations were all from the Far East. Indian carpets covered the floors, Persian rugs were scattered in profusion, swords, shields, lances, daggers and armour of all shapes and sizes hung from the walls and down one side of the hall pictures of every style and background filled the wall. The richness of this huge hall took the breath away.

At one end a fire burnt merrily and, as my host pressed

switches and pulled cords, lights came on that turned the area into a brilliantly lit arena. I confess I had not imagined anything like it in a thousand dreams of glory.

"In Xanadu, did Kubla Khan, a mighty pleasure-dome decree," laughed the old soldier. "We left out the sacred river as being too ostentatious but I think the sunless sea may be Coleridge's way of describing death and we will all see that one day."

"It's handsome," I said, believing I must say something.

"Draw up that comfortable chair and I will get you a drink. What would you prefer? I have a good wine from, of all places, central India, which I press you to try. Or tea. Or coffee." I chose tea since I was hardly a drinker in those days and de Whittlesey spoke into a tube, presumably to the kitchen. "I keep one servant in attendance all night," he said and in a while an Indian lad of, as far as I could judge, about 14 or 15, brought a tray filled with tea for me and coffee for His Lordship and a plate of sandwiches and a brandy.

"Meet Raju," said Lord de Whittlesey as the lad poured tea and placed the other items on a table he found elsewhere in the room. "I found him wandering around Lahore, like Kipling's Kim, but with no English background. He is bright and intelligent and during the day he attends classes with the same tutor who taught my own children in India. At night he is supposed to be on duty but these occasions are rare and he is not exploited. Certainly not as much as he was in the markets of Lahore."

When the lad disappeared we made light talk for a while, mainly about a century I'd taken a few days earlier during a match against Essex. I had found the step up to university cricket from schools cricket, with an occasional game for the York club or Yorkshire Gentlemen, difficult. County bowlers were merciless and for a while I could not get the ball to short extra cover never mind into the outfield. But Essex were no great shakes and they had several lads in the side no older than myself. The hundred took me four hours but I was a much more confident batsman afterwards so that when Yorkshire asked me to play a game or two later that summer I was able to present myself with some aplomb although, as the world knows, my stay with my home county was short-lived and acrimonious.

I sipped at my tea and ate a sandwich but I still could not make out the reason for the Field Marshal's interest in me. It was clear he knew my history and that he had either seen or been given detailed reports of my performances for the University, but why was he so determined to meet me. I could have sworn that he had contrived our meeting although when I questioned him on the point years later he declared it was not planned and that if we had not met by accident he hoped to gain an introduction through the cricket organisation.

Eventually he stood up and turned his back to the fire and, with his hands clenched behind him, made a short speech. "I have been told that you are an outstanding young man," he said. "I know that you learnt Japanese at home from your mother and that your father taught you some Urdu, in a rough soldier's way, and that your examination results were so distinguished that either Cambridge or Oxford would have welcomed you. I hear that colleges vied for your attendance. You are an outstanding cricketer and there is talk that one day you will play for a county, for England and maybe lead them against Australia. Wonderful achievements lie ahead for you. So we must nurture you. It would be unthinkable for you - or others like you - to find yourself in difficulties because for instance you lacked money. So a small group of us, men who have too much of the damned stuff, have set up a fund which will provide funds to keep you flush. Private means are a useful asset. It allows an artist like yourself to live life as it should be lived, without a thought of menial work, without the need to make sacrifices."

He reached into an inner pocket and drew out a cheque. "Here is a sum to start you on the road to success, young man. If you give me details of your bank I will see that once a month a similar amount is placed in your account. Here is my card too. You may need to get in touch with me. Call here and make an arrangement. I am sorry it must be so formal but I have taken advantage of my retirement from an active Army life to pursue other interests. Not least my children and their many grandchildren. So I am not always here. In the meantime, enjoy your time at Cambridge and spend wisely. But I think I do not need to tell you that since you already have all the best and worst of Yorkshire characteristics. That is to say you are careful with your money, although not to the point of being tightfisted. So I hear."

I thanked him as he escorted me to the door. "I have told my young friend to go with you, although you will not see him. He will ensure that your rude assassins do not repeat their intervention." He laughed and pointed me down the stairs. "Go carefully and do not hesitate to get in touch with me. I will talk to you soon, young Collinson."

I had scarcely time to mutter my thanks before I was out in the street, the door closed behind me and I was walking home with a cheque for 200 guineas in my pocket.

All these memories of not so long ago flooded through my mind that late September afternoon as my mother busied herself with one of her main missions in life - to ensure that her son did not die of starvation - while my father asked embarrassed questions about the cricket. Since his arrival in York he had been encouraged by the locals to revere Yorkshire's star players and could not bring himself to understand why I had not been able to stay with the Rhodes and Hirsts, men he thought of as above reproach. So they were. But there was the most distinct racial bias within that club and I knew it as soon as I arrived. Better go now, I thought, and through the good offices of de Whittlesey I was able to move to Surrey after a couple of years achieving a residential qualification.

"Are you certain you have enough money?" he asked. Dad had never learnt the truth of my meeting with Lord de Whittlesey, although he knew I had met his Lordship. "There's a lot of hypocrisy in this amateur business," I said. "Surrey make sure I have enough cash. There's even talk they have a special gate reserved for payments they cannot otherwise acknowledge. I've a nice flat in St. John's Wood as you know. You can walk to Lord's in five minutes from my front door. That's been a blessing since I was made captain of this touring team because I seem to be summoned to meet the MCC committee every other day. There's a lot more to this captaincy business than I realised."

"It would never have happened if you had stayed at Headingley," he said suddenly, with unexpected venom. "Why did you do it, son? It was all I ever wanted. To see you walk out with a Yorkshire cap on your head would have meant a lot to me."

I remained quiet for a minute or two. I let the grandfather clock tick behind me for a full half minute before I answered. I wanted to find the right way of expressing myself and I wanted him to know the truth. Yet I didn't want him to be pained.

"The moment I walked through the gates I heard someone whisper - it may have been a junior player or a groundsboy - words to the effect that only true Yorkshiremen should play for the club. 'We don't need no foreigners' was his expression. Now that would have been acceptable. Whoever spoke that sentence was of no consequence. But when I arrived at the secretary's office he told me that there the concern was widespread throughout the membership. 'You may have a strange reception,' he said.

"I was introduced to the players and received a number of odd glances. I suspect they thought I might have foreign habits, or ask them to bow when they arrived in the pavilion. 'Is it right your mum's, er well, from overseas,' one said as we walked to the nets. 'Yes, mum's Japanese.' He looked at me for a long time as if I had suddenly appeared from the moon. 'Aye,' he said at last, 'next time tha'll find Yorkshire women are best.' I don't believe I have ever felt more uncomfortable. I knew how to deal with the situation. But I did not want to start my life with that great club by having a major confrontation. So I turned on my heel and went back to find the secretary. 'I won't embarrass you any longer,' I said. 'I'll find cricket elsewhere.' He was profoundly shocked and angry. 'What's bloody happened? You've no need to be like this. Come to your senses. You've come to the best county in the world and you're here five minutes and you want to walk out. What'll members say?' 'Judging from what you've just told me and what I've heard outside, they'll give a unanimous shout of 'Good riddance', I said and left him.

"Two days later I got a very unpleasant letter, accusing me of trying to stir trouble but I have no regrets and Lord de Whittlesey soon had a man from the Surrey club knocking on my door."

He interrupted. "There are a lot of people round here who call you a traitor," Dad said. "I must say I'm surprised but I guess you'll blame me for bringing all this on you, marrying your mother. Do you?"

"Not at all," I replied. "I could not have had better parents. And there is more to life than playing for Yorkshire."

"Aye, right," he replied. He didn't sound convinced but he did not raise the subject again although when we walked in the park a couple of lads playing on the grass in defiance of all the notices shouted "Yorkshire are doing all reet without thee, Collinson." So they were - with championship victories as often as not - which meant there should have been no regrets on either side. But they have long memories these Yorkshiremen and even if I win back the Ashes with a score to beat Reggie Foster's 287 and take 20 wickets in the match they'll never forget I lasted only ten minutes with their precious club before walking out.

When my stay finished mum and dad saw me off at York station. They had both travelled enough to know that overseas was not off the edge of the horizon but they seemed convinced that going to India meant they would never see me again.

Dad actually leaned towards me and said: "Fulfilled your destiny with this appointment, Bernard. Well done. And sod all these Yorkshiremen. They know nothing. It's a pity you didn't go to Gloucestershire and take up where the Graces left off, that's all I can say. Good luck, lad." Then he kissed me for the first time in my adult life so that when I got on to the train I was in tears. No kiss from mum, of course. She murmured "itterasahi", the phrase of final farewell rather than "sayonara" which is more in the way of "till we meet again". Heaven knows into what hell they thought India would prove.

As the express picked up speed I looked back down Platform One and saw mum crying too. And, for the first time in my memory, holding on to dad's arm as if her life depended on it.

CHAPTER FIVE
October 27th, 1906.
Bay of Biscay

At 4.30 on the afternoon of October 25, as the evening darkness of early autumn fell over Tilbury Dock, I stood at the bottom of the gangplank waiting for the last of the team baggage to go aboard SS Caledonia. All around me was the hustle and bustle that heralds the departure of every great liner: the farewells of loved ones who will not see each other for years, some faces tearful in grief, some joyful at the prospect of a new life or at least an adventure. Luggage was going aboard, last-minute passengers rushed across the quay, their suitcases half-open and obviously ill-packed; Customs men carried their forms and checked packages with officious zeal; a policeman sauntered here and there suspiciously as if he expected at any moment to have to repel a pirate attack or a new Armada. I was fascinated. To some it must have been an every day occurrence but it was my first trip abroad and I confess I was thrilled.

There were few to see us off. I had said my farewells to my parents in York - and a long goodbye to my lady friend Kate overnight - but only Jake's mother and father, and a whole family group belonging to John Littleboy, the young Nottinghamshire bowler I had bumped into at Lord's, had managed to make their way to see their lads leave the shores. There were also a small group of MCC men in their hideous ties (and one in a matching blazer); photographers from the Press Association and a number of the bigger newspapers; and the handful of reporters I had addressed for several minutes in the dock master's office.

"An important tour, a bit of cricket Empire building, carrying the flag, must show the Indians how the game can be played, looking forward to it, a great chance for the young players, to stake a claim to our Test team etc., etc." It struck me in the middle of my diatribe that I would not see my words in print next morning and then I realised that for the first time I was about to leave England's shores and all that had been familiar to me for nearly 30 years. Quite suddenly I felt tearful again.

I had thought more parents, wives and sweethearts might be present but even those who were gave their men a peck on the cheek and a wave and left long before the due time for sailing. These tours had become commonplace so that families accepted that if father was a cricketer he went on long trips abroad in October and came back with presents, souvenirs and a pocketful of money in the spring. I guess that I had been too much influenced by the pictures of relatives watching troops set off for the Boer War when the dockside was packed with wives and sons and daughters who feared they might never see their menfolk again.

I realised now, if I had been in any doubt before, that a cricket tour comes some way down in the list of important events on a world scale and that not every professional's nearest and dearest had the money for long train journeys to see the head of the family go aboard a ship. As I watched Jake said his final goodbyes to his mother and father; and slipped an envelope into his father's hand, no doubt a few guineas to make his absence easier.

As I tried to persuade a bunch of porters that a huge case with my name on the side really ought not to be left on the dockside I felt a tap on the shoulder. I looked round and there was one of the strangest men I have ever seen. He was no more than 28, it later transpired, but he was stooped, bespectacled and serious, a combination that might have led even the most observant person to think him in his forties. He must have been six foot tall but such was his bowed stature that it was difficult to see what his height might be. In addition he had clearly not received his full complement of neck vertebrae so that his head, topped by lank hair which was cut so that it almost sat on his collar, seemed to merge into his coat. He was dressed in a safari suit which added a further bizarre touch to his appearance in the mists of an English autumn. He had a bag slung from either shoulder and a suitcase at his feet and, from his dishevelled appearance, it was clear he was both late and agitated.

"Excuse me, Mr. Collinson, but" and here he stuttered over his next few words, although whether that was caused by nerves, embarrassment, a determination to find precisely the right word, or a vocal impediment I could not tell at this stage, "I am, er, that is to say, I wish to present myself as the person who will be, if I am any judge, the only reporter, or shall we say, cricket writer, or er, watching over this tour. Eh, hello." He tried to shake my hand but I made him wait. At this point he appeared to wish the ground would swallow him, or that he had never begun this conversation.

"Good evening, sir," I said. "I didn't catch your name. And which newspaper are you representing?" I have never liked reporters, forever asking questions in a flattering way and then running off to write that one is a fool. Or rather that they are one's intellectual superior. Or that if one had considered the lessons of the Punic Wars one would never have declared before reaching the other side's total; or batted on so long; or bowled one's favourite spinner; or failed to rearrange the batting order. Most of them had no more than a rudimentary idea of the practical considerations a captain weighs before he makes a decision. I suppose they add something to the happiness of the human race when they put the venue and start times in their newspapers but I, like most players, pay little heed to their prattlings.

"I am, sir, by name Cedric Mansfield, although in the Daily News I am known, that is to say, my nom de plume is, shall we say, I mean, Keeper, which is, if you follow their reasoning, sir, adaptable for both soccer in the winter and, eh, cricket, which leaves them with a difficulty now that I have decided - no, that is too strong a word - that it has been decided they can afford, or think they can afford, to send me with you." He seemed not only to have a stutter but to be unable to decide on even the simplest word without a debate on its merits in the context of each sentence. It made a conversation with him laboured, to say the least.

He held his hand out once again in a friendly gesture so I shook it. Or rather I supported it. It was more of a slippery piece of soap than a hand and I wondered if, should I chose to pull strongly, his whole arm might fall off.

"So, sir," he said, more businesslike now that the social niceties were done with, "is it possible for me to rely on your good offices from time to time during this trip? May I be allowed to ask questions of your battle plans, so to speak, your team formation, your inside knowledge of what has transpired on the pitch? Occasionally? I promise I will cause only a modicum of trouble."

I was actually beginning to warm to this strange man. "I see no reason why not. We will see how you make out with the players during the voyage and then we may allow you privileged access to the team," I said. "There is a reporter at Surrey who has such an allowance. He writes some notes for each scorecard, to keep the spectators entertained, and we tell him what to expect in the way of news and team selection. Bobby James? You may know him."

Mansfield turned up his nose as if he had been asked to condone the reintroduction of crucifixion for Christians or bear baiting in Trafalgar Square. "Yes," he said, after several attempts to overcome his stammer. "Yes, I know him. Neither Oxford nor Cambridge, I suspect. Perhaps he may have left dame school soon after his first birthday. By the by, I was at Cambridge two years after you. At a rather older, more famous college. We didn't meet." He spoke the last three words as if it was a matter of lasting regret but I rather gathered from his tone that I should be the one with regrets. His combination of diffidence and arrogance amused me.

"Join me for dinner tonight," I said. "In the first-class dining room. Tell the man on the door you are my guest. One or two of the players, including my vice captain Jake Johnson - do you know him? - and the senior pro Morrison and Wilfred Rhodes and Jack Hobbs, who may be a great batsman soon. Never mind that you don't know them. I shall dine with all my players in turn on this trip. I'll soon make you feel at home. Just a word of warning. I don't get along well with reporters as a rule and I know that Rhodes is not fond of the breed either, although you'll like Jake who is a great man and a saviour for me. Don't play the university card with Wilfred. He is adamantly against your sort, and mine, I'm afraid. He knows nothing of the quality of old colleges or new and he damns us all for fools."

Mansfield turned to leave when a thought struck me. "You aren't ready for a little extra work, are you, by any chance? Are you likely to be very busy sending reports?"

"I shall be glad of any chance to earn a little more money. The circumstances in which I have been sent out here are not remunerative," he said, his air of gloom suddenly brightening.

"Well, Mr. Mansfield, we have been sent without a scorer. The authorities tell me that they do not consider the job of any consequence and that they are sure that, for a few pennies, I can hire one in India. That may be true but if you have any expertise in that direction I will be glad to compensate you for your time."

He looked at me as if I had suggested he apply for the next vacancy on the Throne. "Scoring is my passion, sir," he said simply.

It was all I could do not to laugh. "We will allow you to do your best during a practice game and then we will judge you day by day on the rest of the tour. No promises. You stand or fail by your performance as if you might be a player but I think we can find half a guinea a day for your services if they prove satisfactory." His smile, the first of very few on that tour, told me I had found the right man and that if his protestations of passion for the work were correct we might actually have uncovered a small gold mine.

"I am very happy to accept, purely on a trial basis," the strange young man said. He looked relieved. I imagined then, and it turned out to be a correct surmise, that the money was important to him. "I have a new method, telling one more details than the old-fashioned method. I won't bore you with it unless you insist. . ." but he saw the look in my eye and his words trailed away to an embarrassed silence.

"Settled then. We'll see you at dinner. Oh, and by the way, the manager Mr. George Ramsey will be present. Everyone likes George Ramsey, I am told." I may have been wrong to allow my feelings about Mr. Ramsey to be obvious to a stranger but even so early in the tour I found Ramsey's presence irksome and his obvious influence at Lord's troublesome. The fact that he had upset me by betting with one of the players I could forget but a three-month trip round the sub-continent with an over-weight, middle-aged bookmaker and Surrey committeeman who was far too friendly with the players was not an attractive proposition.

Of course, there was also the off-hand way in which I was informed of his appointment. I had been given a list of players and asked to approve and then read in the newspapers that "this team, chosen by the MCC committee, is fully endorsed by the captain who says he could not wish to travel with a finer bunch of cricketers." I am sure that if I had been asked for an opinion I might have been diplomatic enough to put forward this viewpoint - for all the party's quite obvious shortcomings - but no-one had asked me.

The committee had, I learnt when I offered a mild protest, decided that when the list was handed to the reporter of the Press Association, this phrase was worthy of inclusion and that I would "be delighted to see it in print".

No mention was made of a manager and it was not until a fortnight before departure that I thought I ought to know who might be managing the team. I had delayed my question deliberately, hoping that someone would have the courtesy to mention his name to me, but when I was left in the dark for so long I had no choice but to find out for myself.

Lord Harris and I were having coffee at Lord's one morning and he had told me how Lord Hawke had stopped "those cheating little blighters taking a drink whenever a wicket fell" for the hundredth time and we had discussed the make-up of the team for at least the tenth time when I decided I could wait no longer.

"Who will be my manager?" I asked.

"Don't you know?" said Harris, as if I should have found out for myself. "Why George Ramsey, of course. Surrey committee-man. You must know him well. That's why we picked him. Fine chap. Rugby school but, sadly, no university. Some minor disgrace, they say. No doubt connected with his trade on the Turf. I'm surprised he's not been in touch. Go and say hello to him before the boat sails. Make plans, what! He's no stranger to India. Went with the Authentics, I hear. Nice man." And up he got and walked off.

I did have a chat with Ramsey before we sailed and we travelled down to Tilbury together. We also had adjacent first-class cabins on the boat. The best part of the ship according to Ramsey and he told me so at least three times aboard the boat train. Jake and the players were in the next class below - I cannot remember the precise definition but it was meant to imply that one was not quite second-class - and, as I later found out, the wretched Mansfield had only been able to afford some remote place between the engines and the horses. Later I managed to get him into a better cabin somewhat higher in the ship's rating, where he was at least on his own, by telling the captain I needed his goodwill to make the tour a success. When he was seasick in the early days of the voyage his quarters went a long way towards making him feel worse, especially as he had been in a bunk beneath a man "who cares not a jot where he spews."

As for Ramsey I was already beginning to wish he had joined the Authentics on their next tour to the remoter parts of South Africa. I passed him as I followed a porter to my cabin and saw him talking to a very attractive lady of perhaps 35 years of age.

I merely acknowledged Ramsey and nodded to the lady - I was not wearing a hat - but I sensed their conversation was flirtatious, if not downright intimate. Ha, a shipboard romance already, I said to myself.

I made an attempt to unpack for the voyage but soon I felt the ship begin to move and joined the rest of the players as the SS Caledonia left the dock. Ramsey was nowhere to be seen but I thought no more of it as he joined us at dinner in a convivial mood. Mansfield had changed into evening dress like the rest of us and I did not let on that I knew he had been sent back to his berth to change when he first came to the door of the first-class dining room. Better not embarrass so diffident a young man I thought. The words were hardly in my mind when a scene occurred of such cruel embarrassment as might test the tact of one of His Majesty's ambassadors.

We had just begun to sip our wine and to wonder when the soup might be on its way when the door was flung open, the flunkey who stood by it pushed to one side and a red-faced man of around 40 floundered into the room and shouted at the top of his voice: "Where is he? Where is Ramsey the fucker? Where is the man who has fucked my wife and we are not yet out of sight of land?"

It would have been comical if the man had not been so obviously distraught. His face was almost crimson, his eyes stood out like chapel hat pegs, as the devout folk of Yorkshire have it, and a vein in his throat throbbed busily. Agitated is too mild a word to describe his mood and the foul language he was using was a signal that he was in a state of distress since by his clothes he was a gentleman and one who probably only used the words of the gutter in moments of extreme anxiety.

Of course the suddenness of his arrival and the violence of his accusations made it impossible for any of us to disguise Ramsey's place at our table. At the first mention of his name we all looked towards him and the game was up. The man in a temper leapt at him but instead of landing a blow - as I and the others expected - he screamed at Ramsey: "Outside, sir, outside. We have a matter to settle."

To his credit Ramsey sprang to his feet immediately. "Come outside, sir," he said. "We can talk there without disturbing these gentlemen at their dinner." The other man turned on his heel and walked out and, without hesitation, Ramsey followed.

For a moment after their departure there was complete silence. Then the man who had been so rudely knocked from his post at the door announced: "Gentlemen, the soup" as if he meant to say "Gentlemen, The King" and, slightly stunned, conversation resumed, although it all concerned the sudden and dramatic intrusion and its only possible explanation.

I said to my guests: "I saw Mr. Ramsey talking to a lady about the same age as that man who burst in. I suggest that she is the wife he was referring to. I must admit I had not marked Ramsey down as a latter day Don Juan."

"Didn't take him long," said Jake, grinning.

"A bad mistake," said Rhodes as if he were discussing the exact position of mid-on. "Bad thinking. I mean finding a lady for personal gratification is not too difficult on these trips and especially a married lady. Something to do with the motion of the boat, they say. Very willing some ladies. Well, you just have to wait. Otherwise you are lumbered with the lady for the whole trip and that is bound to cause trouble."

"Most unwise," agreed Hobbs, solemnly, as if he had seen a young professional out to the late cut early in his innings.

"Patience and making a thorough analysis of the situation is the best bet," said Rhodes. "Mr. MacLaren gave me this advice on my first tour of Australia. 'The ladies here are very willing,' he said, 'but be careful, my son. It is my opinion that a promiscuous lady is almost always impregnated with a nasty disease'. I have thought hard on his words whenever such a temptation has been put in my way and I feel I am a better man for it."

Jake laughed. "I just dive in. Not too many chances for little wicket-keepers. But if I see the ball going towards first slip I dive across to take it. If you follow my meaning."

I decided to call a halt to this odd line of thinking. "Lets drink our soup and forget about this unseemly incident," I said. "But first, Mr. Mansfield, would you slip out and see if they are knocking one another senseless or merely shouting."

He went willingly and was back before the whole table had been served with mulligatawny. "They are sitting in the bar having a drink," he whispered. "I'd even suggest they were friendly."

I decided that no more action was needed and, although

Ramsey did not return to join us and there were two empty spaces where the angry man and his wife should have been sitting, there was no further reference to this piece of nonsense and the dinner passed in a friendly fashion. Much to my delight Mansfield turned out to be a decent raconteur with a fund of amusing stories about his Press colleagues and in particular what he called "PBI's" or "Press Box Incidents" in which normally easy-going reporters suddenly lost their tempers and committed all sorts of minor misdemeanours.

After dinner, an abstemious one at my table, we took a turn round the deck and then retired to our cabins. I walked down the short corridor, passing Ramsey's cabin on my left and what I presumed must be the married couples' accommodation on my right and wondered how the husband had discovered his wife's infidelity so quickly and how it came about that he and Ramsey turned from enemies to friends so soon afterwards. Perhaps it was all an embarrassing mistake.

It looked as if the voyage, which I had thought of as being a boring one, might turn out to be full of interest, if the first few hours were anything to go by, and I looked forward to recording some of this delicious gossip in my diary when I observed that the door of my cabin was ajar. The faint smell of a good cigar wafted across my nostrils.

I pushed the door open and, to my surprise, found Justin Davenport, the man from the Dominion Office, sitting in my armchair and enjoying an evening smoke. He was as immaculately dressed as ever; an elegant man at his ease aboard ship as anywhere else.

"Good evening, Mr. Collinson," he said with aplomb, as if invading a man's cabin was a daily occurrence. "I thought I had better let you know I was aboard and take this opportunity to have a brief discussion with you about the outcome of my inquiries into the murder of Miss Crossland."

"I'd be just as interested to know what you are doing on this ship," I said, slightly annoyed to find him so obviously in possession of my cabin. "You said nothing of making this trip when we last met."

Davenport took another deep drag on his cigar and blew the smoke across the cabin. "We'll come to that in due course," he said. "But first let me tell you that four Indian gentlemen were arrested this morning for the murder of Miss Crossland and that they will appear in court tomorrow, although only on a holding charge of vagrancy and possessing offensive weapons. Keep them in jail and out of mischief until we obtain more evidence. You may be interested to know that they were apprehended near the docks at Tilbury and it is thought that they may have been lying in wait for you. They were armed with knives and a length of rope such as is often used as a garrote. Of course, they may have been waiting for someone else but in view of this suspicion I was instructed to come aboard this ship and watch over you."

"What makes you think I was their intended victim?"

"I suppose you could say it was our adding two and two together and making five from it," he replied, flicking imaginary ash from his jacket. "There was little enough evidence to link them with you but they were clearly Miss Crossland's murderers. The police had been heading in their direction from the moment you discovered her body. Your man at the apartment recognised one in a photograph and then a police informant offered a clue or two. So when they made a number of inquiries in the locality about this ship we decided to arrest them.

"One of them had a slip of paper in his wallet with your address; they all had knives and one had the garrote. When they were questioned they admitted that they had instructions to seek out a passenger on this ship. They denied any attempt to harm anyone and they would not admit to the murder of Miss Crossland but we decided to take no chances. Their inquiries were so hamfisted that we thought they might be decoys and that another gang, or perhaps an individual, might be here to carry out the mission."

"I know nothing about this work, I have done nothing. Why should they want to harm me?" I asked. I was becoming perturbed about my part in the Government's scheme of things. Being a messenger in moments of need was one thing, but no-one had mentioned I might be killed before I had the chance to act as Hermes.

"You probably have nothing to worry about, my dear Collinson," said Davenport. "Besides I am here and so is a man of ours who will make himself known to you when the time is ripe." He took another pull at his pipe and made himself so comfortable in his chair that I thought it right to offer him a nightcap. "Yes, I'll take a small amount of brandy, if you don't mind," he said as if on my first day aboard ship I might have a full cupboard of after-dinner drinks at my beck and call.

"There's brandy but I am afraid there is nothing else," I said. "Then I will have to make do with brandy," he said and laughed uproariously. "Now," he went on once his outburst of good humour had passed, "what has been happening since I saw you last?"

"Nothing but cricket matters, a brief visit to my parents in York and preparations for this trip."

"And are you comfortable so far?"

"Well, at dinner we were interrupted by a bizarre incident in which the man in one of the rooms on this corridor accused the manager of my team of climbing into bed with his wife before we were out of sight of land," I said, laughing. "Afterwards the pair seemed to be getting along famously. I am afraid I shall never understand human beings and their strange relationships."

"And what sort of gentleman was this cuckold?" Davenport asked.

"Short and rather stout and very red-faced," I answered. "He and his wife are in the next cabin."

Davenport chuckled. "He is my assistant, sent to help me look after you with the help of the lady you saw talking to George Ramsey. Their little act was designed to deceive your would-be murderer - or perhaps murderers. Still I think there is little for you to be scared of." It seemed a very bizarre piece of acting to me but I made no comment to Davenport, having decided some time ago that he understood his own strange business much better than I ever would.

He finished the rest of his brandy, put the glass carefully back on the table and stood to leave. "All I ask is that if you have any suspicions you speak to me. I am in cabin C3 on the third deck. My bad-tempered, bad-mouthed friend will be just down the corridor. And the lady is equally trustworthy if he is not available. I will tell him to present himself to you in the morning. May I wish you good night, Mr. Collinson."

And, with a flourish, he left. I met him again frequently on the voyage which, strange to relate, was completely free of incident in complete contrast to its odd beginning.

CHAPTER SIX
November 20th, 1906.
On the train to Lahore

It was only seven o'clock in the morning when we steamed into Bombay but it was already baking hot. The sun shimmered on the calm blue waters of the bay and all round us tiny boats, some no bigger than the sort of thing I used to row around Peasholme Park on our annual family holiday in Scarborough, and all crammed with dark brown folk and the goods they hoped to sell to us or, more to the point, the passengers on ships leaving harbour. I thought it impossible for these little craft to trade with the massive liners on an equal footing but they succeeded with the greatest ingenuity. Shouts and screams attracted the attention of the passengers - and sometimes the crew - who would barter for the goods on offer and then, with great dexterity those goods would be hurled aboard for inspection.

One of my team, and I shall not mention his name for fear of showing what sort of man he really is, struck a bargain for a parcel of silk. I was standing behind him when he caught it only a foot from his right ear after it had sailed 50 yards like a good throw from the deep. He made to go off with the parcel. "You've forgotten to pay," I chided him, gently since I could not believe he was intending to keep the goods without throwing back the money. "Aye, and why not," he grumbled. "There's nothing they can do." I gave him one of my enigmatic smiles. "You'd better find the money," I said. "Or you might find I decide I can do without your runs and wickets on this trip." He pulled a few coins out of his pocket and tossed them into the water where, from nowhere it seemed, strong swimmers picked them up and distributed them to the rightful owners.

The little flotilla of boats gave way to the liner as we approached the wharf which was already lined with thousands of noisy, excited Indians, all apparently waving their greetings. "We're never going to be lonely here," I said to Hobbs and Rhodes, an inseparable pair already, as we watched the complicated manoeuvres that go with docking. We had been three weeks on the boat and we were anxious to be off, to get to the hotel, to take physical exercise that was not hampered by a rocking ship and to begin our tour properly. Rhodes grunted; Hobbs said: "Yes, skipper."

I think that more or less sums up the pair of them. In the specialised atmosphere of the dressing room they offered wise advice, on the field they were both always ready to make suggestions and when the team met in the evenings they were endlessly encouraging to the young cricketers. In other words they were perfect team men. But neither had social graces or they could not be bothered to use them. In truth Rhodes knew, and with good reason, that he understood more about the game than I ever would, and had probably given Hobbs, his junior in every sense, the same impression. So they did not think it worth their while to hold conversation with me except when they were strictly under my orders. At other times they ignored me. No doubt too that Rhodes misunderstood my motives for leaving Yorkshire and Hobbs, the obedient disciple, misunderstood as well.

Justin Davenport had been the perfect guard or protector throughout the voyage and given me hours of good companionship in which he had talked fairly freely about the difficulties of his work, the need for some ruthlessness in carrying out the government's orders and the way he had had to use every trick, every subterfuge to achieve their ends. He also spoke affectionately of Miss Crossland, whose killers were now in custody, even if their motive was unclear.

She had come from a distinguished family, Davenport told me, been well educated, gone to university at a time when few women were allowed such privilege, and then been recruited by her own father, who had also seen service in the secret government departments, for work such as she had been sent to carry out with me. I gathered there was no requirement for her to climb into bed with her quarry, as she had with me. This easy virtue had worried me immediately after her murder to the extent that I had consulted a doctor but Davenport told me to put my concerns to one side.

"I have no indications that she used sex to obtain her information," he said when in a moment of boastfulness or weakness or, bored by the long days at sea, I told him what had happened. "Miss Crossland did as she pleased," he said without the normal male snigger. "That was her right. If she gave way to you, sir, it was because she wanted to, and why not?" I thought his attitude modern and interesting and we never mentioned the subject again. Jake Johnson sometimes joined us at dinner, or for a drink afterwards, but I was seeing less of him and he seemed to relish his own company and to be strangely unfriendly towards me although I could not guess why.

As for Cedric Mansfield I saw little enough of him. It appeared he spent most of his time in his cabin, especially after he got one to himself, finishing a book on football, and writing articles with any player that would give him half an hour of his time. Occasionally I would make an arrangement to see him for dinner but he seemed not to care whether he attended or not. When he failed to turn up for one dinner I did not extend the invitation again. He seemed to have no idea of the obligations of touring but a very clear idea of how life should be ordered for his own benefit.

He was not far behind us as Davenport and I walked down the gangway. Davenport was still carried away with the idea that I might come to some harm. "I'll rarely be far from you, just in case," he said. "Never know what might happen next in a place like India." Nor did we. Even as I put my first foot on the dockside, a man leapt over the barrier that was supposed to separate the onlookers from the passengers and rushed at me. I saw him coming out of the side of my eye and - no doubt put on my guard by Davenport's words a few seconds earlier - ducked. Davenport swung his fist but the man dodged the blow and reached out to clutch my arm. I expected a knife to appear but instead the man simply handed me a large piece of paper. "Here, Collinson sahib, is the team for the Northern District who will play against you in your first match beginning on Friday." Then he turned and leapt back over the barrier and vanished. Davenport, the failed guardsman, looked crestfallen. I stared at the paper to hide my shock.

As I was soon to learn, India wraps its surprises in strange packages. My introduction to the ways of the country led me to expect the bizarre around every corner. Eternal vigilance is the watchword but, from the Indian rope trick to their way of switching from one language to another and the exotic women, nothing in that delightful, irritating, bulging, hectic country is what it seems. I had more evidence of this contradiction later when I was greeted at the entrance to the Customs House by a delegation from the Bombay Cricket Association at the bottom of the gangplank.

There must have been 20 or more of them, some dressed in the local fashion, some in Western suits, but a tall languid man stepped forward. "Mr. Collinson? I am Ravi Sharma, chairman of the Bombay Cricket Association. Welcome to India, sir. We are here to make your stay more comfortable and to accompany you and the rest of your side to your hotel for the night." I did not immediately pick up the implications of the last sentence. I was much more concerned to get my team into order, to see their luggage was delivered, to go through Customs and Immigration formalities, than to pick the bones out of a speech however perfectly it might be delivered with a classical English accent.

We shook hands with everyone in sight - or so it seemed - as we were hustled through the Customs Hall. "No need for you to go through these tiresome rituals," said Ravi Sharma. "First we have a small ceremony and then you can take your team to the hotel." By now all the team had gathered behind me, smartly dressed but in entirely unsuitable Western clothes, and we walked through several rooms and passageways until we came to a larger hall, already packed to the ceiling with hundreds of the locals. The noise was frightful. Behind me I heard one of the players say something about "a den of monkeys" but I could not identify the voice. I must, I thought, mention such remarks when the team next met, but before I could say anything I found myself on a large platform where a beautiful young lady hung a garland round my neck and dabbed a small red spot on my forehead.

Ravi Sharma then began a long speech of welcome. It was entirely in English and often touched with fine examples of the way the language should be used - but rarely is - but it was predictable and, frankly, boring. My attention wavered and I found that, tightly gripped in my fist, I still had the paper thrust on me by the young man at the harbour. I opened it and read: "The team of the Northern District to play against the team of the MCC in Lahore." The penny did not drop until I heard Ravi Sharma make a reference to "their long train journey so soon after their trip over the seas from England." Suddenly I became aware that, instead of beginning our tour in Bombay, we were to take a train to Lahore. That was not even on the itinerary I had seen in London.

I had to wait until the end of a very long ceremony, which considerably bored the rest of the players, before I could ask Ravi Sharma why the tour began in Lahore and not Bombay. "But you must have a better idea than me, Mr. Collinson. We were asked to make the change months ago in a letter from Lord's. We have made all the arrangements. You will be most comfortable in a first-class compartment. A short journey without changes. Straight from Bombay to Lahore in less than 36 hours. Servants all the way, fresh sheets for your bunk, a chance to see the countryside, excellent food and the opportunity to find your land legs once more before you arrive in Lahore on Friday morning."

By now I was fully awake to the possibilities. "But the match begins on Friday."

"Yes, but we advised MCC of this problem when we informed them we had carried out their wish for a change of itinerary." Ravi Sharma was not getting annoyed but there was more tension in his voice.

"All right, we'll get aboard the train - when did you say?"

"Tomorrow morning, Mr. Collinson. All the very proper arrangements have been made."

We were put aboard carriages and, having pushed our way through the throng to get to the transport, we were not surprised to find that a huge crowd saw us off and that at least half appeared to wish to travel with us all the way to the hotel. The place was no more than half a mile down the road and for every pace of the way we were followed by the hordes.

We were all beginning to get the picture. India was, as those who had been there before had told me, a bustling place but to a degree that astounds any Englishman brought up at what he thinks is a hectic pace but which is a leisurely stroll compared with the racing pulse of India.

The hotel was luxurious beyond our imagining. No need to worry about your luggage. Two servants would bring it to the room, unpack it, hang your favourite suit, instruct you in the workings of a variety of bells and, as they left bowing and scraping, appear delighted to receive the smallest coin in any currency as a reward for their service.

For the rest of the day I left the other players to their own devices. A long train journey, I explained, would leave them feeling tired and they needed all their strength for the match. I told them that I, Jake Johnson, granted an official role as vice-captain by MCC, and Rhodes and Morrison, who should have been my senior pro but was already showing signs of the serious illness which caused him to stay behind in Bombay and eventually be sent home without facing a ball, would select a team on the train.

I asked Ravi Sharma if he had any idea of how the pitch might play in Lahore and what the local conditions would be like but he gave me the sort of enigmatic answer that infuriates captains. "The pitch will be perfect for cricket, I can assure you of that," he said. "The weather will be beautiful as it always is at this time for the year. I suggest a sweater to start the day but after an hour you will be warm enough. As for your famous British rain, you will see none of that."

There is a golden rule in India, I was discovering. Ask a question and you get an honest answer. But if you don't ask the question, you may never find the answer until it is too late. And I forgot to ask what time the train was leaving in the morning until we finished our meal with Ravi Sharma. "Quite early," he said. I asked precisely what time. He said huffily he did not carry time tables; I should ask the bell boys or hotel porters.

I left the dinner table and walked to the porters' desk. The only porter did not have very good English. I looked round for help.

"Mr. Collinson? You look distressed. Can I help?" It was a man from the reception desk.

"I want to know the time of the train my team and I are to take to Lahore in the morning," I said. "That will be the morning train. Quite early I think." He rummaged among some papers. "We have a note to say your rooms will be vacated at 2.45am so I suppose the train will be an hour later. I imagine you have the tickets also."

Of course I then realised I had none. This trip had not been part of the schedule and I had not yet seen the man from the travel agency who was supposed to be looking after us. And 3.45 seemed early - or even "quite early" as Ravi Sharma put it - and perhaps the booking office would not be open or, even worse, there would be no seats on the train.

"This is impossible," I snapped and headed off back towards the dining room only to bump into our manager George Ramsey. "George, this is a mess. Our train is due to go in a few hours, it sets off in the middle of the night and I now realise I have no tickets and I don't even know if there is room on the train."

Ramsey grinned. I hated that grin but only for a minute. "No, Bernard, I've got the tickets. MCC gave them to me in our last meeting at Lord's. They realised by then they were going to have to fit in with the late change in the itinerary insisted on by the Indians and just handed me the tickets. I meant to tell you on the way to Tilbury but it slipped my mind. Never mind, all is well. Managerial skills of George Ramsey, what!

"I've told all the players - bags downstairs at 2am, leave at 2.45, train at 3.45. You and I in first-class and the rest of the side among the also-rans. Not a perfect arrangement but then this is not a perfect world, is it, Bernard? By the way, if you fancy a small wager, I am giving odds of 3-1 that Hobbs leads the grumbles, closely followed at a discreet distance by Rhodes. Couple it up at 4-1 the field for the November Handicap and you have a nice little double. Off course, of course, as I always say, and strictly against the law but no more for that a nice bet. You are not a betting man, are you, Bernard, but if you have any friends who fancy. . . ?"

I pulled him up short like, no doubt, one of his horses. "So are you saying that all the men are aware of the time to go, that you have the tickets and that the hotel will bring down our luggage for 2am?"

"I am, Bernard, and no, I don't want any thanks. 'Take the weight off the captain's shoulders, George,' they said at the MCC and I think I can claim to have been helpful in that direction. Is that right, Bernard?"

"Yes, manager, well done, you have been much more use than I have in this opening day of the tour. Although I would have been grateful for a word on the subject, but I am too relieved to complain at this moment." We parted - as I considered whether it was the right time to ask about his troubles on board ship which had never been discussed by the two of us - and, after I had said farewell to my guests, I went upstairs to find that my luggage had been packed, save for a pair of pyjamas and my toilet bag. A servant stood outside the room. "I am ready to carry the sahib's luggage and to raise him from his slumbers," he said in the tone of a man who does not really understand the words and who has had to learn them parrot fashion. "Thank you," was all I could manage in reply.

We had arrived in a truly remarkable country. I recalled the words of one of those who had offered guidance on this new experience. "You will love and hate the place in the same moment," he said. "You will want to cry some days and laugh at the joy of it all a minute later. It used to drive the old-timers mad, the sun, the idiosyncrasies, the wealth, the poverty, the numbers, the noise, lots of drink of course, the dust and the illnesses. By the way, if you want to stay well, eat their food. They know how to cook it, and that way you may, if you have the right luck, stay healthy. But if you order a salad, or fresh fruit, or eat at the roadside, you had better either prepare for days of Delhi belly or have brought with you a stomach like an iron pot."

Thanks to Ramsey's arrangements we made an easy exit from the hotel - leaving the now desperately sick Morrison behind - only 12 hours after our arrival and a swift journey to the railway station. There the chaos had increased one hundredfold. There were beggars, sleeping wrapped in blankets and water sellers doing a brisk trade since it was still hot in the early hours; porters and more beggars, whores, pimps, dogs being kicked, monkeys trying to steal food, birds under your feet and only a foot above your head; merchants haggling, passengers searching for their platform, railway officials chalking up times and pinning up typed lists of reserved seats; rich and poor, men and women, those with a purpose and those simply looking for somewhere to rest a moment; small children in their mothers' arms, big children complaining, tired children, over-active children, sleepy children. I had thought the crush outside the harbour was great enough and there was constant bedlam in the hotel foyer but this chaos was too much for the ordinary Englishman to endure.

Then, just when I thought I had had enough surprises for one day, came the final piece of madness. "If someone wants to do me an injury, this is the place," I was saying to Davenport when out of the crowd in front of me pops that same young man who had delivered the message about the team at the harbour. This time he was rather more cautious. He jumped in front of me but shouted at the top of his voice: "It's me again Collinson; keep your bodyguard at bay." I held out my hand and he slapped another piece of paper into it. "Please read all of your message," he said and just as suddenly as he had arrived he was off.

"What is it this time?" demanded Davenport. I unfolded the paper and found the sheet covered in train times, hotel names, dates and contact addresses. It was an itinerary much like the one I received from MCC. I turned the paper this way and that but there seemed nothing else to be read. "I'll read it again on the train and compare it with the original from MCC," I told Davenport. "Lets get aboard."

We struggled down the platform until we found George Ramsey and the other players who were arguing over the lists of passengers. "You're all right, skipper," said Hobbs immediately. "You're in first-class. We're in third." He did not have the temerity to ask me to join them, to see how the other half of the world conducted its travel arrangements, but I could tell he was not pleased with his lot and that insubordination lay just beneath the surface. And Hobbs is, I have to say, one of the more obedient souls on the circuit and not in a position to argue since he has spent a long time qualifying and must know that, for all his ability, his place with Surrey depends on goodwill from those in authority.

"Take me to see your accommodation," I said. We walked back down the platform and found their carriage. Basic, wooden slatted seats, cleanish and empty apart from my players. "Fine," I said. "I could make a point and George and I could come to be with the rest of you, but that would only mean less room for you." Then I remembered the cash MCC had given me.

"George," I said quietly to Ramsey who was standing at my shoulder. "I want you to inquire if there are enough first-class seats for the rest of the party. I've been given emergency funds so I'm quite happy to pay. Don't make a lot of noise about it because if the men see there's a chance of getting better seats and then there's nothing doing they will be disappointed. And here's a few rupees to grease palms if you think that necessary."

Ramsey was off in a flash and back too quickly to have had any great success. He returned my money with the bad news. "Nothing doing I'm afraid. Someone had just taken the last few seats. We could have squeezed in there too. Still. . ."

As he was finishing his sentence a small, squat man who could only be described as ugly but none the less immaculately dressed in a black suit. touched me on the elbow. I find it difficult to say just how ugly this little man was but his wretched visage was not his outstanding feature. On top of his brown, sweaty and shiny head was the worst wig I have ever seen in my life.

"Collinson?" he asked.

"Yes, I'm Mr. Collinson," I said, with a touch of pomposity, since I have never liked being called by my surname at school or by my county captain. Too many Indians fail to understand the difference between a given name and a family name and even though I had been in the country such a short time the fact had already begun to irritate me.

"I am your travel agent, sir, by name one de Silva."

I misheard him or misinterpreted his meaning. "Well, Juan," I said, "you are late for duty. Why weren't you at the docks this morning, or at the hotel?"

"My instructions, direct from our branch in London, insisted that I meet you here - see," he said and held out a piece of paper covered in the same figures that had just been handed to me by my own mysterious messenger.

Right across the top in bold capitals were the words "Meet at Bombay Central Station 2am." Did he write that instruction on his copy of the itinerary himself? Alternatively, whose mistake was it? At 2.30am on my first day in India, I did not even dare inquire.

"Right, Juan," I said, "welcome to our little party. Can you see if you can do anything to help us put all the players in first-class. Third-class may be all right but it would be better if they could all be with me. Oh, and here is a few rupees if that helps."

"Yes, sir. But I have just purchased enough first-class seats for you all. As soon as I realised you had - mistakenly I think, sir - been separated I decided that it would be better if you were all together and I bought enough tickets for you to travel in comfort and together. I am glad I anticipated your need correctly. And I look forward to being recompensed for my initiative."

Just in case I misunderstood him he offered a receipt which I paid immediately. Another moment of Indian trickery, I thought. Afterwards I came to the conclusion that he had bought unsold tickets cheaply as the train was soon to leave and that I might have bartered about the price.

I walked back to the compartment where Juan's lower orders were sitting and, quite frankly, sulking. I ignored their dirty looks and brought something like cheer to their faces with a short speech. "Pick up your stuff and follow this gentleman" - I pointed out Juan or de Silva - "to your new lodgings. And you had better be nice to him because for the journey back here next week we will need his good offices again to get you better accommodation." The party moved into the new seats with some good grace - although as George Ramsey predicted Rhodes and Hobbs grumbled softly to each other all the way - but just before the train moved out of the station we were settled down and I could begin to relax or even take a few hours' sleep.

CHAPTER SEVEN
November 25th, 1906.
On the train back to Bombay

I think we all felt better for a good night's sleep and most of us dozed right through until noon when we were only a few hours from Lahore. I had a meeting with Jake and Wilfred - while George Ramsey, who should according to MCC thinking have been a major part of the selection process, poured the coffee - and we chose the strongest team available for the first match. Our idea was that we did not know the conditions and that only the best side might be able to overcome whatever unusual circumstances we found. We were already without the steady Morrison and I hoped his absence would not be felt. I gave the team to Cedric Mansfield, who had by some mysterious method found his way into the first-class seats, to use as he pleased. True enough, as soon as we dismounted at Lahore he headed off for the telegraph office and was not seen until his duties as scorer began.

Of course we had to head straight for the ground and arrived with only half an hour to spare ahead of the match. I had changed into whites and a blazer, immediately went to the home side's dressing room and handed my team to their captain Mahmood Baig and invited him to the middle for the toss. It was my first as England captain and I wanted everything to be right; and I was very excited. But first there was a new discovery. My little committee and I had spent hours on the train, not only picking the team but discussing what tactics we might use on the matting wicket.

Lord Harris's advice had been to bat first if we won the toss, to take our time making runs so that the Indian side, whoever they were, would become frustrated. We must, he said, try hard for the first few overs of their innings to bowl a few out when we might see a total collapse. He did not have a high opinion of their morale; "but watch the buggers, they are up to endless tricks," he said, sniffily, as if he had never tried a trick on a cricket field in his life.

Well, we came up against the tricks long before the game began. I saw as soon as I reached the pavilion that no mat had been laid and asked the nearest official why not. "But, sir," he said, as a grin spread from one side of his face to the other, "surely you are aware that we no longer have matting wickets in this part of India. In Bombay and Madras and Cawnpore I am sure you will still find mats but in Lahore we have had natural pitches ever since the Authentics left behind one of their men to instruct us in this art. We have prepared for you one of the finest pitches you will ever see, sir. Go to the middle and win the toss, sir. And bat for two or three days if you wish." He was a tall, distinguished man in a turban and wearing a magnificent set of whiskers and I guessed he had been a cricketer in his youth. So I decided that, as one cricketer to another, he was telling me the truth.

So keen was I to inspect the pitch that I hardly noticed Baig's actions but Rhodes told me afterwards that he practised tossing his silver rupee several times and then left it lying on the pitch. When I finished my inspection, which taught me little since I was not able to judge whether the cracks in the ground might keep their hard edge or aid the spin bowlers late in the game, I invited him to make the toss and, according to Rhodes, he did so with a second silver rupee. He must have had a great store of these coins for he tossed it as high as he could and distracted me by pointing to the coin on the ground. "See how it lies," he said. Behind my back one of his players caught the second silver rupee and quietly put it in his pocket. So I was told by Rhodes at any rate. I was aware of absolutely nothing amiss.

Rhodes stuck to his story even when I told him that I had won the toss. "I don't understand that bit, skipper," he said. "This is a funny country and no mistake." This little incident left us both mystified.

"We'll bat, skipper," I had said to Baig in the time-honoured phrase. Baig shook his head solemnly. "Not in the sub-continent, Mr. Collinson, whatever W.G.Grace has said on the subject. Not here, sir. However, if that is your desire. But next time, you will remember to bowl first and take advantage of the dew" and he shrugged his shoulders as if he wished he had given me this piece of wisdom an hour earlier. My brief look at the pitch had detected no dew or anything else that might induce me to bowl first. I was so flummoxed that I put my hand down on the wicket again to search for any sign of wetness. The pitch was as dry as Baig's handshake.

On my way back to the pavilion Rhodes, who had been standing 20 yards behind us during the toss told me of the little trick that had just been played on me. He chuckled as he spoke and I suspected that he was already working on a similar idea to be carried out next summer at Headingley or Huddersfield or in one of those other spots where Yorkshiremen practise their black arts.

I sent Rhodes and Hobbs in to bat and put myself at No.3 and told Jake he was in charge of the rest of the batting order, to send the non-players to find a net and asked George Ramsey to sort out the hotel. By now it was a lovely autumn day, the sun just below its zenith, a cooling breeze from the north-east; perfect conditions for any human activity, game, war or race meeting.

We had another shock at the start of the second over. The first came from Baig himself at little more than medium pace: middle-age trundle without the nasty venom, as Jake put it. But the second over was bowled by a giant and he worked up a pace that made both Rhodes and Hobbs hop about. No fast bowlers in India, are there, I thought. I wonder how many other differences we will find here?

Still nothing came of these surprises and by lunch the pair had reached 80 in an hour and a half, at tea they were both approaching their own centuries and at the close I was batting and fifty not out from 325 for two. Rhodes had gone, more because he was too hot and bothered than because of the bowling skill and Ken Hutchinson from Kent got a nasty ball that kicked off one of those cracks. Hobbs was long past a century and looking as if he might be the most prolific run-scorer for years as we had all suspected. He returned to the pavilion red-faced, blowing slightly, but far from weary without a mistake to his name in five hours.

As for batting first, I had clearly made the right decision. The fast bowler had soon lost his pace and not one ball had seriously misbehaved all day. What's more, I detected in the faces of the fielders were discontent with their lot and I suspected Harris was right. We would bat as long as we could and then let the quick men off the leash and see how much steel was in the Indian backbone.

"No danger of us losing this one," I said when Mansfield came to ask me how I felt the day had gone and he studiously wrote that down in what looked like a schoolboy's new exercise book. I suspected he was not quite the mighty force with his newspaper that he pretended. Yet on the voyage out he had conducted an interview with me that showed some perception, although when he approached the subject of my mother and leaving Yorkshire he was clearly at a loss to know how to express himself properly. Somehow all the inhibitions of his past at public school and Cambridge prevented him understanding how the rest of the human race lived and there were times when his attempts to select precisely the right word delayed his questions intolerably.

He carried his scorebooks as if it might be a Shakespeare first edition signed by the author and told me that the scoring had been instructive since it had allowed him to meet two local men. "I knew they would be good scorers as soon as I saw them since they sat bolt upright like soldiers on parade. They missed nothing, they must have the sharpest eyes on the planet and when some of their relatives came into the scorebox they allowed them to stay only on condition that they were quiet. I think," said Mansfield, once again afflicted by his difficulties with the mot juste, "that quiet is, shall we say, or maybe I can put it this way, a comparative term in the, er, sub, er, in these parts."

After the day's play they invited him to their home but he said he might wait for another occasion and pleaded much work back at the hotel and tiredness. "I may have offended these nice gentlemen," he said wearily, "but I am worn out and a long sleep will be more helpful than a heavy meal and the need to maintain social niceties. I think you will find the same." He sometimes spoke to me as if I were suffering from some sort of brain disease even though my degree was a better one than his own. But in his eyes going to an older college was so much more important than the result of three years at university.

I went to the hotel wishing nothing more than a simple evening meal, a chance to study those two notes handed to me in such a strange manner at the landing place and the railway station and a long sleep. But fate had other plans.

The new hotel was nothing like as luxurious as the palace in Bombay but the rooms were more than adequate, the servants just as numerous and the crowds outside just as attentive, clamorous and determined to secure autographs and handshakes. I got down from the carriage that brought us from the ground and

97

had to force my way through the throng, all of whom seemed to know my name - "Collinson, Collinson" they shouted - until I was glad to get into the calm of the inner courtyard. Stern policemen or security guards kept them behind a line with those long thin canes they call lathis and every so often picked out one noisy client for a few blows just to encourage the others.

Inside the scene was slightly more subdued but I went straight to my room - with Davenport's assistants in the room next door - to find, once again, that all my unpacking had been completed. I had hardly been in the room a few minutes when there was a knock at the door and in came a very pretty maidservant, accompanied by her own servant or bearer. A third man stood outside; presumably he was the bearer's bearer. The maidservant wasted no time in demanding that I ask for her by name - which I now forget - if I wanted anything. She was, it seemed, especially assigned to my room.

She also let me know that her brother was a cricket enthusiast and that he would be attending the remainder of the match if some kind person would only give him a ticket. "I wish I had one to give him," I said. I thought that leaving England for India might rid me of the burden that goes with the belief among so many people that the captaincy of a side brings hundreds of free tickets in its wake. Obviously not.

My maid gave no reply except to hand me another large sheet of paper like the one the lad gave me in Bombay. "This paper was left for you at the desk," she said. "The bearer said I must tell you to read it carefully." With that she swept out of the room, taking her servant with her.

I decided to take her literally since I had received the same message from the man at the railway station. I fished out the other two sheets of paper and examined them every way I could. Still I could find nothing except the most obvious message.

Finally I took all three pieces of paper to the paraffin lamp to see if I could detect any clue by holding the paper in front of the light. Suddenly words began to appear. It was the oldest trick in the world, beloved by science masters and schoolboys alike, a message sent by onion juice which only becomes visible when heat is applied. I made haste to jot down the messages but I did not have to work long. They were, thank heavens, identical and it was clear that someone had been concerned that I should get the message and was prepared to send it to me again and again until I understood.

It began: 'Collinson, This will be our method of communication in future. There is nothing for you to do at the present so enjoy your cricket while you may for shortly a great conflagration will begin which involves every nation on earth. Watch out for Mahmood Baig for he is a cunning devil and will lay a plan today that will trap you a month later. Yours, The Captain.'

As I thought out the meaning of that extraordinary note a knock came at the door. It was the maid once again, with her troop of attendants, explaining that she now understood that I was the captain of the team, a great man in my own right, and that I must be able to obtain a ticket for her brother. I said firmly that I had no tickets, that they were in any case very cheap and that she must seek elsewhere. She went away without a word.

I had arranged to meet Jake Johnson, Justin Davenport, Wilfred Rhodes and John Littleboy, the slow left arm bowler from Notts who had been at Lord's the day I was ordered out of the committee room while the mighty men picked the party for this tour. We would start in the bar and then take a leisurely dinner. Young John was not playing in this match but I had hoped he might find Rhodes had time on his hands and pick up a few hints.

Rhodes had been suspicious of him at first but he could not resist the temptation to show off his tricks and his assertion, often repeated to young Yorkshire players, that cricket "is not just about batting, or bowling or keeping wicket or fielding but about ALL aspects of the game" was one I felt Littleboy might do well to note. It was an important tour for the boy and I wanted him to get as much out of it as he could. Funnily enough he had seemed to get along with Cedric Mansfield better than anyone else. Mansfield could tolerate mortals without education if they were talented cricketers. He seemed totally unable to deal with anyone of his own high standards of education.

First I took a stroll out on to my balcony and watched the great moving mass of traffic out on the road. I had taken the opportunity to read a little of Kipling's work before I reached India. From his pages you can smell the dust and the dirt, hear the noise, see the people; here I had the chance to witness the India of Kim, which begins in Lahore, pass in front of my eyes.

As I walked down the long, broad corridor towards the bar my maid was there again. She repeated her message in a different vein. Surely I must know someone who would provide her brother with a ticket. I referred her to Ramsey who deserved a little excitement in his life.

The bar was ornate and welcoming after a long day in the field, but the beer was nothing to make us reach readily for a second glass and we soon adjourned for dinner next door where we were served by enough waiters to staff a whole British restaurant. I chose the Indian menu, bearing Harris's advice in mind and advised the rest to do the same, but the died-in-the-wool Yorkshireman Rhodes would have nothing save steak, although he ate as if he were being charged by the mouthful. He pronounced it tough and no doubt it was, but I had nothing to complain of either in my rice or curry. I made a note to inquire further about Indian food in detail and to try a variety of dishes.

The meal passed quickly but my hopes that Rhodes and Littleboy would form a greater alliance were clearly too optimistic. Rhodes talked to the boy but you could see the canny man had decided that he had to serve an apprenticeship and that he would do nothing which might turn him into a rival for an England Test place. How short-sighted, I thought, but Rhodes like all the professionals, needed to earn a living by his cricket and it would have been surprising if he had opened the gate for a youngster to deprive him of a wage packet no matter how far into the future.

We adjourned to the lounge for coffee and sweets, a delightful finale to our dinner and, not for the first time on this trip, I noticed how quiet Jake Johnson had become. "Got something on your mind, Jake?" I asked when the others had gone, either for a walk around the terrace or immediately to their beds.

"No, skipper, I'm at peace with myself," he said. There was an edge to his "skipper" so I persisted. "We don't see much of one another," I said. "Is there a problem?"

"No, but I am worried about my father who was taken ill just before we left and I guess I would be reassured if I had a letter from him."

"You could send a cable via MCC," I suggested. "They told me their secretariat would be helpful if there was such an emergency. Is your father seriously ill? I can despatch a message in the morning and, such is the miracle of modern science, and the time difference, you might have a reply in 24 hours."

Jake seemed to perk up. "Cable, eh. Um. Would you be so good as to try it? How does it work, skipper? I'd like to see that in operation."

I paused and tried to recollect what the lady in the office at Lord's had told me. "You simply write out your message and it goes much like a telegram back home," I said. "Lets try it in the morning. I don't suppose their offices are still open. Better still, lets consult young Mansfield. He has spent most of the evening sending his reports back to England. If he is being paid half a guinea a day by all those papers he has picked up in the last few days he must be worth more than you and I put together."

Jake laughed and once again there was an edge to his voice when he said: "He'll have to work bloody hard to accumulate more money than you, skipper."

I ignored the remark and called over a porter who happened to be passing. "Ask Mr. Mansfield to come to see me," I told him.

It was some time before Mansfield appeared, still wearing his perpetual and by now crumpled safari suit, looking disgruntled and constantly glancing round as if he suspected he might be followed.

"Ah, Cedric, Join us in a cup of coffee, or something stronger if you would care for it." Mansfield grunted an acceptance of a brandy. He was clearly not pleased to be disturbed and had the bad grace to make it obvious.

"Look, Cedric, you can be of great help to us," I said. "Jake here has a family problem. His father is ill and he wants news. Tell how this cable stuff works. Is it satisfactory? Is it efficient? What does one do to put a cable through to Lord's?"

Mansfield was lost between his desire to show off about his work and his annoyance at being asked such a trivial question when he wanted to be elsewhere. "Simply go to the porter's lodge and hand him your message, properly addressed," he snapped. "I have sent half a dozen messages today - and I might add I have two more to go - and all but one seem to have arrived.

"Indeed I have had confirmation" - and here his desire to be properly modest, not to state his own case too strongly, and his wish for the world to know that he was a highly successful reporter, made him stutter furiously - "and I may say, or perhaps it is wrong of me to be so bold, or, well, a couple of what I can only describe as congratulatory notes."

"So you had no trouble in despatching your reports?"

"I think that overstates the case somewhat, but in the main it is a simple process that anyone, even, someone without experience could accomplish." It sounded as if he had been caught half way through a thought that even an idiot who had been to the wrong college at Cambridge could send such a message and deciding that no-one ought to talk to the England captain in that way. Really, this was the most irritating man. But there was no question about his skills. If only he could accept his ability and not want to demonstrate it repeatedly. Thank heavens he was not one of my cricketers or I might have had to spend more time on his foibles than on the rest of the team together.

Jake joined in. "We'll try this method of yours in the morning, Mansfield," he said. "I'd certainly like to know how Dad is progressing. My father had enough strength to see me off at Tilbury but my mother rushed him away as soon as possible with the intention of sending him straight back to bed. He insisted on being at the ship. Why do they all think they will never see us again?" he grinned.

"My parents declined my invitation to go to Tilbury," said Mansfield, suddenly vulnerable. "They said that my uncle Edward made a dozen trips to India in the days of sail and that they were sure I would be as safe there as I had been at school. Father said the food would be better and that I was unlikely to be beaten for wearing the wrong cap. I'm afraid my parents regard their children as a necessary nuisance; someone to leave their money to." He began to stutter even more. "I don't think they like us very much, my sister and I. Still, she did come to the station with me." Then he subsided into his chair, cringing almost as he considered whether he should tell us so much of his family.

Jake sprang to his feet. "To bed, or rather to a short run, a few press ups and so to bed. I'll call on you at 7.30 in the morning, Cedric, so be ready to talk me through this cable business." In a flash he was off, the fit athlete bored with the conversation and ready for action.

Mansfield did not linger. "I'll see you in the morning, Bernard," he said formally. "Provided Johnson leaves me with enough energy I will be back on duty. I may say that, thanks to your invitation to be your scorer, it looks as if this trip may be profitable for me in many ways. In addition several newspapers besides my own have observed my presence here and asked for reports. All different, of course, which is a problem since they all have to be typed and taken to the cable offices where a certain amount of cajoling is necessary to produce action. My friends in the scorebox were helpful in this little matter. When I said to them that some of my reports seem to lie long in the in-tray at the cable office one of them - Aktar, I think is his name - went with me and delivered a long speech in Urdu. He said it was to the effect that they were letting their people down but he then suggested that if I left two rupees on the small dish at the front of the cable office it might help and, true enough, my cables went without let or hindrance afterwards."

"What about the Daily News?" I asked. "Do they mind you working for other newspapers?"

Mansfield became expansive. Once into his stride his inhibitions and his stutter were forgotten. "They have only insisted that my identity should not be compromised," he said. "The sports editor sent an immediate cable saying I would be sacked if reports appear in other newspapers but he may have had second thoughts, or perhaps wiser, more economic considerations were brought to bear. He sent a second cable agreeing to my working for other papers, although he also laid down that I must not despatch anything to their main rivals. Since I am the only reporter here I can, first of all, pick and choose and, secondly, the greater public has no idea who is doing what. The rest of the press will, sadly, have to make do with agency reports and those will not be many I suspect."

I remembered a journalistic offer of my own as he spoke. "Pelham Warner suggested I might, without a contract, and when I pleased, send back a weekly letter to the Daily Telegraph and that he would ensure I was paid for my efforts, but I shall see how the burdens of this new job sit on my shoulders first," I said. "I cannot undertake too many commissions and there is already an offer from the Wisden Almanack to consider when I return. I like to write and

I keep a journal and I may call on your scoresheets but it is a burden to those who do not practice the art every day."

Mansfield stood up. "I must return to what you are good enough to call my art," he said. "Two reports were still sitting in the cable office when I left. It operates day and night but I must be as sure as I can be that my works of art are not left lying around where the greater public is unaware of their existence. That way will not lead to riches," he said and off he went, although he hardly had the speed nor the grace Jake had shown in leaving. His short neck and his hunched appearance would never make him elegant. I thought I must read some of his writings and see if I could persuade myself to like him better.

Before I went to my room I made sure I identified the cable office but, since it involved a long walk down a dark lane - "go past the vultures sitting on the wall and be careful since there are sometimes snakes although they will not harm you unless you sit on them and, in ten minutes . . ." but I had lost interest at this point and retired to bed.

The maid and her bearer were waiting in the corridor and, as she stepped forward to ask me for the fourth time if I might have acquired a ticket for her brother while I was at dinner, I saw her wave to the bearer to go to open my door. I said she should ask me again tomorrow night, bade her good night and swept straight past the bowing bearer and through the open door into the bedroom.

As I made my way forward the room was suddenly plunged into darkness and I felt a sharp tap on the back of my head. Even now, several days later, I can still feel that blow; strange how sharp the memory is in these extreme moments. I plunged forward unable to see where I was or what was happening to me but I can also still feel the way I was bundled up into a soft covering and, as I lost consciousness, carried away at high speed. I also wondered where, at this important moment, Davenport and his assistants might be.

CHAPTER EIGHT
November 25th, 1906.
Still writing on the overnight train to Bombay

I felt sick. I did not know where I was. I felt as if I might be hanging upside down; as if the world was a dipping, swaying place designed to make me desperately ill. I was hot and bothered and it was a while before I dared open my eyes. When I did the true horror of my position was all too clear.

I was strapped to the back of a camel and facing down. As far as I could judge, and this was not easy since I was tied and blindfolded and covered from head to foot by a huge swathe of cloth, we - that is to say the camel and I - were heading uphill and from what I could see of the ground beneath my eyes we were crossing very rough ground. It was certainly not a well defined road but it might even have been the wildest desert. I closed my eyes again and prayed that life would change for the better.

My worst affliction was the headache that started at the back of my skull where I had taken the full force of whatever some muscular brute had used to hit me and continued throughout my cranium. Hammers beat inside my head and cruel streaks of light burst across my eyeballs. I was thirsty beyond measure and I was certain that my life was still able to take a slide towards oblivion because I wanted to vomit and at the same time in desperate need of a lavatory. I cannot remember feeling so ill after having my tonsils removed as a six-year-old child - on the lap of a very unsympathetic doctor, using tools that would now be laughed at if they had been the weapons of a medieval torturer - and although I did not cry for my mother I was pretty close to crying out for help. Except that now I was gagged as well.

I had, of course, no clue where I was. All round me I could hear native voices but their language meant nothing to me. There were words I learnt to define as cursing whenever the camel stumbled - and from my upside down perch across its back I could see its feet splay outwards followed by an extra lurch and a blow from its driver - but nothing to tell me where I was heading nor how far I had been conveyed from the hotel.

I could not have stood much more bouncing around when the camel suddenly halted in the midst of screams and shouts and more cursing. The great shawl was pulled from my back and a dozen hands lifted me down from my undignified position and placed me on my feet. I staggered too and was roughly hauled back into place; my blindfold and gag were torn off and I realised that it was still the middle of the night and that we had probably been travelling no more than a few miles. As my eyes grew accustomed to the moonlight I thought that in the distance - and not too far away - I could see the lights of a city. Lahore, perhaps? I thought so and wondered why we had stopped so near to law and order and the possibility of detection for the miscreants and rescue for me.

All round me were men who could only be described as ruffians. They wore exotic headpieces, clothes wrapped round their faces to prevent recognition; they all carried long rifles, bandoliers of ammunition and short curved daggers such as one sees in schoolboy yarns. It occurred to me that I was taking part in such a tale, many miles from the Khyber Pass, the natural setting for such adventures, but much more realistic and much more frightening.

There was no obvious leader for these dozen or so men but they all crowded round me, with their eyes gleaming, and poked me as if I might be a creature from another century or some such. One took me by the arm and led me roughly aside, unfastened the rope that tied my hands and gave me a pitcher of water. When I had drunk he signalled to me to piss if I needed to, which I did gratefully. He watched intently and after a while shouted something - from the smattering of Urdu I have from my father I deduced it was vulgar - before hauling me back to the camel. By now I felt a deal brighter but as my head cleared I decided there was no point in attempting to escape. Where, after all, was I to run to and could I run faster than their bullets? It seemed unlikely. All these men were lean and clearly used to an outdoor life and keen-eyed. I did not imagine I would get a dozen yards before one of them shot me down. Besides it was far from clear that they intended me any harm.

They seemed to guess that I was too hurt and too sensible to cause trouble but they tied my hands again and loosely fastened my feet together and then signalled me to sit in the shadow of the camel. The ropes round my ankles were fastened to the camel's head and the bonds round my hands loosely linked to the camel's feet.

Thus I could not escape without raising the camel from its grumbling slumber. It was a bizarre arrangement but I had to admire the mind that figured this method of keeping a prisoner tightly under control but, thanks to the carpets they had arranged under me, not completely uncomfortable. There was nowhere I could go but no complaint I could make. Some sort of political compromise I thought as the men around me chattered away in an incomprehensible tongue.

Clearly we had to wait; what for and for how long was not so obvious. The guards sat round me and stared. Nothing was said for a long time until one of them stood, walked right in front of me and, taking a rather unorthodox guard, essayed a stroke that might have been made by a very bad village cricketer. I laughed. The rest laughed. The mimic resumed his seat as if nothing had happened but I think I read the runes correctly. They knew who I was which made my plight all the more dangerous.

We had hardly got over this lighter moment when there was a clatter of hooves and round the corner flew three horsemen riding as if they had learned their equestrian art in the Arabian Nights. All three leapt to the ground with a dramatic flourish and one stepped forward to address me. He was tall and lean but I could not see his face for the wrappings. "Collinson," he said, and once again I bridled at this unnecessary use of my surname, "we need to keep you in this camp for a few days. You will not come to any harm, my men will treat you with respect and courtesy and we ask only one small favour. Please do not try to escape or we will ensure that your legs are so badly broken that they do not set in time for you to resume your career in cricket at any time in the next five years. I shall not repeat this threat but Abdul here" - and he pointed to the biggest of his followers who leered at me through his face coverings - "used to be the executioner in Faisalabad and he knows a thing or two about inflicting death and pain over a period of time. So from now on your hands and feet will not be tied quite so tightly but a guard - Abdul, actually - will always be with you. If you need any further explanation please ask when I make my next visit to this camp on the evening of the day after tomorrow. Then we will allow you to go, unharmed and untroubled. Farewell."

It is difficult to see how he could have spoken more plainly if he had spent all his life in England so I settled down, in

107

the company of the good Abdul, to pass the next 48 hours or so, wondering in the meantime what this palaver was all about. It was not exceptionally worrying although of course I would not have chosen to spend the second and third day of the opening match of the most important England tour of India so far removed from my troops and in the company of men who appeared to be among the most unsavoury I have ever met in my life. I tried speaking to them in English and then in Urdu - I could only remember the greeting "Asalaam alakam" which did not get us very far - and as I received no reply I desisted. The order about lighter bonds seemed to have been forgotten; but, as I said before, I was not uncomfortable. Food seemed to be out of the question.

We were located in a short valley with steep sides and only one entrance. The band set a guard but you could tell they did not expect to be disturbed and, once Abdul installed himself so close to me that I might have been his shadow, the day passed in a relaxed way. That night we slept when the sun went down and it was not long before Abdul, having made sure I was comfortable but secure and given me a blanket, went off to join his pals.

I slept easily. After all I had had a draining day, a bump on the head and a great deal of worry. I guess I had gone to sleep for more than an hour when I was woken from a very exciting dream involving my lady Kate, a pile of rugs and an empty house. Someone had a finger pressed over my lips. As I opened my eyes I saw a figure above me, head to foot in black, her face covered with the cloth the women all wear in this Moslem part of the country lest their innocence be destroyed by lustful men staring at their beauty. Her eyes signalled me to be quiet.

"Have you come to rescue me?" I asked. She shook her head vigorously. "No but I have a message from one in England," she answered. "You are to stay here and know that your life is not in danger. Do you understand?"

I nodded. "There is a second part to this message. It goes thus. You are part of a greater scheme of things that you cannot understand at this moment. All will be detailed to you in Karachi. Do not worry if the cricket goes badly."

Once again I nodded. I was pleased to hear that someone was concerned for my welfare. But who?

"Who sends this message?"

"One Lord Harris although the message has passed through many lips since it began its journey to the cable office. He says I must be careful to tell you the next part in full. 'The cavalry have left their stables and are on the way to take the burden from your shoulders.'" She giggled. "And I am to be helpful in any way I can." Again a giggle.

"Beware, there are guards," I whispered.

"I know. No matter. If they find us together I shall take your manhood in my hand and pretend I am a foolish virgin come to comfort you." Suddenly I knew the voice. Who else but my room maid. The lady who could not live unless she had a ticket for her brother.

I was still excited by the dream, I suppose. "Can you take my cock in your hands anyway," I asked.

"Aye, if the sahib asks, can an Indian maiden do anything but obey. Especially when she has a helpless manly victim, bound to a camel, at her feet and is able to do with him as she wishes." She put a cloth in my mouth and said: "Please be quiet while I deal with your needs, man. I can convince the guards if they find us but there is no need to do so unnecessarily."

Maidens do not, I think, behave as this lady behaved in the next few minutes. It would not be seemly to take advantage of her kindness that night by describing her actions in full but I will say that she demonstrated that her hands were not just for dusting my hotel room nor was her mouth only to be used for asking favours of the guests. She was an accomplished performer of the art of giving a man pleasure and she had not read all the instructions in a book. In a short time the joy she gave me excited her and she had used what she could make of my erection for her own pleasure. At just the right moment she snatched the cloth from my mouth and applied it to her own but even so there was a groan that might have woken anyone save a sleeping former executioner.

My own pleasures were multiple and the final ejaculation I shall remember for as long as I live. I suppose the delights were the more acute since my hands were tied and I could not reach out to hold her when I most needed to and I have to say that I understood at last the needs of those men who cannot enjoy a woman unless one or the other is bound and helpless.

She murmured something sweet in Urdu or Hindi and

then, as suddenly as she arrived, she was gone. Perhaps I slept in the moment she made her escape, perhaps it was another Indian rope trick. I do not know and at that time I did not care. There were questions I wanted to ask but she was gone without telling me, for instance, how she came to be chosen for the task of carrying Lord Harris's words to me. Sufficient to say I slept until I was roused by Abdul who sniffed the air and proclaimed: "So the sahib can still attract the girls even when he is bound and, no doubt, gagged." How he knew I cannot tell.

The next day went by without incident. I had no means to make trouble; they knew I was tied to their side since I did not see how I could escape nor that I needed to. Abdul reminded me in the most subtle ways of his former life. On one occasion he mimed the hanging of a man and produced a whip with which, it seemed, he had practised on those who had offended the authorities. He sometimes spoke, but only in his own language which of course I did not understand. Neither of his little demonstrations provided pleasant moments but I took his point exactly and never stirred, although I made a note of his face, his height, his colouring (which was much darker than the other men around me) and his tiny, dull brown eyes. I have a fair memory for faces and I thought I might recognise him again.

The worst of this obviously ill-planned crime was that there was no food and precious little water and certainly nothing in the way of medical supplies to tend to my head. Whenever my hands were free, which was not often, I felt the painful bump and what I thought must be dried blood on the back of my head but there was nothing to be done but hope that I would soon be back in the hotel and able to obtain a doctor's help. The gang had brought their own food, or perhaps some of them slipped away to obtain it, but they seemed to have no plans to include me in their daily meal. I was given ample supplies of water but that cannot sustain a fit young man and I could feel my strength slipping away by the hour. Call me a baby, or an athlete who believes he cannot live for more than a few hours without nourishing food but I found this a trying part of the ordeal.

At least this interlude gave me time to think. I wondered where my supposed guard Justin Davenport had been when I needed him most. I wondered why this nasty charade was being played out, why it had been necessary to knock me unconscious. Most of all I wondered who was behind my kidnapping and what was going on back at Lahore cricket ground, who had taken my place at the crease, what tactics Jake might be adopting in my absence. I supposed he might have gone to the crease himself, that my MCC team might have reached 450 and that, judging from the way the pitch played, the game was heading for a draw. And for a while I meditated on the possibility that my talkative maid and her bearer had been part of the plot. Perhaps she was aware that the villains were in my room and her signal to her bearer was as much a warning to them as for him to open the door to my room.

In the end I was delayed longer among the ruffians than I expected but at about noon on the third day, there was that clatter of horses' hooves again and once more the dramatic descent from the saddle by the group's leader. This man, who seemed to have great authority and some style even if he did have much too great a sense of theatre. This time he sprang in front of me as if he might be about to declare war and announced: "You may go, Collinson. Return to the city by walking to the end of the defile, turn left and in about eight miles you will be in the outer parts of Lahore. Take a carriage to the hotel. By the time you get back your team will be there and ready to depart for Bombay. I trust you have enjoyed your stay with us and let me say that it has been a pleasure and a profit to have you among us." Then he gave a great laugh and leapt back on to his horse and led his small group away.

By that I took him to mean that a ransom had been extracted from the team and I wondered how they had raised the money so quickly. I had not had time while I was in Lahore to ask if there was a high British official in the city; such concerns were far from my thoughts. Perhaps they had been helpful, perhaps there was such a regular spate of kidnappings that money lenders regularly handed out sums to rescue the victims, perhaps Davenport was carrying large sums with which to pay for souls like me who were foolish enough to get themselves spirited away.

All the gang then leapt on to their horses and rode off in the same direction I had been instructed to take. (The camel, incidentally, had vanished as soon as it had finished its task as prison warder). I walked after them, thinking dolefully of the long trail back to Lahore after two days virtually unfed, after a crack on the head and a disgusting camel ride; two days tied up and unable to exercise; but I need not have worried. At the end of the short track I turned left on to the Great Trunk Road, as it turned out to be, but before I could make a dozen steps down the road I heard a carriage draw up alongside me and a driver call on me to take a ride with him. I was so grateful I did not notice the man sitting inside.

Justin Davenport laughed out loud when he saw me, scruffy, tired and injured. I was glad to be out of the hands of the kidnappers and into the safety of a cab with someone I knew but his attitude was jocular and that irked me. "My dear fellow," he guffawed, "my dear chap, it's you. I came out for a ride in this direction and who do I find but our dear missing captain. Where have you been?"

I had thought at first glance that he might have been out searching for me, that perhaps he was the advanced guard of some mighty force devised to find me and bring my assailants to justice and that he might have eased my concerns about how the team had fared in my absence. But no. The secret agent from the government had turned the whole business into a joke and he clearly had no intention of running helter-skelter after the mischief makers.

It was most displeasing that he seemed to infer I had been off on some jaunt of my own, boozing perhaps, or with a native girl, or possibly searching for an ancient treasure. I was furious. "I was hit over the head when I retired to my room and held, with no more than an occasional drink of water, for two days in the heat and the dust under the threat that some ruffian would hang or flog me if I tried to run for it. Or that my legs would be broken into several small pieces. I am not amused, sir, to hear you go on as if I had taken a week-end pass without so much as a by your leave."

My tone stopped him in his tracks. "But," he stuttered, "you left a note for Johnson 'the team's all yours, declare and press for victory, I'll be back in no time'."

"Don't be so bloody silly, damn you!" I shouted, nay almost screamed. "No captain in possession of his full senses would do such a thing. That is a ridiculous suggestion. Are you telling me that Jake believed I would just nip off and leave him in charge in the middle, not just of the team's innings but when I was not out 50? I hope he still has the note so that we might identify the culprit."

Davenport was crestfallen. "I am sorry to say, Bernard, that we were all taken in by this deception. I can see by your appearance that you have not been on any sort of holiday and there is matted blood still on the back of your head." He leaned out of the carriage and addressed the driver. "Hey, lets go straight back to the hotel, please."

The driver looked round and nodded in that peculiar sideways motion the Indians affect. "Certainly, sahib," he said. Davenport said: "There is no hurry. The travel agent has arranged for us all to travel to Bombay tomorrow by the mid-morning train. Touring at our leisure, he says, from now on. No more midnight trains, no more hurried departures. The early finish to the match today means that the rest of the team have been able to attend a reception and they will not yet be back at the hotel. You can repair the damage to your body, have some food and a drink, see a doctor if you feel the need and attend the return of the other players in an hour or two. George Ramsey has gone to the reception in your place and is no doubt making your excuses." You can tell the state of my anger, my confused state of mind and my general lethargy at that moment that I did not think to ask the result of the match. I simply imagined from his good humour that MCC had been the victors and by a wide margin.

We took no more than an hour to return to the hotel and I went straight to my room while Davenport went straight off to find a police station and report the incident. For once there was no sign of the maid and her assistant so I ran my own bath and sat in the hot water for what seemed to be the most blissful 15 minutes of my life. The aches and pains of the past few days ebbed away and when I eventually dragged myself away from the soothing water I felt a different man.

I still needed attention for my head and looking for help I spotted that one of the half dozen or so bells near the door was labelled "Medical assistance - emergency." Why not, I thought, and pulled the rope vigorously. To my surprise, since I had viewed the label with some suspicion, there was a knock at the door in no more than three minutes and a small Indian with a doctor's bag and the air that the professional always adopts was standing outside.

"Mr. Collinson?" he asked. "Davenport sahib sent a message that you might need my help and I have been waiting for your summons. Allow me to look at your head. Yes, a nasty little bump, but there is nothing to worry about. Self-healing has taken place under the blood clot. Wash your head, sir, and allow the process to continue. You have a headache? Take one of these pills. Think to yourself that you have had a bump on the head such as might occur in any of your sporting encounters and I suggest to you that all will be well in a few days." He left smiling as I ordered the first food I had eaten in what seemed to be a lifetime.

Once another fine Indian curry had been demolished I was fit to face the world and to think properly about my circumstances and, incidentally, to fill this journal with an account of the happenings of the past three days. As far as I could tell nothing had been stolen from my room which was left much as I remember it.

I was prowling round the room making sure that everything was in place when there was a knock and I found Jake at the door. "Skipper!" he said, "I have just met Davenport and he has told me the most extraordinary story. That you were kidnapped. That the note was a forgery. I am most terribly sorry for the way. . . "

I interrupted him. "I think Jake, it would be better if we both begin at the beginning and that you start. What Davenport has told you is a brief version of the truth and I will tell you the rest later. For the time being I will tell you that after a hot bath, a little advice from the hotel doctor and a meal I am as fit as may be expected. Tell me your side of the story."

Jake looked solemn. "I came down to breakfast yesterday morning and when you did not appear by 8.30 to go to the ground I asked for you at the reception desk and they handed me a note. Here it is."

He pulled out of his pocket a sheet of paper much like the ones I had now begun to accumulate. This one was written in the same hand that I recognised from the others. Jake should have known I could never have written this note.

"Jake," it said. "I'm taking this opportunity early in the tour to have a day or two off. I'm leaving you in charge and instructing you to declare immediately and press on for victory. Rub their noses in the dirt of their own natural wicket and so establish a reputation for ruthlessness early in the trip. I will be back long before you have won the match and I may even resume charge on the final day. Yours, Bernard."

I was astounded. "Does that sound like a note from me, Jake?"

"Well, of course not, Bernard, but what alternative did I have. We had runs in our pockets, they looked like a weak side, and so I did as instructed although it would not have been my inclination and it was not the tactic we discussed on the train. Big score, bowl them out twice in the last day and a half was what I understood.

"But I did what the note said, what I thought you wanted, and of course you know the result."

I still did not understand the significance of his remark. "And the result, Jake. What was the result?"

"Oh, don't you know. We lost."

"You what!"

"Their batsmen went off as if they had a whiff of grapeshot behind them, hit out, had huge slices of luck and passed our total within the day. Completely different pitch on the third day, the little spinner who bowled only three overs in our first innings got among us, took seven with no trouble at all, and in 40 overs we were all - only ten men to bat of course - out for 120 and they needed 80 to win. The game ended just after tea this afternoon. Comprehensively beaten, skipper, by eight wickets. Shook hands with that nasty man Baig, short speech of congratulations in front of a crowd who, to be fair, seemed stunned by the result and gave us a nice round of applause as we left, and back to the hotel before going to the reception. Very unpleasant atmosphere there I am bound to say."

"What do you mean?"

"As soon as I got in the door I was approached, violently approached actually, by a fat man with a huge red beard who called me a cheat and rogue and threatened to write to MCC. He's the local bookmaker, it appears, grown fat on rich takings at the racecourses and who, so it is said, accommodates those who wish to bet on the cricket. Not the serious side of his business, if you know what I mean. More of a hobby. Loves his cricket, can't resist continuing his trade at the same time. So the locals said afterwards. Anyway he was at the cricket on the first day and picks up a bet or two and at the close of play is asked if he will offer odds to a lot of rupees Northern Districts to win. He says what odds do you want to his client, someone he never sees before, and the man says he is after 20 to one and my big friend says 'done' thinking there is every chance it will bring him another large meal. Not that he is in desperate need of another large meal, if you follow me.

"Of course when we are seven or eight down he suddenly remembers this bet and lo and behold there is his client sitting next to him waiting to be paid out. He pays promptly because he does not have any choice and he will not be writing to MCC. For the same reason. Betting is strictly taboo in an Islamic society and, although he is tolerated because he fills a need and does not make too much noise and just goes about his business quietly, he knows that if he does kick up a fuss he will be hauled off to jail and given whatever passes for punishment out here. But his message to me is that he is sure the team and the 'betting gang' as he calls them are in cahoots and he is not happy." Jake comes to a halt and I go quiet while I try to absorb all this information.

"There is worse news, by the way," says Jake after a couple of minutes of silence.

"You'd better tell me, Jake."

"The man who placed the bet. He was a European."

"So effectively one of us?"

"Wearing dirty flannels and a spoiled and very old MCC cap."

"You asked this bookmaker to identify one of the players?"

"I did."

"And?"

"He failed. He said they were all too young, that the man concerned had a beard and an elderly manner. Of course you have to ask if they can identify us easily. We find it difficult to tell one of them from another."

I began to feel sorry for Jake. Not only had he the worry of his father's illness when he was too far away to help him but he had been left in the lurch by my kidnapping and now he had been accused of deliberately losing a match.

"Did the cable trick work? Is there any news of your father?" I asked him.

"Well, thanks to young Mansfield I sent off the cable

without any difficulty and by some device he discovered it had arrived but there has been no reply from either MCC or my mother. Perhaps the new fangled electrics is too much for all of them," he replied.

I sat quietly for a minute or so. There was too much going on for a young head to unravel all at once. "What next, Jake?" I said. "Have you any more news? Good or bad. I am now fully prepared for a note from MCC telling us to pack and go home."

"Well," said Jake, looking more serious than ever. "That is not beyond the bounds of possibility but I think we must look nearer to home for the next trouble. I was in the middle of the players when the fat chap made his accusations and of course they are not best pleased that you left us in the lurch as they saw it and some of them are blaming you for the defeat and the charges of dishonesty. I think the next trouble will be in the dressing room."

"Thanks, Jake," I said. "I don't need any more trouble but I'd better meet this bit head on. Call a team meeting and drop the word that I am back and want to make a short speech. We'll meet in this room in 20 minutes. Oh, and by the way, tell young Mansfield I will want to see him afterwards. We must get him on our side straight away."

Jake saw the sense of what I was saying and headed off to round up the players while I sat down at the desk and began to write down a few sentences that I could read to the players. By craning my neck in several directions at once and using two mirrors at the same time I found that there were still enough signs of my injury to look convincing but I realised that unless I made a good fist of the speech I was as likely to be scorned as believed.

I had just finished when I heard the noise of the players gathering and went to let them in.

"Come in, men, there's been a misunderstanding and I have something to say that will clear up all these matters," I said as I ushered them into the room. "Come in all of you, we've got to clear the air," I said.

I had arranged some half dozen chairs in a semi-circle and asked the rest of the players to sit on the various settees and on the floor. I wanted the atmosphere to be informal and far from heavy.

I stood at the front. "Good evening, everyone," I said. "You will all have been concerned about my absence for the last two days and no doubt some of you will have put it down to the captain's right to bugger off and have fun whenever he pleases leaving the Poor Bloody Infantry to do his work for him. I was the victim of something similar at Surrey a couple of years ago, before I was captain, and I know what damage that did to team morale.

"So let me try to explain. I'll be happy to answer any questions and anyone who wants to point the finger and say I was in the wrong need not fear the consequences. Just say your piece and lets get all this out into the open because nothing, in my opinion, does more to hurt a team than rumour, uncertainty and dishonest behaviour."

I then went into a brief account of the events that followed the dinner and drinks two nights earlier, cutting out all the detail and asking Jake Johnson to fill in with his version of what had been going on while I was away. I was received in absolute silence but at the end Wilfred Rhodes got to his feet and said: "I am the senior among the players, skipper, and I want to say you have our support. We think you're a straight man."

And with that he sat down. A long silence followed.

"Is there anything else?" I asked. I saw that if Rhodes was on my side I would have the team behind me. I thought there would be no more comment of any sort when without any warning John Littleboy stood up.

There was no embarrassment about the young man and he spoke without any hesitation. "Mr. Collinson, I want you to know that my family have been miners for generations, messed about by colliery managers, owners, pit head bosses and only the good Lord knows who else. We don't stand for being deceived, or put upon even though in some cases it has cost us wages we could not afford. 'Better say what you think and be damned for it than keep quiet' my dad says and he learnt that from his dad and no doubt grandad learnt it at his dad's knee. They always said you can tell a decent man because he asks you to question what he says. That's what you did tonight and so you've not just got the backing of the senior man but you've got the belief of a young man who has the wisdom of his ancestors in mind at the same time. I have only one quarrel with what you said. You said that there would be no consequences as a result of what anyone said here tonight. Well, I don't care if there are."

118

When he sat down Rhodes turned to him and said: "You're too young to hold such big opinions. Let your seniors speak for you in future."

I held up my hand but Littleboy got in first. "I'll thank you to keep out of my business, Mr. Rhodes," he said. "If I am old enough to fight for my country and to be sent on a three months' trip to play for my country I am old enough to speak my mind. You should also note that I am on your side and that I am a fine friend and a fierce enemy." I did not know Littleboy had such a good brain nor that he was able to stand up for himself so convincingly. The boy was a man but I could see from the look in Rhodes's eyes that he might think a long time before he gave his apprentice any advice on the art of slow bowling.

They both sat down slightly red in the face and I thought I had better close the debate before it got out of hand.

"I thank both of you for your support but I want you two to shake hands in private when you feel able to do so," I said. "We are in difficult circumstances, in a foreign country which is already making fools of us since we do not understand either the laws or their customs and it is easy for us to take the extreme actions of a small group as representing the ideas of the majority. I am sure there are good people in this country as well as the not-so-nice we have met in our first few days. But I feel there is a conspiracy to unsettle us. We must not give way to this plot, we must remain as one and, if we are to come out of this tour with any increase in our reputations we must concentrate on our cricket and try to ignore everything else.

"What I will ask you to do is simple. If you find yourselves in any sort of difficulty, discuss it with your team mates, with me, or George Ramsey, or Jake Johnson and bring it out into the open. Let us not harbour our grudges, our worries or our ignorance. We will always be stronger if we lean on one another than if we try to act as individuals.

"Incidentally, some of you may be asked to speak to the police since Justin Davenport went to report this incident. Tell them the whole truth, about the match as well as what happened to me. Lets get it all out in the open. I propose to speak to Cedric Mansfield shortly and let him know what has happened and invite him to write about it extensively. Any comments?"

Rhodes stood up. "We trust the reporters we know in Yorkshire," he said, "but do we know this lad well enough yet?"

"What would you do if he was a young player, Wilfred?" I asked. "You'd put him on to bowl when the going was tough to see if he could stand up to the fire, wouldn't you? That's what I'm doing. We will know him after this nasty piece of work, that is for sure."

They all passed Mansfield as they left and gave him ready smiles. I think they knew he was trustworthy and I hoped they were right, as I let him into the room and began to fill him in with details of the sort of story he can never have expected when he joined us at Tilbury Docks less than a month ago. Nothing of the lady of the night, of course. Newspapers would never carry that sort of detail, no matter what.

CHAPTER NINE
November 26th, 1906.
Past midnight on the train to Bombay

I spent half an hour with Cedric Mansfield, and nearly an hour with two of the most efficient policemen I have ever encountered - every bit as courteous, and cynical as Sergeant Maynard when Miss Crossland was murdered - trying to give them every detail of my abduction. Davenport attended their questioning and pronounced them talented policemen. "They have been well taught," he said. "We must hope the British can take some credit for their professional attitudes."

There was only one definite clue. I could not identify any of the rogues in the camp - "dacoits" the policemen called them - but I said with great firmness that I could recognise the voice of their leader anywhere.

Jake Johnson told them his version of what had happened at the match and discovered that they were suspicious of any event connected with the fat bookmaker who turned out to be "one Abdul, son of Ali, a notorious dacoit of these parts, and grandson of Abdullah, noted for thieving from the Sind to the Khyber Pass and beyond." They had never caught the bookmaker doing anything wrong but they wanted to desperately; and this betting business nagged at their consciences because it was, at the same time, illegal yet allowed to flourish because it was useful to powerful men with a weakness for gambling.

When they had gone I asked Davenport to stay behind and we had a long discussion about the events of the past few days. I suggested he stayed in Lahore when we had gone and talked to the police as their investigations continued and to the local cricket authorities and tried to find the older man who had seen fit to wear flannels and MCC cap to make his bets. We thought it might be a ruse to cause confusion when questions were asked later and we were not sure of the age but we guessed that Abdul Rahman would have sensed the man was a European even though the mix of races here means there are many different shades of skin.

By now it was nearly midnight and I was desperately tired

but I had one more mission. I slipped down to the cable office in search of Cedric Mansfield, past the vultures crouching on the wall only a foot above my head and past all the snakes - if there were any - until I saw a light. Inside the busy office I spotted Mansfield immediately, waving a piece of paper and arguing violently with the man who appeared to be in charge. I pushed my way through the crowd at the barrier to the part of the office where the work was conducted to see if a word from me might be helpful. In the noise and concentrating hard on his own part in the debate, Mansfield did not see me until the last minute.

His reaction was extraordinary. He grabbed the piece of paper in the hands of the overseer, and stuffed it in the pocket of his now even more crumpled safari suit. "Well, damn you," he shouted at the overseer, "I'll take no for an answer. I'll send this material from the station in the morning. You have been nothing except obstructive throughout my stay. Here, take this tip for your men" - and he flung coins on the desk offering me the aside "they are fine operators, all of them, Bernard, but made less efficient by this fool of a foreman."

With that he barged out of the office, red in the face and clearly at the end of his tether. I later learnt to identify this state as "the Indian sign" and thought it came from the trying heat and dust and, sometimes, the trying behaviour of the locals. It was a funny thing, but throughout the stay in India I - and other members of the party I spoke to - never felt 100 per cent as one might in Britain. There was always some snuffle, some little headache or some trivial complaint. And those were the good days. At other times, when the dreaded Delhi Belly struck, one often felt that death was a happy option and that it could not come too soon.

I would have followed Mansfield, save that the overseer caught me by the arm, and launched into a long complaint. "I hope you are his chief, sir, and ask you to reprimand him and perhaps teach him some manners in the most traditional manner, sir, for he has done nothing except tell me to 'bloody' this and 'damn your eyes' for several days now. Working with this gentleman has been the most unpleasant experience of my life, sir." I will cut short my description of this homily which went on at length and meant that I missed Mansfield completely.

After I walked back to the hotel, with the vultures still

watching me lest I sat on a snake and therefore became of much more interest, I found the irascible man had gone straight to his room. I followed him but the servant nearby said Mansfield had given instructions he was not to be disturbed until eight o'clock in the morning. I thought it unkind to override this order and went to my own room.

I was walking through the reception, with the vague feeling that something was irritating me. Suddenly, I realised what it was. I had not seen my friend the room maid since I returned from my great ordeal. I felt we might have something to discuss; like the reasons for her turning up so suddenly with a message. I also wanted to know where she came by the message, how Lord Harris trusted her, a room maid of all people, to carry such an important message and perhaps something of her willingness to make a man happy. Where was this persistent woman?

I asked at the desk. They said, irritatingly, that I must consult their dhobi people - what we might call the laundry - but I was tired and left all such matters to the morning. By which time they had gone right out of my head.

December 12th, 1906. Bombay.

Let me admit with some shame that I have had little time for this volume in the last week. I suppose that nothing has happened beyond the cricket and that the inspiration to write has been missing. Not a murder, not a kidnapping, not a seduction, not a robbery. And I was beginning to think that cricket tours were made up entirely of such events. Instead I have been fully occupied with getting my team into the best possible shape, playing in two matches of three days each (both ended in draws since our attack is sadly proving under strength and the good Rhodes, patient man, has not been able to bowl out the Indians on his own since the great skill of their batsmen is in playing spin).

I have long ago come to the conclusion that my team is not strong enough to compete with the newly-improved Indians. It is a curious mixture. Hobbs, Rhodes, Jake Johnson and I can play against anyone with some success, but Ken Hutchinson, John Littleboy and George Thompson are not yet come to their zenith, while Douglas Tidy and John Sharp had only agreed to take part when their soccer clubs agreed to their release. (Those two have suffered from illness more than the rest; I cannot imagine why since they are undoubtedly the fittest of us all). As Tidy was our only bowler with genuine pace I was often faced with the prospect of opening the bowling with either Rhodes or Littleboy or asking Hobbs to use the new ball for three overs. Rhodes had to bear an intolerable burden but he loved bowling and he saw in some of the local batsmen worthy opponents. Morrison's return home in the first two days was a major blow leaving us desperately short of numbers.

There have been one or two curious incidents. During the train journey back to Bombay, a most comfortable experience since I knew there was no match for three more days and I had no more concerns about the arrangements which were being organised by de Silva, our travel agent. He had proved a more than competent man, and notable for his ability to anticipate problems.

I was able to bring this journal up to date and write letters, first to my parents and then to Lord Harris, outlining events from my point of view. I knew that Cedric Mansfield had placed reports of my kidnapping in several newspapers and eventually, after more persuasion than necessary, he had consented to show me copies of his stories which gave a fair account, even if he had a tendency to allow his imagination to run away with him.

"Really, young man," I rebuked Mansfield at one point, "you seem to have exaggerated the dangers that faced me. I was there less than 48 hours, they issued not a single threat to me except some horrible fate if I attempted to run away - which I did not - and apart from lifting me from that camel when I was unable to do so myself, no-one laid a finger on me. Yet you make it sound as if I was under pain of death from the start."

He barely gave me time to finish my sentence. "Bernard, please allow me to write and I will make no comment when I see you penning your no doubt thrilling missives home and applaud loudly the next time you reach fifty," was his answer. My God, but he had an arrogance about him. I must say he was a hard-working lad. I always thought of him as much younger than me, although his stay at Cambridge just behind me (and in a far superior college, as he reminded me repeatedly) showed that he must be only a couple of years my junior. Just as a precaution I sent a long letter to Lord Harris explaining exactly what had happened. I wanted him to have the truth before too much damage was done. I had also sent a complaint about the strength of the team.

We arrived in Bombay without trouble and the next two days were spent in setting ourselves up for an encounter with what was called the President of the Indian Cricket Board's XI match. That was to be followed by a game against the Bombay XI and then we had to travel off to Cawnpore for a match against the best players of the Central Districts.

I made my way to the same room I had occupied on my previous stay and was immediately set upon by another room maid who knocked repeatedly at the door and eventually made a typical request for tickets. This time it was for her uncle. I shooed her away, telling her that if she repeated her request I would inform the management but I made a note to consult George Ramsey, who was in constant touch with the Indian authorities to see if they could let me have sets of tickets for each match. After all, if that was going to have the same effect as a gratuity, we must take advantage.

The match passed without incident, save that we had another grand exhibition of batting from Hobbs. He will be a master in a few years, mark my words.

He came from the field at tea time on the second day having just made 143 after we had bowled out the locals for 125 before tea on the first day. There was something majestic about everything he did, including the way he walked off and the crowd, who can barely have known his name when he arrived in the country, cheered to acknowledge that they had seen a new champion. He walked straight past me and into the dressing rooms; here was a man sure of his destiny, knowing already that most bowling would submit to his bat.

Not so the next man in. Bill Gardener, an amateur plucked from the depths of Suffolk to take part on this tour after perhaps half a dozen games with Essex, followed Hobbs at the wicket and, as we feared, lasted for half an hour that was embarrassing to watch. His method, if such it was, appeared to be a defensive stroke followed by a mighty heave. It might have worked in some remote town in the Fens but against clever spin bowling such as the Indians produced it was hopeless. Gardener, a sheep farmer, was clearly out of his depth and, not for the first time, I wondered why MCC had chosen him. Perhaps because he was happy to pay for the privilege of travelling to India to make half a dozen runs.

The rumour ran round the dressing room, so I was told, that Gardener was the child of a senior member of the MCC committee who was simply looking after his own. Jake said: "If he were Lord Harris's son, from either side of the blanket, he would be a better batsman than Bill so we can discount that tale."

Gardener did not even go into the pavilion to remove his pads when he was out but sat down next to me in front of the dressing room and asked: "What am I doing here, skipper? I did not ask to come on this trip, and to be fair I am not making the most of the opportunity. I cannot even say I am enjoying it."

I had to give him a straight answer. "All I can ask is that you keep yourself fit, that you fight it out when you get to the middle and that you field as you did yesterday when I thought your catch had the signs of great promise. I had no say in the selection of this team and, to be frank, I would not have chosen you, nor Jimmy Lane-Wood, nor Thomas Abbey. You have done nothing to prove yourselves in county cricket - indeed Thomas is fresh from University - and to be blunt to the point of rudeness you do not look as if you are going to be much of a help to me on this tour. In addition it was always likely that you would be made unhappy by your failures and so be an additional burden to the team.

"But let me say this to you. Cricket is still a team game and if you field well I will have no complaints. Remember one or two of you and maybe all of you will have to play in what they are already calling a Test at the end of this tour and there will be a lot of prestige at stake then. A small score of perhaps 15 or 25 might make all the difference. One wicket might too and a catch can always turn a game. So please do not be depressed by the circumstances that surround this tour. Do your best and you will find my report at the end is a fair one."

He smiled for the first time. "There is talk in the dressing room of this tour being made up of 'dead beats' and 'no-hopers' with yourself and Hobbs and Rhodes here to keep us in order. It is said that MCC did not want to undertake this tour and sent out a poor team as a consequence. Is this true, skipper?" he asked. He was a big, brawny and clearly honest lad and I saw that he preferred the truth to a white lie.

126

I looked at him for a few seconds. "I will be frank. I have thought the same. We do not have many top rank players and if we are not careful the Indians will beat us in that so-called Test. In addition to our lack of skills, there is a definite feeling that one or two things that have happened have been organised to unsettle the side.

"My kidnapping, that sudden change of itinerary, the way the pitch changed overnight while I was absent in Lahore . . . they all spell trouble. So you have a point. But, if I may say so to a young batsman making his way in the game, there is a great chance for you to make a name for yourself. The greater the adversity, the greater the triumph. But I am glad you have come to me with your worries. As I said in Lahore, troubles shared are troubles halved. If you would be good enough to encourage the young players to do the same I would be much obliged."

Gardener went silent. He looked at me for a long time. "Come on, man, spit it out!" I said. "You have another worry, don't you."

He laid one hand over the other at the top of the handle of his bat and stared at the ground. "Uncharacteristic," he muttered. "That it was. That second innings at Lahore. Uncharacteristic, I say."

"What happened?" I asked.

"Well, it was this way, skipper. As you know it was easy batting on that first day and if we had not been feeling our way, testing out the bowling, a bit shocked by the way that big bearded chap got it to leap about, sort of trying to see what might come next, we'd have scored a lot more. So the thinking that said declare was all wrong." He looked at me accusingly.

"The note - left for Jake - was a forgery," I said. "I would have batted longer. Perhaps even until lunch time."

"Anyway, their opening pair fairly let fly, skipper. Fairly let fly. There was a little left-handed lad, no more than 18, he just drove at everything and, given a bit of luck, he could not go wrong. It was a pure bash from beginning to end and when he got to 150, and the whole crowd stood up and cheered, I said to Lane-Wood 'That's the worst long innings I have ever seen.' But by that time they were beyond 300 and, of course, the next morning they whipped us out without a pause. Hobbs got one that kept low,

Hutchinson, next ball gets one that flies and then they put on another kid and he pitches some off breaks just right and we all tumbled out.

"But I could not understand the innings played by Jake, skipper. You know he can bat, and what he lacks in skills he makes up for in pure donkey obstinacy. But he goes in and starts to play shots straight away. When a draw is our only option. First ball he hit through cover point like a bullet, skipper, as if it was Hastings at Festival time and nothing to play for.

"Of course the kid with the off breaks just pitches one higher and wider and Jake goes off after it and it turns back on him and he is stumped. Neat, skipper. Nice bowling if you happen to be on their side. Poor batting if you're one of us. But why, skipper? Why did Jake go rushing down the pitch? I asked him at that reception but that big fat bookie chap got hold of him and started shouting cheat and all the rest of it and it didn't seem appropriate afterwards. But I was not happy with his batting, particularly with three poor tailenders to follow. And him captain for the day, too, so to speak.

"Anyway, I guess it didn't matter because they got off at such a rate to get the few they needed to win we had no chance. Poor Rhodes, he did not know where to pitch it. They just clattered everything." I guess it was one of the longest speeches of his life and it was certainly a sign of his concerns about that match.

"I appreciate your honesty, Bill, but what's the worry. Jake plays a bad shot, goes a bit wild. Not the end of the world." I was tempting him to say more.

"No, skipper, fine, if he wanted to play that way but it was a remark made by George Ramsey I didn't like. I said something about the innings to George and he said 'Just trying to secure his future, Bill' and to be truthful, skipper, I did not like his tone of voice."

Gardener had plucked off his gloves and spent most of our conversation playing with the elastic, pinging it off his fingers in a quite distracting way. I could see he was nervous and upset. Perhaps that is why he found the courage to speak out. Few men would have dared talk to the skipper about his deputy in this way.

I said: "Let's forget it all. There's no need to worry about a single defeat at the start of this tour."

He left me for the dressing room and I pondered the meaning of his conversation. It was clear he worried whether Jake had pushed the game towards the locals once he saw it was doomed by his early declaration and their rapid scoring. He had also opened the second innings with Rhodes bowling but that ploy had not worked and their little left-hander had, according to the score chart kept by Mansfield, done fearful damage.

In guiding the side to victory in the two games in Bombay, and the long journey across to Cawnpore where we drew, I had enough on my plate so that I had forgotten much of what had happened by the time we reached the next stage of our journey to Karachi.

The best of the long detention outside Lahore was the time I was able to devote to reviewing my position so far. I had not had pause to consider any of the events since the death of Miss Crossland; I had simply been too busy. But once I had time to assemble all the facts many new ideas presented themselves.

I asked myself a number of questions. Why was Miss Crossland killed? Not surely because she had spent time alone with me. How had a number of Indian criminals become involved? How had the police, baffled for several weeks, according to their statements during my many interviews with them, suddenly been able to pounce on them outside Tilbury Docks?

There was no immediate answer except that provided by The Captain who had chosen such a strange method of delivering his message while I was held by kidnappers so careless that they allowed her to visit me as I lay in captivity. Look at it any way you may, it was a very odd business and the more I applied my brain to the subject the more bizarre I found it.

I had revealed the curious tidings and their irregular method of delivery to no-one. Who could I talk to? Justin Davenport was now as often absent as he was with me, for all his vain talk of being my bodyguard. He had not been present when he was needed and I still had not found a decent explanation for his fortuitous arrival a mile from the valley in which I had been detained to give me a lift back to Lahore.

Still, once I was back at the hotel I had taken the opportunity to sneak past the vultures once more and, carefully avoiding the snakes, sent Harris a cable. The next morning, by the miracle of modern telegraphy, he had replied. The Captain, who I gathered was the man who preferred to remain anonymous at the meeting with Grace and all those politicians, was already on his way to meet me.

No doubt explanations would be forthcoming. Meanwhile I had a cricket tour to run.

CHAPTER TEN
Christmas Day, 1906.
Grand Hotel, Karachi

I found today trying. Sentimentality comes into it. Christmas at home is crisp, cold and dry. Once in a lifetime a bit of snow. Never very much. I spent the festive season at home every year and we had great times because Mum made a big effort to understand and Dad loved Christmas. Still does of course. Main day of his year. Even when he was making his way, before he had gathered the small fortune which allowed him to retire early in comfort, he would lay a special event on for Christmas. Something to do with spending so much time in the Army, away from home, and longing to be back if only at Christmas.

One year he took Mum and I into Wensleydale and showed us the bands playing at Hardraw Force almost underneath the waterfall. We stayed overnight at the Green Dragon Inn nearby. I was ten at the time and thought myself very grown up to sleep away from home in a room of my own. Another time we were off to Scarborough; another time - after I had begun to play for Surrey - he asked if we could spend the festive season in my flat provided he and Mum carried down all the trimmings of Christmas. They arrived a day before I expected them and found Kate still in bed after I had gone to the city to meet the Surrey players for lunch; and made no fuss nor pretence about what such a beautiful girl might be doing in my flat, half naked three days before Christmas when we were - hush, whisper it softly - not even betrothed.

Of course, Mum turned it into a great romance and demanded to know when we might be married and all the rest; but she also took a shine to Kate, and asked her to visit them in York as soon as we were engaged which was the last thing in Kate's mind. The upshot of this unorthodox introduction was a fine Christmas, perhaps the happiest we had together, since Mum had a daughter to treasure for once and the two chattered happily as they put up decorations and iced a cake. If the exchange of gifts required a few late adjustments, we made a riotous party for several days. Well,

Kate and I were a new pairing at the time, and in love with our affair if not entirely in love with each unfaithful other.

I turned all these happy times over in my mind as I struggled to make myself get out of bed on Christmas morning in Karachi. Everything was as unlike Christmas as I could imagine. Hot. Up to eighty-five degrees. I looked out of the window and saw not a single tree, much less one covered in snow, or frost or tinsel. My room was bare of bunting. I wanted to cry. Home seemed beyond the farthest horizon. The great tie with my loving parents was broken and with it all that had been precious to me.

For a while I dozed in bed, knowing that I must be up and about my duties as a substitute Father Christmas. George Ramsey had been out and bought each man a gift and a Christmas card and I turned some of my MCC money into a small bonus for the professionals and a half bottle of champagne for the amateurs. Ramsey had spent lavishly out of his budget for a lunch at which champagne, the reward cricketers rightly demand on these occasions, would come by the gobletful and we had called at the office of the British District Officer and invited them to send along any particularly lonely or unhappy young man, one perhaps who might be spending his first Christmas away from home. We felt very virtuous, almost Christian, as we called on the office.

The response was not exactly what we hoped. A superbly dressed, very autocratic official, received us with no grace whatsoever and said the man he referred to as "the chief" was away in Rawalpindi but he would consider the request when he returned. "Good," I said. "When will that be?"

"The District Officer will return on Wednesday," this officious soul replied.

"That's two days after Christmas."

"Yes?" as if he might be talking to an idiot.

"Then you are telling me that you are declining our invitation?"

"I would not dare be so bold as to anticipate the District Officer's answer to your - if you will not object to my saying so - unexpected arrival and presumptuous invitation. I am afraid you will have to wait." I wondered if I might call him a pompous ass to his face or if I might lose all chances of a knighthood if I did. "You are a pompous ass, sir," I shouted as loudly as I could and was gratified to see a wide grin spread across the face of a young chap working at the far side of the room.

George, giggling, and I, fuming, left forthwith. We formed a pretty low opinion of these people of the Raj on our trip round the country and this little incident did nothing to improve our notions about the men who represent Britain abroad.

I was dressing and mulling this little story over in my mind, and trying to improve on the way I had conducted myself and how I might have produced a more devastating answer when there was a knock at the door. I feared it might be my new chambermaid, an old and slow lady certainly not among my first choices for a moment of passion beside a camel. She too wanted tickets for her - let me see, I believe it was her father - and she also made a point of putting in a request each time she came into the room with her accomplice who was, I suspected from his eager attention whenever she mentioned the subject, the real recipient of the tickets. By this time Ramsey had come to an understanding about tickets with the Indians and we were able to distribute them freely. They were gladly received even though they were worth only a few pence each.

I shouted: "Come in" but the knocking was repeated and I had to go to the door. There, to my momentary amazement, was the figure I recognised as The Captain, with Davenport and Mansfield in attendance. I ushered them in. I had not seen Davenport for a day or two and as for The Captain, I was flabbergasted to meet him again. I simply had no idea what brought Mansfield to my room in such company.

The Captain was brisk in tone and precise in manner. A man who took charge. An officer not an NCO. Yet there was an underlying sadness about the man. I had not been able to make a study of him as he sat among the shadows in the little house at the back of Lord's but I recognised him now. He looked, as Yorkshire folk say, as if "he had lost a pound and found sixpence" but he presented himself as a strong, determined man for all that and as I looked up and down his long lean figure I saw in his smartness years in the Army and a fierce pride.

"My dear Bernard," he said extending his hand. "I am acting - heavens what were the words Harris said he had used . . ."

"I think you mean the cavalry leaving the stables," I said.

"Ah, yes. The analogy of the hunt. Or the battlefield. Or a mixed metaphor. I remember. Harris always had this romantic streak even when we were in India, in this very city actually, and I was his aide-de-camp. Great man, very kind man, great man at encouraging youth, as you will find Bernard."

"He has treated me well, sir."

"Not sir, Bernard; Captain will do nicely. My nom de guerre as Harris would no doubt put it since I played at Oxford. I'd be obliged if you would stick to that title, Bernard. Indulge me, please."

Quaint, I thought, yet his manner was still that of a soldier. How strange to insist on such a title.

"As you please, Captain."

He drew himself to attention, turned and grabbed a chair and made a gesture for us all to sit. "A few words of explanation will be enough, Bernard. The house in which you met the Prime Minister, Foreign Secretary, and the rest is the house I occupy, a grace and favour residence offered when my wife died leaving me and my adopted daughter on our own, by MCC in return for certain offices. I am their link with parts of the world they are estranged from. The Government is one department they deal with through me. The Church when that is necessary; the Foreign Office; the Secret Service in all its many guises; the Police.

"Surprising where cricket gets, Bernard. Surprising how many men of the High Church think of cricket as their relaxation, how many cricketers are believers. There is also a society of friends working to improve the world - popularly known as the Masons - who have many cricket people among their society. I have acquaintances in all these areas and when cricket needs to speak to them I am often the conduit. That is to say MCC speak to me. Counties tend not to deal with me direct. Proper channels."

I nodded. I was a bit confused but I guessed that such was the power of Church and the Freemasons that I had better not reveal too much ignorance of their part in the cricket world.

"So it was through me that first the War Minister and then the Army and the Navy then the Secret Service decided that cricket, and particularly its Test captain, might be a useful adjunct to their work. Davenport here," nodding at Justin who looked as if he had heard the lecture before and might just be resting his eyelids, "is my direct link with the Dominion Office so that when we go to Australia, or come to India, he and I liaise. Right, Justin?"

"Exactly, Captain." Davenport almost turned over and went to sleep but then seemed to remember something and became much more alert. For the rest of the conversation he stared at me intently.

"Mansfield here is a cousin, aren't you,Cedric and, like you, he is being tried out to see if the Press can perform a useful function in reporting back or carrying messages. We have worked together before. His skill in the ways of communication by telegraph, not to mention a capability with Morse Code, has given him an advantage and he has shown great promise." Mansfield looked, as always, as if he wished the ground might swallow him. In my own turgid brain many facts began to fall into place. I also began to wonder when I was going to meet someone who was not involved with the British Secret Service. I decided I must take greater note of who was driving the next train, who brought in the food for lunch; and wondered if that abrupt man at the District Officer's place had been another spy in disguise.

The Captain went on. "So you see that since I took over these roles there has been a strong conjunction between cricket and what I might call the government forces. No doubt there are other men of my position doing the same service in, for instance, the world of horse racing. I'm not sure, but I guess so."

The Captain paused. "Clear so far, Bernard?"

"Yes, Captain."

"Let us not say any more about the death of Miss Crossland except that I became immediately more involved in your life, Bernard. I have had daily reports from Davenport here, from the police in London and in India, from the Foreign Office, the Dominion Office and, to quote one minor example, the shipping line on which you travelled out here.

"Just before you sailed I heard of the arrest of those rascally Indians near the boat. I am afraid that I did not take quite the same line of thinking as Davenport. I saw only a direct link with India and I reached a conclusion which will surprise you.

"I saw that the death of Miss Crossland, the attempt to attack you and the movement of certain shadowy figures in the

London criminal world as being a direct threat not to you, Bernard, but to cricket."

I was astonished. "Indeed."

"I am sorry to say that what I first imagined to be a scandalous way of turning matches upside down, to predetermine the result is, instead, the work of a gang of international saboteurs. They will stop at nothing and they are ruthless enough to, for instance, murder Miss Crossland."

At this moment the voice of this precise, cool and dedicated man broke and it was all he could do to bring himself back under control.

Davenport looked across at me and seemed about to speak when The Captain regained his grip on his voice and said: "No, Davenport, I will tell Bernard. You see Frances was my adopted daughter, the apple of my eye. I recommended her for the work after her brilliant success at university and she obeyed her father rather than her instinct for work as a doctor in some Far Eastern country where such services are in short supply.

"It was my order that she should approach you in Baker Street and decide if you were the trustworthy, discreet man we needed for this work. She came directly to me at home after she had met you and said she had no doubt that you were the epitome of care and that you would not let us down. She left the house the next morning and a few hours later she was dead.

"That evening I received a telegram before the police had even informed me of her death, which said 'See how far our tentacles reach, Captain.'"

It seemed from his long speech and his manner that The Captain had no idea of the level of intimacy his daughter and I had attained in a short time. I was pleased.

"I'm sorry to hear that the death of Miss Crossland was your personal loss," I said. "I should be dealt a mortal blow if I brought up a daughter for 20 years and then saw her snatched away. I don't know what to say. . ." but I was brought to a halt by The Captain.

"It is my loss to deal with," he said. "No man ever had two ladies so good as my wife and my daughter and I have had the misfortune to lose both early in my life. I cannot think of a greater loss for any man to bear. I must learn to put it to one side, but it is hard. Much harder than all the losses of friends and comrades I had to bear fighting the Boers."

Davenport, feeling the need to fill the silence that followed this shocking revelation, said: "The Captain was at Spion Kop, Bernard. He has an award for his gallantry."

This reminder seemed to shock The Captain into life again. "Enough of that, man. Let's turn our minds to what has happened here. I would be obliged for a full account of your kidnapping, Bernard."

I told him about most of the events of those incredible days and he listened without interrupting. At the end of my account, which largely followed what I have written here, he snapped: "You tell that story well, Bernard, as if you had recounted it often. I don't suppose you are foolish enough to keep a journal, are you?"

"A brief note of the main events of the day," I said. managing to divert my eyes from this diary which lay in a travelling case only a few feet away.

"Good," said The Captain. "MCC will not be best pleased if at the end of this trip you produce a sensational book of these events and I am sure the government of the day will view it with disapprobation. What happens on these tours is not for public consumption, Bernard. Please remember that if you want to continue in your present role. Meanwhile, back to the business in hand. Do you have any idea who is behind all these tricks? A kidnapping of an England captain? It's unheard of. And what about this bet in Lahore, the strange behaviour of Jake Johnson when he was leading the side in your absence, Bernard. What do you make of that? Foolishness? Lack of experience as captain? Or was there a deeper motive?"

"I have known Jake since he was a boy, sir, and I will swear by his honesty. He came from a poor family in my neighbourhood, but by dint of hard work his father accumulated enough money to send Jake to Cambridge at the same time as I was there myself and he is able to play for Surrey as an amateur. He lives in some style. I cannot believe he has done anything except make a few errors of judgement. And remember, sir, he was in receipt of a cleverly written note which suggested I wanted him to declare on that second morning."

"Ah, yes," said The Captain. "So you have come to no particular conclusion about who might have been responsible for this outrage, if that is what it was?"

"I admit I am still puzzled. Davenport and I, Johnson and I and the other senior players have discussed it frequently. It makes little or no sense except that someone made a small amount of money - a few thousand rupees, but not much in pounds - when my side lost."

The Captain shook his head. "My plan now is to stay with you for most of the rest of this trip and see what may occur. I shall not initiate any investigation myself. That seems to have been done most thoroughly by you, Justin, and by the local police. I hear from London that the Indian men who were found in possession of those murderous weapons near the ship will only be charged with lesser offences since the charge of murdering Frances is apparently unsustainable in a court of law. A long term of imprisonment awaits these scoundrels. It may even be true that they are not the killers. I leave such matters to the police and the courts, although I would happily see her assassins go to the gallows."

I could see the man, for all this military bearing and his dry eyes, was still grievously affected by this enormous crime. "Perhaps it would be as well if you went to your room," I said. "You will join us for Christmas lunch?"

"Yes," he said, once again the officer remembering his duty. "I will sit among your men and perhaps they can direct some light on to that game in Lahore. Be good enough to introduce me as an MCC member who has happened to drop in on his way somewhere else."

He marched to the door and said: "I'll see you at lunch, Bernard. Perhaps you could knock on my door 15 minutes before it commences."

Davenport and Mansfield stayed behind. "I have known The Captain for 15 years and I was one of his staff officers at Spion Kop," Davenport said. "I have never seen him in this mood. Usually he stays silent in any discussion and lets others put forward the arguments while he draws the conclusions and makes the decisions. He is greatly disturbed and I wonder if he is not on his way to some sort of breakdown."

I nodded. "I am only pleased that he has no idea what

took place between his daughter and I. It would only add to his burden. Look, I have duties to attend before the lunch. I will see you in the dining room at 12.30 and we will toast Christmas before the main event. I can take a little in the way of drink since our match does not begin against an Indian eleven until later in the week. It is, if you read the local papers, assuming all the importance of a Test but we can wait for a while before we prepare."

As he and Mansfield turned to leave I called them back. "Just tell me one thing," I said. "I am not happy that there seem to be more infiltrations into my team than I can cope with and I have a lot of thinking to do before I can work out exactly what has been going on around me among people like yourselves who claim to be on the same side as me. But, do tell me, is it entirely necessary to bring a room maid into the scheme of things?"

They answered almost in unison. "What room maid?"

"Never mind," I said. "We'll talk it through some other time. But, if you would give us a moment or two, Davenport, I'd like a word with Mansfield on his own." Davenport left, a little reluctantly I felt, and Mansfield, flustered as usual, stood at the door.

"This won't take long, old man," I said. "I am only going to express my disappointment that, after I had made you more than welcome into this party, you did not see fit to confide in me."

He fairly snapped at me. "I am not in the habit of confiding in people."

"But I could have made life much easier for you if you had said something about your duel mission. Don't you see that. We are supposed to be on the same side."

I cannot recall having seen anyone so unwilling to concede an argument. "I think you are talking nonsense," he complained. "I believe, and I told The Captain so before we came here this morning, that he should have left me in place as an invisible man, so to speak. Much more would have been learnt and probably much more achieved. But he was insistent."

"So what else have you been doing that I was not aware of?" Something was irritating me as I tried to recall a conversation or phrase he had used.

"Nothing. I have not written anything, nor done anything" . . . but I stopped him with . . . "except read my diaries!"

I had called his phrase to mind "writing your no doubt fascinating bits of tour trivia." I had thought at the time that he had been referring to my letters home to the Daily Telegraph and then forgotten his words. Now I realised that he had found the diary in some way and read all that comment on his own personality.

Now he was angry. "Only because you were gone from your room. Remember those of us aware of the danger that faced you at Tilbury, those of us who knew the truth about what happened to The Captain's daughter, those of us who had been sent, in effect, to ensure nothing ill befell you, were concerned about your disappearance from the start. I thought there might be an indication, a clue" . . . but by now I had lost my temper and would not let him continue.

"So you thought it proper to read a man's private papers," I shouted.

"Yes, and to wade through hundreds of ridiculous words about oneself, most embarrassing, not the sort of thoughts anyone should be so crass as to put on paper. . ." but once again I brought him to a halt.

"You seem to forget," and by now I was fairly bellowing at the lad, "that private papers are called private papers because they are not intended for anyone else's perusal. These papers were not intended for anyone's eyes except my own. Do you understand!" These last words must have been heard, certainly by Davenport standing outside, and probably by the cooks in the kitchen 100 yards away.

"This is most unpleasant," Mansfield complained and I cooled down. "Well I hope you will put much of the content to the diaries to the back of your mind."

"How can I?" he bleated. "You have defamed that wonderful girl Miss Crossland with your nasty suggestions. You don't seem to realise, in your gross, unthinking, sordid cricketer's mind that this lady was to be my fiance when I returned from India. I had already discussed a proposal with her father, I had had the honour to escort her to the opera, we were, before her tragic death - never mind your disgraceful rumours - to be married."

"Did you discuss this marriage with her?" I was still boiling but this latest revelation had knocked me sideways and I was rapidly cooling down as I considered the effect those diaries must have had on Mansfield.

"No, I had not been so bold as to mention my feelings to her, but simply said to her father that I was, how shall I put it, that I had the feeling, that one day, perhaps . . ." and he was back to the old fumbling, wordshy man who I had first met.

"So you had no idea if she reciprocated your feelings?"

He looked at me in astonishment. "She very willingly went to sundry places of entertainment with me," he exclaimed. "Eh, dancing, the music hall."

"And you had no other hopes than that. A night in the ballroom and you expected to base a life's unity, a family, on that?" I was beginning to realise that, for all his brain power, Mansfield had little understanding of what made the world go round. The journalist-romantic in him saw no barrier between what was in his mind and its attainment.

He put his hand on the door knob, clearly ready to go. "Shake my hand, Cedric," I said. "I did not know Miss Crossland for all I have written and you may console yourself that whatever I have written I had no intention of seeing her again. In a brief space of time. . ." but now it was his turn to lose control.

"Damn you, damn your eyes, will you be good enough to stop reminding me of your filthy trick, damn you," he shouted and threw open the door, much to the surprise of Davenport who was so near that you could not help thinking he must have had an ear to the keyhole. Once a spy, always a spy I suppose.

Not surprisingly Mansfield made no appearance at the Christmas luncheon. I felt it my duty to send Jake to his room but he was working, Jake said, and unable to attend and sent his apologies. I suppose he was still in a temper and felt he might spoil the party. I also kept a close eye on The Captain but I need not have concerned myself.

He offered a toast during the meal, he told one or two heroic stories of days in the Veld and his experiences in India and he made it his business to talk to each member of the party and encourage them to defeat the Indians "so that these blighters know that English cricket is still on top of the world."

I suspected, although I was at the far end of the table, that he also inquired about the match in Lahore and when I saw him in a long conversation with Bill Gardener I knew he would be aware of the feeling in the dressing room that Jake had made a mess of things. Gardener will never play for England except in circumstances too unusual to contemplate but now his tongue was loose he could talk for a combined England and Australian side and the expression "mum's the word" had no meaning in his book.

Not that I was taking a lot of notice. I had had a fair amount to drink, trying to forget my Christmas Day sorrow, the conversation with The Captain, and the stormy meeting with Mansfield. And I had spotted in the reception area a lovely, not to say beautiful lady, dressed in the most modern style and with a constant smile. Now there, I thought, is a lady worth knowing and hoped I might bump into her accidentally.

CHAPTER ELEVEN
Boxing Day, 1906.
Karachi

I had time today to head for the old Karachi market to see Dunne Sahib, the Englishman gone native Lord Curzon had spoken about, for no other purpose than to satisfy my own curiosity. About Curzon, The Captain and precisely what was going on around me and my team that caused a large bet to be laid, me to be kidnapped and a curious air of distrust to have grown between us and the Indian players.

It troubled me since I had been sent to India with a second purpose; to foster relations with the Indian authorities, to spread the game and to leave with a clean sheet. Instead there seemed to be a conspiracy to turn the game into a political weapon. I hope that Phillip Dunne would point my mind in the right direction so that I might be able to think more clearly. Especially if anything else went wrong.

Finding him was remarkably simple. I hired a carriage with the aid of the hotel porter who gave the cabbie directions. The cabbie set off down the wrong street but only so that he could meet a chum who gave him a much clearer picture of my needs. There was a lot of giggling, gesturing and smiling but I did not understand what all the chattering meant; nor had I picked up the strange glances that I was given at the hotel when I asked directly where I might find Dunne Sahib in the market. I was soon to learn what I had let myself in for; but as I set out on my innocent journey I was only concerned to know the way. Once that was settled we made good progress and only half an hour after leaving the hotel I was being driven through the market stalls at a rate I found too quick for the alleyways into which my man took his horse.

But then that is India; home of the unexpected. The best driving I have ever seen in my life came from a man handling two camels pulling a giant load of hay on the back of a cart in the centre of Lahore. The cart itself was so narrow you could hardly see it yet he wove in and out of horses, oxen, donkeys, asses, dog carts, walking porters and running boys; men with huge burdens on their shoulders, women with pitchers on their heads; and not only kept these difficult beasts moving but seemed to time his moves through the crowded streets as if somehow the traffic was flowing to his tune, rather than as if he had to fit into the general pattern.

I bow to none in my admiration of the London cab driver but they would not easily win the Karachi Derby run through these narrow streets.

Eventually my speedy driver brought his horse to a stop on a busy corner and signalled for me to get out. I told him to wait and he gestured for me to move inside where I was greeted with the most remarkable sight.

Curzon had told me of the degree to which Dunne had gone native but he did not prepare me for what I found as I stepped out of the bright sunshine of the main street of the Karachi market into the gloom of his establishment. It was, according to your taste, your upbringing and your imagination, either the most voluptuously sinful place on earth or the entrance to Hell.

Every inch of the place was hung with drapes and each one moved as if blown by a breeze. Perhaps the wind was caused by a mechanical device turned by some slave sitting in the background, or it may have been the natural movement of the wafts of air that permeated from the street, but as those curtains moved so did the figures of the naked men and women depicted, and so did each kneeling, bending, erotic figure seem to be taking part in an orgy of sexual congress.

As I moved further into the establishment these happenings appeared to be increasing their tempo so that it was impossible to stay divorced from the cameo delights. Within a few seconds I was fascinated, aroused and unable to tear my eyes from the groping hands, the fornicating bodies and the couplings and triplings that appeared before me at every turn.

I was so engrossed that the booming voice that emerged from behind one of the veils shocked me to the core of my being.

"Well, Mr. European, do these strips of adventure delight you, stimulate you, encourage you to pay a small fee for a further trip into the Pleasure Palace in my next room?" the voice asked. "I have to say that you are a rare visitor for few men of North West Europe know this address. May I know your name, sir?"

"I am Bernard Collinson, sent by Lord Curzon and

looking for Dunne Sahib," I answered, more stiffly than I should have done, since I was, first, shaken by the exotic nature of the establishment and, secondly, certain that I was speaking to Dunne.

A huge barrel of a man strode from behind the drape picturing one of the floating nymphs who was performing an act rarely seen in chapel on a Sunday morning with, I suddenly realised, a lion whose face twitched with pleasure as his drape twisted and swayed in the half-lit shop. The man was taller than I and a great deal fatter and he was dressed in an eclectic collection of clothes; part European, part Indian, and all thrown together as if he had just risen from his bed.

"Hello to you, my dear Collinson. I am Phillip Matthew Elsworthy Dunne, and you, sir, are the captain of the MCC team due to play a match of monumental importance in this city in the next few days, are you not?"

"I am, sir. Lord Curzon sent me with a note of introduction which I have in my . . ." but I was cut short. Dunne grabbed me by the arm, simply saying he had Curzon's note, that he had been expecting me and that if there was anything "legal or illegal" he could do to help me I must say. He led me through the drapes into a smaller side room where a lad of perhaps 14 years of age and a girl who looked as if she might be three years younger grappled on a couch.

"Come on, out of here, you two. Off to your room; you can do what you like up there. Ali, keep an eye on the shop. Nasimah, is there any work you can do? Go and find some to keep you occupied. Off, off, off, the pair of you." His clapping hands drove them from the room; the lad noticeably in a state of undignified arousal, the girl giggling.

"I have to earn a crust," Dunne said with less of an apology than if he had had to admit to being a market gardener. "The front of this establishment is to my own design, and it brings my guests to a state of frenzy so that they can enjoy the pleasures of the flesh all the more. There are other delights. You can see them if you wish. Partake of them if you so desire. But later. You have rather more important subjects to discuss."

"I want to know what the devil is going on," I said. "Since I came here I have been kidnapped, my team has been beaten in circumstances which arouse suspicion and there is a scandal of the most terrible kind involving bookmakers and causing my team to see traitors in their own midst. Is there anything that you can tell me that will help me sort out this mess?"

"I'll do my best," said Dunne, urging me to take a seat and clapping his hands for chai, which was already giving off a wonderful perfume. An even younger girl emerged with a tray and two cups of this delicious beverage. "Put it down there," said Dunne, indicating a table which, true to the rest of the area, had ornate carvings of men and women attempting to add to the population.

Dunne nodded as he followed my eyes watching the girl walk round the room. I have to say she was, at whatever age, extremely pretty. "Too young," he said. "Much too young. Six months, maybe a year. Then - but you won't be here," and he picked up his cup and sipped the hot liquid. He might have been discussing a new bloom in a flower show, a puppy in a litter.

I felt ashamed of my own diversion into his culture. "I was not thinking," I said, "that I . . ." but again he interrupted. "No matter what your honourable intentions might have been," he said. "I know what you were thinking. Another day, sir; some other time." He shrugged with the worldly air of a man who has seen too much of the faults of others.

"Let us return to the subject of Curzon and the activities surrounding your team. Curzon was here for several years and realised the importance of India in a strategic sense. So he left behind men - some like me, with an ear to the ground, some in high places, some in the Indian upper classes - who could be relied on to send him information about what might happen here next.

"He chooses well and he pays well. I could not have established this business, which enables me to find out the most intimate secrets of the Indian hierarchy, without his money - or rather the British public's money - and he must think it well spent. He is also the mind behind this tour of India by you cricketers. He thinks it will make the Indians feel they are accepted back home and that they will one day be allowed to send a team to compete against the best MCC can produce in our country. That would be considered a great honour here and this tour is a step along the way.

"However, he has had the misfortune to chose a bad moment. The rumours in the bazaar talk of an uprising, a new man who is to lead a great movement of the people - although no-one knows his name at the moment - and a fight that will eventually mean the end of the Raj. Of course, we all see that as inevitable in the long run and it could be 50 years away, but there are bound to be pinpricks along the way." Dunne seemed happy to be lecturing the new boy on the ways of India, but he was not helping me sort out the problems of my team.

"How is this going to affect our team?" I asked.

"Please don't waste your time thinking about it," Dunne replied. "They will bring you no harm. They love cricket here and treat the players like gods. The local population would rather harm themselves than one of your men. If there is any problem for you, it must be coming from your own country."

"So tell me about Curzon and The Captain. Do you know who I mean by The Captain?"

Dunne laughed. "I was at school with him; he was my subordinate when I was in charge of the Government Inquiry Agency, as it was known, in Delhi. That is to say we were spies, looking for trouble, trying to stop trouble on the North West Frontier. He did all the field work, with one other agent, and I co-ordinated their lives back in Delhi. Then I - well, how shall I put it so as not to offend against all the laws of decency - got into trouble and left. He took charge and would not even give me a single day of work when I was on my last legs. If it had not been for Curzon, life would have been really difficult." Dunne had a far-away look in his eyes. His gratitude to Curzon, who had not struck me as a particularly likeable or generous man, was obvious.

"What sort of trouble?" I asked the question in a restrained way since it clearly brought about a serious dilemma.

"A boy who was too young to be in anyone's room at 3am suddenly raised an alarm. I had no explanation, my 'reputation' meant that everyone believed the worst. And rightly so. Except I never quite understand why the boy, who had raised no objections before, suddenly became alarmed."

"You had a suspicion?"

Dunne paused. "I can tell you that The Captain, sick of being my underling, was at the back of the whole thing. Watch that man, Collinson. He is not a pleasant fellow, although he may seem to be at the first meeting. He is a cold, ruthless man and it is not an act. Curzon is the opposite. He plays the generous role when it suits him as it did with me. Underneath he is just as ruthless as The Captain."

"What's The Captain's background?"

"He was the son of a noble family who made a fortune supplying British troops in the wars against the French at the start of the last century. His grandfather left a large estate, but his father was the second son, and he in his turn was the second son. So, thanks to dear old primogeniture, they had to earn their own livings. He still thinks he should be Lord Crossland instead of his stupid and indecisive older brother and he treats anyone he considers less than his equal with contempt. He has access to other dangerous men; lean and amoral men who do not know the meaning of either fear or conscience."

A thought struck me. "You know he's here?"

"Well, Collinson, if he is in India, and particularly if he is in Karachi, he will come knocking on my door before very much longer." He cocked one ear. "I thought I heard a knock," and laughed. "I suppose I should hate the man because of the way he invented stories about me. It was a disaster for me. I was given no time to justify my own actions. Simply sent away and told not to darken anyone's door again. The story swept right across the sub-continent and I was effectively blackballed."

I had heard such action within cricket and I was hardly surprised to see it repeated on a wider scale. "But you survived?"

"Oh, yes," Dunne said, waving a pudgy paw, around his erotic den. "There is a call for this sort of thing. I take in a few pence, I have my little joys and smaller boys and I can watch through this device" - and here he drew open a slide in the wall above his desk and beckoned me to watch.

At first I could see nothing but then I realised, as my eyes accustomed to the dark, the unmistakeable motion of two people in the writhings of love. "Be quiet, and you will have a bigger surprise," he said. He pulled a cord and gradually more light filled the scene we were watching. "They concentrate so they are not aware that I have opened a curtain slightly," he whispered.

I realised at that moment that one of the figures was unmistakeably George Ramsey; the other had a boyish figure I did not recognise. "You know this gentleman?" Dunne asked.

"My manager, George Ramsey," I said. I was shocked but not too much so. Ramsey on board ship, Ramsey ever since, had an eye for the ladies.

"Who is he with?" I asked.

"A young girl in my collection," said Dunne. "He came with several requests. I think the second is about to be realised."

I turned away from the opening. "I'll leave him to his pleasure," I said. "He is harming no-one, except himself."

Dunne laughed. "You may remind him of that scene and tell him that the owner of the brothel has a picture of his less seemly moments. If the moment arises."

I said: "I don't think I will taunt him. He has, to be truthful, done me a series of favours on this tour, helped me when I was in trouble, and never interfered with my moments of disaster. I think he will prove a loyal manager throughout."

"Perhaps," said Dunne. "Now, are there any other questions? I think you see the point I have to make here. The Captain is serving several masters. MCC are his main paymasters, but the British espionage system has him in its thrall, and he is, I suspect, trying to earn himself a knighthood or some such so that he may rise to the position in life he believes he deserves.

"But he is not behind your kidnapping, nor the knavery that went on when you lost the game in Lahore. For that you must look to your vice-captain Johnson and the gambler who placed the bet in Lahore and who has been seen with Johnson on several occasions since. Johnson buys gold in the bazaar, and he loves to spend time in a house of love, as the Indians call it, down the road. Not a cheap place to waste three or four hours, so I am told."

I was struck by a horrible thought. "You have not had any of my players in this . . ." and my voice trailed away.

"I can tell you a lie if you like," said Dunne, grinning.

"Tell me the truth, damn you."

"Rest easy. None of your men have been here."

The conversation lagged and my thoughts turned back to this extraordinary place. Quiet above the hurry scurry of the bazaar. Exotic curtains blowing in the gentle breezes; erotic young children wrestling on the settee; Ramsey's pleasures.

"I'll leave you here a minute or two," said Dunne in his booming voice. "Here's a magazine. Flip through that until I return.

Drink up your tea." I have no idea what happened in the next few minutes, nor indeed how long I was alone in his den.

When he was gone I picked the magazine up idly and turned the pages. A soppy poem caught my eye and then a story about a Crusader away from home. An erotic sentence or two crossed my line of vision which appeared to be out of focus, I seemed to doze until I could have sworn that a beautiful young girl came into the room, let her sari fall to the floor and made love to me as I waited. A dream no doubt; or was it?

What happened in those few minutes I will never fully understand but I awoke with my head clear and an absolute certainty that I had at least one answer to the puzzles that had dogged me on this tour. The voice I had been listening to all afternoon was the voice of the brigand who had made such dramatic dismounts from his horse when his men kidnapped me and kept me hidden in the valley outside Lahore. I told the police I would recognise him anywhere and I was right.

I was brought back to full awareness by the return of Dunne. "Refreshed? Pleasant dreams?" he asked. "Feeling better after your little sleep? Amazing what the sun and the seaside air does to the human body, isn't it? Have you thought of any more questions?"

He beckoned and I followed him through the room of swaying curtains and out into the street. It was almost dark but my faithful cabbie was still waiting. "Take Collinson Sahib back to the hotel. Here is your fare - do not dare to ask him for a penny more." He shook my hand and said, with a very serious face: "One thing surprises me about your visit here, Collinson."

I hardly had the strength to answer. All my limbs seemed to be outside my control. "What surprises you, sir?"

"Only that you have never considered the power of hypnotism when allied to a small amount of a drug placed in a tea cup?" He laughed - a cruel laugh I thought - and waved the cabbie off.

I caused the cabbie to pull up and leaned out of his carriage to say a last sentence to Dunne. "You may also wish to reflect on another matter," I said. "I have realised in the last few minutes where we met before. Outside Lahore. I am right, am I not?" Perhaps I should have kept quiet but, to be frank I had had enough of people telling me what I should do, from Mahmood Baig, to The Captain and Cedric Mansfield. It was all too much and, as I may have indicated already, in India the smallest trouble grows from a molehill into a mountain immediately. Being told off by Dunne was more than I could take and I thought it time that I answered back instead of allowing myself to be constantly criticised by men whose characters I did not respect.

Dunne turned on his heel and strode off. I needed no other confirmation that I had spotted the right man, although what his motive may have been I had still to discover.

CHAPTER TWELVE
Boxing Day, 1906.
Eve of our great match, Karachi

Back at the hotel I had the good luck to walk through the main door and bump into - quite literally - the attractive young lady I had seen and been so taken with the night before.

One stride into the foyer of this opulent hotel and the lady, who had been sitting on one of their gilt chairs at the side of the swinging door, stood up so that for all my neat sidestep I could not avoid colliding with her. She slipped, grabbed at my trouser leg and, in her panic pulled me down on top of her.

Now the effect on me, after I had spent the afternoon in the midst of whirling rampant ladies and gentlemen at Dunne's palace of delights and had the dubious pleasure of watching manager Ramsey cavorting through a peephole, was utterly predictable. I was very pleased to see this lady and I have no doubt that, because of my experience in ingratiating myself with other members of her sex, I did rush the fences somewhat.

"Good evening," I said, as I pulled her to her feet and tried at the same time to dust myself down. "I am very sorry for my clumsiness. I tried to get out of the way but, well, no matter for this gives me an excellent opportunity to introduce myself. I saw you last night and I had hoped for a chance to meet you. I'm Bernard Collinson and I am in India as captain of the MCC cricket team. I believe you are Miss" - and here I plucked a name out of the air which I do not now remember - "and that you are here on your first trip to this country."

Of course I had no idea if she might be the Queen of Sheba but any sort of excuse is better than none. However I soon discovered that she was not a fool and that she was also not going to be deceived by any old piece of nonsense.

"Good evening to you too, sir," she said, looking straight ahead. "You are right in one sense at least. It is my first trip to India but only if you take into account the fact that I was born here. And, once again, good evening sir." And off she flounced, dusting herself down the while, just to underline the fact that she had been in this minor collision. I stood, not at all at my ease, floundering as if I had just fallen flat on my face. Which in one sense, as madam had just put it, I had.

If you ever make a complete ass of yourself you can bet that not very far away is a friend who will not only laugh out loud, but come up and give you false sympathy and then immediately rush off and tell all your companions that you have just exposed yourself to great folly.

"Hello, skipper." It was Douglas Tidy, the quick bowler, and the wit of the party. "You seemed to get a bit of a brush-off from that lady. I spotted her too last night and thought 'she looks fast - I bet the skipper chances his hand there.' And she's gone and brushed you off good and proper. Not like you to lose a chance like that, skipper."

"Too quick for me, Douglas," I said. "Good evening, I said, good-bye she said. Put it on the wrong side of the ledger. A failure, one of my bad days, go back to the planning department and start again but not a step further forward."

"Don't give up, skipper. A young lady with that degree of composure has seen a bit of the world and I have no doubt that a reasonable amount of persistence will have its reward. Or you can recite the old team motto, skipper. If at first you don't succeed, another tart will be along in a minute." Tidy was having a marvellous time.

He was teasing me now and I knew that within a few hours, certainly by the time the players had dined together, the story would be enhanced a thousand times, the young lady would have slapped my face in full view of everyone in the foyer, thrown me over her shoulder or called the police. Or, more likely, all three.

"Well, Douglas," I said, winking at him lest he took the remark too seriously, "you'll have plenty of time to think it over doing your 12th man duties in this match. Me, I'm off to help Rhodes pick my team for me and I'll have to do some fast talking to get you, or your twin, into the side."

Tidy sobered up. "I've hardly taken a wicket so I don't expect to be in this match," he said. "But Tom, he's batted well in the nets and I'm sure he's worth a shot." The pair were the biggest pals in the party, Hobbs and Rhodes apart, and they both had the same shaped moustache, the same lean bodies and the same odd walk. They were also born on the same day 25 years ago but while Tidy first saw the light of day in Darlington of a coal mining family Tom Abbey had come into the world in a village in Shropshire.

The stories Tidy had invented to cover this chance similarity were hilarious: that they were both sired by the same father and, as he told the story, that father was W.G.Grace, or two of the Grace brothers, and, on one occasion, the present king, a noted ladies man who, according to Tidy, had an expert knowledge of the train timetables so that he could impregnate both Mrs. Abbey and Mrs. Tidy on the same day and still be in London for a night of jollity and further conquests by the evening.

"Tell us how you and Tom were conceived." That was the shout after many a team dinner on this trip and Douglas always obliged and always told a different story. But, funny raconteur that he was, Douglas was also a great team man and very loyal to Tom Abbey, whose skills he greatly admired. I have to say he was not alone in that admiration, even if Abbey had not been an obvious choice at the start of the tour.

"You may be right," I said. "Tom Abbey has had few chances to shine on this tour and when he had played the luck seemed to have gone against him. His name will come into the discussions but in the end I guess Ken Hutchinson will get the place, and rightly so, since he has more experience."

"And fewer runs this trip," said Douglas, taking advantage of the clown's right to speak his mind.

"I'll see you all at dinner," I said, not wanting to get mixed up in too much discussion ahead of the selection meeting in my room in a few minutes' time. "I guess George Ramsey will have put the word round, but we are having a private room for our dinner and we will settle a team and discuss how this match might go during the meal. So no time to tell us one of your long tales, eh?"

"It's good practice for me," said Tidy. "When this tour is done I will advertise myself as being available to speak at dinners, lectures and the like for a small fee and so earn a little extra. I think I have something to keep an audience amused and mixed in with the tales of India, the elephants, the poor people on the streets and the dirt and disease, I may be worth listening to."

"How do you feel to see the poverty, Douglas?"

"It's those dusty hands with no fingers that affect me worst, skipper. But I keep myself cheerful by remembering the story I was told almost as soon as I disembarked," he answered. "A young man arrived in India and was taken on a tour of Bombay where he saw many disfigured beggars, many homeless people on the streets and many babes in their mothers' arms crying from want of food. His guide asked him 'Isn't it a pitiful sight?' and he replied it was.

"'Some of them have no other place to live, but spend the whole of their lives, eating, drinking, sleeping on the streets,' said his guide.

"'Don't be ridiculous,' said the young man. 'If that was the case, how on earth do they get their mail?'"

With that Tidy departed and I set off for my room where, as I guessed, my selection committee were waiting. "Hello, Ramsey," was my first greeting to the little group outside my door, "pleasant afternoon?" Of course I did not expect a guilty reaction and he merely nodded but I saw no reason why I should not have a private laugh over his little excursion into the Indian underworld.

We trooped into the room and spread ourselves around its vastness. When we played a match in Jaipur we stayed at a hotel in which Tidy measured out what he called "the business end of my run-up" in the room he shared with Tom Abbey. "I woke in the middle of the night and there he was, demonstrating to himself that he could get in the last 12 yards of his run and still have a bit of space for three walking paces," Tom told us all many a time.

"I said 'What the hell are you doing Tidy' and he grunted 'When I get home I may cut down my run and see if I can't bowl off-cutters because that will save me a lot of trouble and sore shins.' He's quite mad, of course. Full of plans that come to nothing, boastful and making a fool of himself all the time. No wonder he's a fast bowler."

As captain I had the best of the rooms on each stay, so we had no need of a team room and many a night the whole party gathered in my suite - it was furnished as if I was at least a maharajah - and, without causing any other of the guests the slightest inconvenience, had our parties as far into the night as we pleased.

Coffee and tea, on silver trays large enough to plan a war, soon arrived and Ramsey took charge of our refreshments. It was, so far as I could see, his only purpose in being at these meetings, since he neither contributed to the discussions, nor was of any value otherwise but in the letter of contract that MCC sent me it was laid down that "the manager must attend all relevant selection meetings and discussions." So that he could write an end-of-tour report on my behaviour, I used to think in my black moments.

Our meeting on this occasion was short. Every member of the party was fit and well and Rhodes, who said little except to Hobbs on the whole trip, but never missed a trick, pronounced that morale was high. "The lads know it's one more match and then off home," was his only comment.

Jake Johnson, as vice-captain, chipped in that he was impressed with the batting of Tom Abbey at the nets and, without warning, Rhodes said: "I wish to say that, although I was not in favour of young Abbey when we arrived here, I have changed my opinion and I think he might well play in place of Ken Hutchinson. He is hitting the ball nicely at the moment, as Mr. Johnson says."

That settled matters. Hutchinson had not scored many runs and none that were important, either in the first innings or in winning or saving a match, and so we left him out and gave Tom Abbey his chance, with consequences none of us could have visualised.

Before the meeting broke up I thought it wise to have a few words of my own. "Tomorrow's match is on the schedule as An Indian XI v MCC," I said, "but the local newspapers and every Indian I speak to says it is the first Test between England and India. Now we know that is untrue, and we also know that MCC and history books, not to mention Wisden, will not regard it as such.

"But while we are in this country, while this atmosphere prevails, we must consider the Indian reading of events. In other words I want everyone in this room - and I shall say exactly these words to the whole team later on this evening - to consider they are playing for England against India. I shall tell Mansfield too so that the message returns to the people back home.

"Not least important is that it will motivate the players and simplify matters in their minds. We have the beating of the side, if it is the one I see referred to in their newspapers, but they have the idea that they have national pride behind them and we must match that pride blow for blow."

They all nodded solemnly but without the slightest enthusiasm and I hoped I got a better response when I spoke to the players, but as my small committee of Ramsey, Johnson, Rhodes and Hobbs, who had as usual said nothing throughout the meeting, trooped out I felt depressed by the way my short speech had been received.

I walked to the door with them and there, to my surprise, was the lady I had knocked down with such little gallantry that afternoon and who had, to be frank, floored me in return.

"Are you busy? May I talk to you for a moment? I will not keep you for more than a few minutes." What could a gentleman do but invite her into his room and ring the bell for afternoon tea. The time passed as I took in the full details of this young lady. She was tall and well-made but trim and with, as far as I could tell under her long dress, legs that, as Tidy has often said, "seem so long they must reach to heaven and probably do."

But it was the smile that fascinated me. Something seemed to amuse her every moment of the day. Her blue-grey eyes lit up and her wide, generous mouth split across teeth she must have cleaned whenever she had a minute to spare. When the tea boy argued because it was our second order for tea to my room within an hour she seemed to find the scene hilarious. She still had a faint smile when he left, protesting even though he was richer, if I am any judge, by a full week's wages.

"Now Miss . . ." I paused to allow her to fill in the details.

"I am Annabelle Jameson, and I have lived here in this part of north India - as I so rudely told you during our brief, what shall I say, er, our tumble together in the foyer - all my life." At the word "tumble" that smile lit her face again. Fascinating. I could not have been more taken with a lady.

"And you visit this hotel frequently?" I was making desultory conversation, trying to find out anything about this Mona Lisa that might give me a reason for her presence, her abrupt rudeness and her visit to my room now.

"My father is the manager, my mother is his right-hand man, so to speak and now that I am 21 I am his helpmate too. Poor Daddy. He is so hard worked and with no other European on his staff he is pushed to keep going. A full team of cricketers is a worry but then so are a maharajah's retinue and a king's band of rascals and we have all three here at the moment.

"But I am sure you are wondering about my presence. I have come to apologise to you for my behaviour this afternoon. As soon as I had spoken to Mama about it I realised that it could not have been all your fault and that I must take some of the blame. So" - and here she held out her hand - "let us shake on it and be friends, Mr. Collinson!"

We shook hands with great propriety and I took care not to hang on lest I appear to be the sort of male bully whose only wish in life is to hold some part of a lady's anatomy. I admit my thoughts had strayed in that direction; but more of that later I told myself.

She sipped delicately at her tea. "An excellent cup, if I say so myself as runs this hotel," she smiled. The pleasure she got out of life was incredible and the warmth of her enjoyment spread everywhere around her. I was desperate to know her better by now. I must see more of this girl, I thought, and, for the first time since I fell for the washergirl at Archbishop Holgate School, aged 12, the thought of marriage, children, home by the fire and a cat on the parlour couch, crossed my mind.

Miss Jameson rose and headed for the door. "Do not see me any further, Mr. Collinson," she said and left the room, pausing only to give me one last smile.

Ten minutes later there was another knock at my door and I found a young porter from the hotel desk with a card. It announced that Major Hugh Potter of the 16th Rifles was hoping he might have an hour of my time.

On the back of the card he had written: "I have been here 20 years and I may be of help to you and your men in their forth-coming battle." I glanced at the clock and found there was little more than an hour before our dinner but I told the boy to bring him along and five minutes later, as I sorted out my dinner jacket, a clean shirt and my shoes for the evening, Potter was with me.

He was a straight, lean man in his late forties but it was difficult to tell that he had served his time anywhere save England for under his broad-rimmed hat he was paler than any Yorkshire yokel.

"I have read reports of your men's distress in the heat and I wondered if I might offer some advice, especially as I also read that the Indians think this is some sort of Test," he began.

I admit I was cautious. I felt Potter might believe he had worthwhile information but that his true motive in coming to visit me was to obtain a ticket for his wife's second cousin, or to gossip about us in the mess that night, or to seek an autograph or two. I was wrong.

He went on. "I have spent the whole of my career in the Army and the last score or so years in this part of the world. Nothing exciting, mainly teaching young officers how to keep their men alive and well in the heat and under the mental strain - which can be as real as any physical ailment - that goes with being in a foreign country. Have your players gone through such problems?" he asked.

"I call it homesickness - you can call it what you will," I said. "My major concern has been the traditional illness - often called Delhi Belly - but I am afraid that few of my men have missed that illness, including myself. You must know as much about it as any man on earth. Is there a cure?"

"Yes, the local doctors know the remedies and you can trust them. Yes, if one of your men is overtaken by this nasty trouble you must tell them to eat nothing for roughly 24 hours, only to sip liquids and then to go on to a diet of black tea, perhaps a banana and plain bread for another 24 hours.

"There is a prevention and although it is late in your tour I recommend to you the simple process of eating the local food, cooked by local men, and refusing to consider such ridiculous statements as 'I'm English and I never eat foreign food'. Of course, I have much greater authority over my men than you have over your cricketers but if I had come to you a few weeks ago I would have said you must insist that hot Indian food cooked by men who know how to keep their materials fresh is the only answer." He banged his fist on the table a couple of times and I guessed what sort of officer he might be. Not a sympathetic one.

Potter went on. "Tomorrow will be hot, even exceptionally hot, according to those who make a few pennies by forecasting the weather in the market places and I suggest that your men drink as much water as they can comfortably hold before they go out to play and replenish it whenever they have a chance. I suggest that, even though they have been out here for several weeks, they cover up and particularly the back of the neck."

Major Potter fished squares of cloth from his knapsack and offered them to me. "If your men get these sewn on to their caps so that they hang over their necks they will miss the worst of the sun. Here is another aid to conquering the heat. I have brought you some salt tablets. Not too many mind. A couple a day is all you will need if your men lose moisture by sweating; another might be a help if they have to piss. Men differ in these needs."

I liked the man. Utterly direct, without a scrap of side and prepared to help because, he said, his son had wanted to be a cricketer and it turned out he was not good enough. "Sad, but I have learnt to accept the disappointment," he sighed. I wondered how the lad felt but he probably had no idea he was living his father's dreams.

I thought I might try to put some of his disappointment behind him. "I think there is one further favour you might do us," I said. "We are about to hold our end-of-tour dinner combined with our team meeting ahead of this important match tomorrow. Would you be good enough to attend the dinner, talk to my lads about their health tomorrow and make suggestions to them about the Indians and their habits. We know them as cricketers but not as men and I am sure you might help us correct this omission."

Potter agreed as if he had been offered the chance to attain some personal nirvana; indeed being behind the scenes with a cricketer was probably his idea of heaven. I went into the dressing room of my suite, leaving him to finish his tea while I put on my dress suit. He was in uniform so he would not be out of place and he declined my invitation to wash and brush up.

By the time dinner was done Potter proved to be the life and soul of the party and all those who had the chance to talk to him - and particularly the new lads or "raw recruits" as he kept referring to them - seemed to spend most of their time smiling, which is always a good sign. I had told him to take a back seat while the team was announced, but he had the commonsense - the humanity indeed - to pick out poor Ken Hutchinson as the most distressed man in the room and go across to talk to him immediately afterwards.

Hutchinson had, poor lad, been left on his own when the other players realised that he was the one to be dropped and that Thomas Abbey would be their team mate. They crowded round Tom and rightly tried to make him a member of the family. Ken was left on his own but Major Potter realised his misery and went over with a few kind words so quickly that I had barely the chance to assure him that his career was far from done because he was not in this team.

Potter, who I introduced to everyone as the guest of honour of the evening, had no trouble in making conversation; indeed he had a sort of genius for opening up everyone save Rhodes, who clearly decided he was above such stuff and Hobbs who would not be drawn on any subject. "Rhodes is a thinker as befits a man named after such an island of poets and philosophers and Hobbs's powers of concentration make him seem remote," he said, without appearing to be offering an excuse for his failure to communicate with the only truly great players on the trip.

He talked at length to Jake Johnson and briefly to Mansfield who had become an integral part of our social life in the three months. "That man is untrustworthy," he said after his first talk to our only reporter; but I could not agree. Mansfield had betrayed no trust, shown at times that he was capable of carrying complicated and difficult messages back home and proved himself highly trustworthy.

I am wondering as I write this note whether I misunderstood Potter completely and that he might have been talking of someone else; but as you will soon discover I have had little time to consider anything since I completed the dinner by telling my "troops" as Potter would have it that they were to consider they were playing for the full England team tomorrow.

Two hours was enough to end the dinner and I drifted back to my room with no great purpose in mind, save to give Major Potter a last drink, a small MCC tie pin - of which we had many - as a keepsake and make a short speech of thanks. On the way I passed my new housemaid and said: "Good night, Sharda" but Potter interrupted me. "That is not Sharda," he said. I said glibly that I could not tell one Indian from another.

"Don't forget that they cannot tell us apart either," he said and the thought stuck in my head for all I had no special reason to remember it. It is whirling in my brain as I write this chronicle now.

As we arrived at my door there was a commotion from a crowd of Indians running towards us. "Collinson Sahib, a terrible event has occurred. Collinson, help us, Collinson." I held up my hand for silence and slowly the most smartly dressed man in the crowd emerged to tell me what had happened.

"Sir, Miss Jameson has been kidnapped and the brigands have written an impertinent note to her father which says that unless he pays 10,000 rupees within a week she will be killed." A dread feeling gripped me as I wondered if this latest piece of devilment was aimed at my team rather than her father.

"Her father wants your help, sir, because he knows she was in your room today and thinks you may know something of this terrible crime," the man went on.

"Bring her father here and tell him I will do what I can to help," I ordered. Potter said: "If there is anything I can do I will, but I feel this is a matter I must leave to you." I accepted what he said, thanked him for his good services, shook his hand and bade him good night. The tie pin would have to wait.

I stepped inside my room and found a note on the floor. Big sheet of paper, sprawling writing, no date and no signature. "Lose the match or the girl will lose her virginity, her fingers one by one and finally her head by a single blow," it said.

Not much choice there. I sat down in my room and waited for her father, sure that once again my tour as England captain was going to end in disaster.

CHAPTER THIRTEEN
December 27th, 1906.
Karachi

I thought it best to send for Justin Davenport to see what he could do to help. Our chief spy and defender of yours truly had been about mysterious other business in the past few weeks, assuming that the tour had settled, that I was not in any danger and that there was nothing for me to do for the government.

By the time he was found Mr. Jameson, the hotel manager and the father of Annabelle, had also joined me and shortly afterwards we were telling yet another tale of kidnapping to a new set of Indian policemen. They nodded their heads solemnly, read all the notes and compared the details we offered of my capture and release with the present circumstances, listened to our stories of the betting coup and looked, to be fair to them, totally mystified. But so were we.

It was long after midnight when the meeting was finished and I still had to sit down, as I always do on the eve of any match, and try to prepare my own mind for the day to come. What happens if I win the toss, who is to bowl first if I lose the toss, what are the opposing batsmen and bowlers likely to try, how will my fields look. What shall I say to my men, which bowlers must I try to rest and is there anything in particular to remember about the opposition. Those are the common thoughts of any captain.

On this day I had a unique problem. I also had to consider how I should go about losing the match if Miss Jameson were not freed before the end. Her father was beside himself with worry about how to find the ransom money - 30 years' salary, he said with a rueful grin - but I told him that his daughter would be returned without any injury if the second note was obeyed.

The police had promised to send out their spies and I had dispatched a note by hand to Dunne Sahib asking if there were rumours of a betting coup around the bazaar but these were desperate measures by desperate men and we did not hold out much hope of success.

I could not sleep for several hours as I worried over the consequences of winning this match. It might bring the death of a lady I admired for the second time in a few months. Equally if the game were to be lost my career and the livelihood of several of my players might be in jeopardy. Imagine the likes of Rhodes and Hobbs returning home and being asked how they had contrived to lose to a bunch of Indian amateurs. Their fellow professionals would laugh in their faces, the selection committee of England might look elsewhere for players to beat Australia and the county committees would wonder if it might not be better to cancel the contracts of such incompetents.

Eventually I snatched a few hours' sleep on my settee - which was wide enough for the average elephant to make itself comfortable - but by six o'clock I was listening to the cries of the street below my window. I could not resist looking out and saw as remarkable a sight as India ever presented. Four men were transferring live chickens from one cart to another. The chickens were bound tightly with string and being passed in the manner of those games of Rugby I used to witness on the Knavesmire as a lad. Poor chickens, no doubt heading for a pot and spending their last few hours being chucked with great dexterity as if they were bags of flour.

I dressed in my cricket gear, packed my leather case and went to breakfast. On my way I asked that extra flagons of water should be taken from the hotel - which has astonishingly clean water for this part of the world - to our dressing rooms at the ground. I paused at the hotel door and watched the sun rising over the sea; the dawn of what sort of day I could only imagine.

During the night I had decided feverishly that I would do nothing untoward by way of fixing the result of this match and that I would have to contrive a defeat on the final day if Miss Jameson had not been found. In other words if the game went against us I might not need to take any steps that clashed with my conscience.

Only Jake Johnson was at the big table reserved for the team in the centre of the breakfast room when I sat down.

"Couldn't sleep, Jake?" I asked.

"Biggest game I ever played in, Bernard," he said. It was a shock. He had not called me Bernard since I was appointed captain and sometimes his ostentatious use of the word "captain" or "skipper" had been irking. Yet he had seemed pleased enough when I told him back in August.

"An unforgettable match I guess," I said. "Any idea which way it might go. I think we must be the stronger side by an immeasurable amount."

I think I caught him off guard, although I did not intend anything of the sort. "I was talking to my. . ." and then his voice trailed away. "That is to say I was talking to my friend in a little place in the markets here where you can take a Turkish bath and he told me that in the bazaar you could not get a bet on England and that when you asked the price for the Indian team the answer was 'what price would you like?'"

"That will only spur on the Indians," I said. Jake laughed out loud.

"Those we have played against so far did not look great fighters and we have won every match except the first when all that nonsense took place and I do not see any way we can lose," he replied. I noticed he was eating the hot Indian food that had been largely ignored for most of the tour. Potter's words were having an effect.

"Perhaps," I said. I confess I was puzzling over his slip of the tongue. He had obviously not intended to finish the sentence in the way he did and I wonder who he had originally intended to add to his possessive pronoun.

He changed the subject. "Who will open the bowling? Rhodes again? I also heard last night from your friend Major Potter that it would be damned hot today and so I guess that the slow bowlers might be required to do a lot of work."

We pushed the subject backwards and forwards and came to no great conclusion. Three hours before the match was due to begin there was no sign of great heat and it seemed to me to be cooler than usual. I asked a waiter but his conclusion was so contorted that, frankly, I lost patience and sent him about his business.

The others joined us one by one, with Rhodes coming in last. He is normally the most punctual of men and although he was not last he was later than I would have expected and not looking at his best. "A bit peaky, Wilfred?" I asked rather anxiously.

"No, skipper, a touch of the collywobbles in the night but

I'm fine now. Don't worry I'll be there morning 'til night, bowling into the wind, with the wind, uphill, downhill. . ." It was not his complaining voice so we took no notice and soon we were all gathered together and ready to make our way to the ground.

Cabs were called, equipment loaded aboard, the hotel servants came to wish us good luck and we were off on the last great adventure of our tour of India.

I have to say that, although some of the grounds we used were in less than perfect condition, the Indian authorities had made a big effort with this match. The ground itself looked in fine condition with marquees, those open tents they call shamianars and flags flying bravely from the pavilion. Inside it was clear they intended us to be welcome. The dressing rooms were clean, the latrines fairly clean and, thanks to the negotiations conducted by George Ramsey, food was being sent from the hotel too.

One or two of the younger players, led by Hobbs, went on to the ground to knock up; Tidy, who was not playing, ran several circuits of the ground at a quickish pace, leading Abbey who was nothing like so good an athlete while the spectators cat-called and the Indian players looked on in amazement.

Half an hour before the start their captain Baig was at our door inviting me to go to the middle for the toss and once again the sense of excitement surrounded me. "Come with me and see fair play, Rhodes," I said, because he had been the one who spotted the trickery in Lahore. But he sent Hobbs in his place and at that point I should have suspected something was more seriously wrong than he would admit.

I had my own plan. As we reached the middle, I offered Baig the golden guinea which has been called my lucky coin, and said: "Do me a favour and toss with this coin. It is a great keepsake of mine and I would be honoured if you would use it for this important game."

He made no attempt to dissuade me but handed me his own coin. "Exchange is no robbery, eh," he laughed. "You will see there is no deception in my coin, Collinson, but I will happily toss with your money." I had not intended to allow him to keep my coin but his gesture meant I had to take his silver rupee for my gold guinea. Not a great rate of exchange, I know, but I cannot believe that a man who could have bought Buckingham Palace with his loose change needed such small amounts of money.

For whatever the reason, my exchange worked and my lucky coin came down heads just as I called. The sun was a lot hotter now, the wind had dropped, the pitch looked firm and dry and I did not need to think long and hard. "We'll bat, skipper," I said and shook his hand. I think I felt it tremble. Winning the toss on that pitch, in the coming heat, was a distinct advantage and he must have known he faced a long day in the field.

I broke into a trot as we neared the pavilion and announced to my men breathlessly that "We're to bat. Pads on Rhodes, Hobbs. But where is Rhodes?"

"You find him outside, skipper. I reckon the old lad is not too well," said Tidy.

"Damn," I said as softly as I could. "You're all right, Jack?"

"Fine," Hobbs said, concentrating.

"Tom Abbey?" I called.

"Yes, captain."

"Go in first with Jack. Have a talk with him first. He likes to get off the mark early and I don't want you run out first ball. All right?" Abbey was already buckling on his pads and there was a look in his eye as he strode across to Hobbs that I thought might indicate a few runs from the lad.

Rhodes came out of the latrine looking dreadful, green as a garden pea and already thinner in my imagination. "Sorry, skipper," he said. "I wanted to say something before you announced your team but I felt all right and then suddenly everything came up."

I took him by the shoulder. "Ken Hutchinson will take you back to the hotel and send for Major Potter. No, he won't. Potter is here. I've just seen him across the other side of the field. Douglas, go and find the man. He's with a group of Army chaps. Put your running to some use and get that nice man across here promptly." He ran off immediately

I turned back to Rhodes. "Did you talk to Potter last night? He will fix you up in no time, give you the right advice, see you are fit as soon as maybe. If you can get well by tomorrow and bowl for us we'll be very grateful. If not, it will be someone else who has to bowl from both ends." I was so pleased that we had young Littleboy in the team, a lad brought up in hardship and only kept in the shadows on this tour because Rhodes was batsman, bowler and brain. Now Littleboy's turn had come.

Rhodes was in safe hands and I could look to the rest of the day. "Right, is everyone listening? Wilfred is ill and I've announced him in the team so we're a vital man short. Hobbs and Tom Abbey will start, I'll go in next and then it's the order as before. We are hoping for long innings. No need for anyone to hurry. Slowly does it. This match can go into the fourth day and that should be plenty of time for us to win. As I said last night this is a Test in their eyes and we must consider it in the same way. Except that none of them is Spofforth or Giffen or Billy Murdoch and we shall win."

I don't normally make what are often scornfully referred to as "Ra Ra" speeches but the lads looked more cheerful afterwards and by the time Hobbs and Abbey went out to bat there was a much more spritely attitude in the dressing room. The noise level had risen and that is always a good sign.

By the time I had finished talking Major Potter had been located by Tidy and taken Rhodes off to a quiet corner of the pavilion but he could not promise he would be fit to play by tomorrow. He had sent for an Indian doctor who he said "rarely kills more than one patient a day." Unfortunately Rhodes heard this remark and looked as if he would rather be in the Yorkshire Dales to receive his medicine.

Of course, this day's play has been extensively reported in the English newspapers, thanks to the industry of Cedric Mansfield under a variety of nom de plume, so that Hobbs' great double century and the support of Abbey and the rest is already well known. The pair of them played beautifully on a pitch that might have been made for batting. Hobbs was imperious; Abbey merely industrious but it served our purpose nicely and I knew by lunch, when they had 95 runs to their credit and not given a sign of getting out, that we could not lose and that, given ordinary luck, we must win.

My own singular failure, caused by a thoroughly careless shot to my first ball which went off an edge on to my stumps, did not even cause a hiccup. After all 199 for two is not a bad score and by the end of the day we had piled up 360 for eight. Sadly, there was still no prospect of Rhodes batting. Their attack was not first-class, the captaincy of Baig was optimistic - he had close fielders after five hours of non-stop attack - and my batsmen took advantage.

In a sense the illness of Rhodes was an incentive for the lesser batsmen to shoulder the responsibility and they showed how well they were able to take charge when the call came. I was as proud of them as any captain might be. "We're going to win this one," I told them at the end of the day and when Mansfield came to ask me for a summary of the day's play I hinted at as much again. "And pass that message to your Indian reporter friends too," I told him.

Unfortunately it did not help us to discover when we returned to the hotel that there was no sign of Miss Annabelle Jameson and it began to look as if we might still have to think fairly quickly if she was to be saved.

Justin Davenport was nowhere to be found, there was no answer from Dunne Sahib on his bazaar gossip and all the hotel manager could say was that he had not seen his daughter since "as I told the police again today, she made an entirely unofficial and unnecessary visit to your room."

By this statement this poor man, greatly upset at the absence of Annabelle, seemed to be implying that I had played some part in her disappearance. He had my sympathy but his line of reasoning was doing nothing to help discover the whereabouts of his daughter nor apprehend her kidnappers.

I dined with the whole team once again and the conversation revolved around the condition of Rhodes who was slowly recovering, but weak since Major Potter had given him little save liquids all day and not allowed him tea with milk which was like depriving a Yorkshireman of his birthright. "Black tea is not what God intended man to drink," he said when I paid a visit to his room, but Potter was adamant and Rhodes admitted the worst of his sickness was over and that he had not made a violent rush to the lavatory since he left the ground.

Potter was far from optimistic about a recovery in time to take part in this match. "We'll see in the morning," he said.

CHAPTER FOURTEEN
December 28th, 1906.
Karachi

I had decided during the blackest moments of the night that I would declare immediately and so give the Indians the chance to draw level with us and provide me with the opportunity to throw the game in their direction even if it meant taking the team into my confidence. So far the story of Miss Jameson's kidnapping had not leaked out and neither my team nor the opposition knew anything of this crime. My lads were blissfully looking for ways to settle the result quickly.

Rhodes could not keep his mind off the match and he had summoned young Littleboy to his room and given him detailed instructions. Since I was only captain of the team I was not allowed to know what these might be but that suited me. I had other things on my mind and thought it better not to ask until we got out on to the field. After all Rhodes was the owner of one of the best brains in the country, he came from a highly successful Yorkshire team and he had a long background in Tests. To say he knew more about cricket than I might ever hope to learn was to underestimate his prowess.

Once again the day dawned brightly and I confirmed my intention to declare when I ran into the Indian captain Mahmood Baig as I arrived at the ground. I was being polite but once again he chose to go on the attack.

"I admire your courage," he said with one of those enigmatic sideways nods of the head typical of the Indian and irritating to the Englishman who has not the faintest idea what the gesture implies.

"You think me the bravest of fools?" I asked with a smile.

"No, Collinson, I think you have made a poor tactical decision and particularly in telling me so early in the day," was his answer. Sometimes Indians can be as blunt as any Yorkshireman and to no purpose.

I reached the dressing room to find Rhodes sitting on a

canvas chair waiting for me. He still looked pale under his tan and his naturally lean build seemed skeletal.

"How are you this morning, Wilfred?"

"Getting better, skipper. Major Potter has the right answer - and a very natural cure if I may say so - and I feel better but terribly weak. I don't suppose he would expect a soldier to get straight back on to the drill square after such an attack, much less fight a war and I don't feel as if I could bowl more than half a dozen overs. Still, we must see if the lad Littleboy can earn his corn. I have given him a few useful pointers." He nodded sagely as if he had managed to pour all his vast knowledge into Littleboy into a single cricket lesson.

"What have you suggested to him?"

"Only that he might bowl one spell of fastish stuff. Of course, it is not my business to tell you what to do Mr. Collinson but if I might suggest you use him to open the bowling with his usual mixture of slow deliveries but in the next spell allow him to bowl as quick as he likes. He tells me that he began as a fast-medium bowler something after the style of my team mate George Hirst and I have not seen that type of bowling since I arrived in this country. It requires a different technique from a batsman and, no matter how talented, these inexperienced Indians may find the quick left arm variety of bowling over the wicket is too much for them."

"Good point, Wilfred," I said. "You know I am to declare?"

"I have spent most of the waking hours of the night - and those have been many - considering what you might achieve by an early declaration," Rhodes answered. "If you batted another hour you might put the game beyond their reach even at this early stage. You are giving them the chance to win but you cannot expect many runs from the rest of the side and you may as well press on with the game. After all, as yesterday's play demonstrated, we are far too strong for them and I think if I had been batting they might be facing a first innings total of 500."

I gathered the players round and told them we were to declare immediately and that I was pressing for victory even though this was only the second morning. There was still no news of Miss Jameson but I thought I might still be able to swing this match around on the last two days if that decision was forced on me. I have to admit I was still reacting like a cricketer and the very idea of tossing the match to the Indians, whatever the circumstances, revolted me.

By now there was only a short time before the start of play and players were fidgeting with their whites, their equipment and, in the case of Jake Johnson, going through the fitness routine that he had maintained in India just as he did at home.

The concentration grows inside a dressing room as the time for play approaches; you can see the tension in each player; and it makes a fascinating study. But the study can only be carried out by those deeply involved in the game.

A stranger might not observe this intensity but a cricketer walking into any dressing room in the last few minutes before play might smell the atmosphere, sense the well being or otherwise of the side and, just as important, detect who might be the leading players, who might be the disruptive forces and who might be likely to dominate the day's events.

These thoughts were forming in my head, perhaps for the thousandth time, when there was a loud knocking on the door. I walked across and found an Indian, dressed in the uniform of their Post Office, and carrying an envelope. "Here is mail for Collinson," he said.

I was on the brink of telling him to take it to the hotel but I suppose curiosity got the better of me so I simply thanked him and took the letter. "Mr. Collinson, MCC cricket team, India" it read. The postmark was a British one and only a month old. Ominously it also bore the words On His Majesty's Service.

You will wonder how it found me across India's vast continent but you will send yourself into a tizzy asking such questions. Call it a miracle, call it a new version of the rope trick, call it a piece of magic or think it may have arrived on a magic carpet. You will never find the answer.

Still trying to work out the complexities of this letter's markings I tore open the envelope and found inside a letter with the imprint of the Dominion Office at the top and Lord Curzon's signature block at the bottom. There was a second unreadable signature too. There was only a single sheet, typed no doubt by the rude woman in his outer office and not wasting a single word.

'22nd November 1906.

Dear Collinson,

You agreed in our previous meeting that you would carry out the government's requests from time to time and now you are to be tested by your first mission.

It is absolutely essential for the sake of a trade agreement which is to be put in place shortly that we have the full confidence of the Indian people and that a good atmosphere is created in the country.

In order to facilitate this agreement I am instructing you to lose the final match of the tour against An Indian XI. I recognise that you may think this an unusual request and of course it goes against your nature as a captain to consider defeat. However this decision has the full backing of the Prime Minister and I have taken the precaution of getting him to sign the letter as well.

I trust you have enjoyed your trip and that you made the acquaintance of Phillip Dunne as I suggested.'

(His signature and that of the Prime Minister followed.)

Well, well. My, my, I thought. Here is a pretty kettle of fish. One that smells too. What trade agreement? With whom? India? What piffle.

I was pulled back into the real word by the sound of Jake Johnson's voice. "Come on, skipper. Time to field." And off we marched on to the ground, listening to the roar that greeted us from God only knows how many Indians. As far as I was concerned they might as well have been whispering. I had just read the strangest letter I have ever received and I did not have the faintest idea how to react.

Looking back on things as I write this day's entry late at night in the hotel I suppose I should have seen my course of action immediately but the shock of receiving the letter and all the other events of recent days put my head in a whirl. How I managed to set a field for Littleboy I have no idea; if he had started with his right arm I doubt if I would have noticed.

He had bowled half his first over, slow spin round the wicket and keeping a nice length straight away, when I came to my senses. I had been so out of sorts that I posted myself at mid-off instead of slip, just to find time to think.

Then it came to me in a flash. I would not do anything. I would ignore the letter, throw it away if necessary and pretend I had never received it. What sort of a life would I face if I deliberately lost this game, presented whoever was betting on it with a huge sum of money. Even if my actions did save Miss Jameson's life - and I had no guarantee of that - it would not stop these ruffians, whoever they were. They would simply be encouraged to try the same trick again.

Besides, it was not my responsibility to obey kidnappers, or to rescue their victims. My duty, as I saw it, was to play a responsible game of cricket for the paying public. If they chose to bet on the matches they should have a certainty that both sides had been trying their utmost to win, or draw. After that, whatever I had promised the government, I should not try to alter the result of a game.

I also remembered what the Prime Minister had told me at that meeting in the little house behind Lord's. He said that the government would not ask me to do anything which interfered with the playing of matches. By that, he explained, he meant that he would not "ask you to lead your men against the Boer warriors" or some such phrase. He would not whisk me away from a match to talk to another Prime Minister. In other words my primary duty would be to the match in which I was playing. Only if it was convenient would the government use my services.

Standing at mid-off while the young Indian batsman who had made such an impression on my players with his innings in Lahore prodded the ball down the pitch, I had another thought. I had no idea if the letter from London was genuine. And who could I ask? The Captain was nearby but I had not seen him for a day or two. Davenport had vanished too and it would not be a shock if the two were together on some mission. Dunne Sahib seemed to have no desire to communicate with me further, if his failure to reply to my request of two nights ago was anything to judge by.

In short I was on my own and it was down to me to make my own decision.

I made one immediately. "Come on, young man," I shouted to Littleboy. "Let him have one quick and short and I'll put a man under his chin. Tom, go to short leg for the last two balls of the over." The trick worked like a dream. The young opener who had been content to defend suddenly found himself forced on to the back foot, the ball skidded off bat and pad, and straight into Tom Abbey's hands.

The lad, who clearly had no English or he would have understood my intentions, walked off with some reluctance and I suspect he felt that, although the umpire's finger went up promptly, he was not out. Straight off the pad perhaps, but no matter. They were one wicket down for nought in the first over and still nearly 400 short of turning this game into anything but a walk-over for us.

Mahmood Baig came in next and batted for the rest of their innings. At least he had the strength of character to ignore the disasters at the other end and when they were all out for 118 he had 54 and was still batting. I did not like this strange man who, for all his fabled wealth, his English education and his background of privilege, could still not bring himself to treat his players with decency. I heard him barking orders at his bowlers, sending his fielders on long trips at the end of each over and complaining all the time. But I have to admit that he was a fine batsman, that he had more courage than the rest of his side in total and there were times when I sympathised with his contempt for his underlings.

I ordered them to follow on and once again Baig treated me as if I might be a congenital idiot. "Why are you taking this course?" he asked; headmaster demanding of a stupid pupil why he imagined two and two might make minus three. "There is more hot weather to come and if you batted a second time you would tire us out and demolish us easily in our second innings. Why don't you think of these things? You deputy made mistakes in Lahore and now you are not only repeating his errors but creating a difficult and dangerous situation for yourself."

I did not reply but left him to his arrogance. I did not have to live with him for more than a few hours of my life; he had to live with himself 24 hours a day. I wondered how he coped.

December 29th. Karachi.

The second innings went nothing like so successfully as the first. The Indians had a deficit of 242 and they had to bat for the last third of the second day and the two following days to save the game; or make enough runs in their second innings to set us a difficult target on the fourth day in the final innings when conditions might be different. Perhaps the ball might turn, or cracks appear in the pitch; who knows?

Their first salvation came, not from bad bowling by us, nor from great batting but from the weather. One moment we had heat still around the century mark and the next clouds rushed in from the sea and we had rain that prevented any further play on the second day.

Back at the hotel there was better news. Wilfred Rhodes was improving as rapidly as could be expected and Major Potter, who had been as diligent as Florence Nightingale in keeping Rhodes' morale high and his food intake low, suggested that his patient might eat a little light supper and see if he could keep that in his system and then we would judge his fitness in the morning. If play resumed and if Rhodes was fit then the tide would definitely turn our way.

Justin Davenport was in my room when I arrived. I was tired from the emotional strain of the day and not relishing company but I thought to take advantage of his presence and asked him to read Curzon's letter.

"My God!" he exclaimed. "This is a pretty puzzle." He sat there staring at the letter and then said: "I think this may be a forgery, Bernard, but I cannot be sure. Let me consult Mansfield, to see if he can get a confirmation from the Dominion Office that Curzon has sent you this missive. In the meantime, what do you propose to do?"

"I am determined to press on for victory," I said. "I have decided that a mere cricketer cannot be held responsible for trade agreements, nor should anyone obey the orders of a kidnapper. Is there any news of Miss Jameson? I wish her no harm but the matter of her abduction is far from clear and I feel I would be wrong to assume her disappearance should concern me."

Davenport put his thumbs behind his lapels and considered the ways of the mysterious world for a moment.

"The police have no news, Dunne Sahib has heard no rumours and The Captain, who has been in touch with me this afternoon, says that he hopes the death of a second young lady will not mar this tour. He is clearly deeply upset by the demise of his adopted daughter, particularly in such a dramatic and horrible way, and I think his judgement is affected when he thinks about her.

"I think you should press on with your match in any way you see fit. I too am puzzled by the note from Curzon. How can he have judged a situation weeks ahead? If I had access to a note of his I might see if the signature had been forged - or, for that matter, the signature of the Prime Minister too. These are great men and it would be easy to copy their handwriting. Someone, like Dunne Sahib for instance, who had worked with Curzon and no doubt seen notes from the Prime Minister, would not have any trouble in identifying a forgery."

I said: "Or getting a forgery made?"

He paused a long time before he answered. "What are you suggesting."

"Only this, Davenport. I met Dunne this week and I know he is the man who led those brigands who kidnapped me. His voice is exactly the same and when I put the matter to him he did not deny it. But why, Davenport, why?"

"Any number of reasons," he replied, putting on his best imitation of a spy in a foreign land. "A reason of state. Not difficult to guess that there are many things going on we do not hear about. Treaties, trade agreements, the sins of the mighty. Who knows what little secondary plot lurks in every decision that comes out of Parliament, or the Cabinet, or from one of the Palaces, and I guess Dunne is privy to many of these matters. Perhaps he is playing a very deep game."

"And I thought all this naughtiness was simply a matter of a few Indians putting on a bet or two," I responded.

"Maybe," he said. "But this letter, forged or not, indicates that there is something more afoot. We may be in the midst of a big event, or we may simply be in the middle of a cricket match of no consequence." With that pronouncement Davenport went off in search of Mansfield, our perpetually busy, frequently distressed reporter.

My day was not finished yet. Within a few minutes I had a knock on the door that revealed George Ramsey, who reported that Littleboy had been taken ill with the same upset tummy that brought Rhodes to his knees, and then came another knock from Jake Johnson to say that Tom Abbey was also ill.

"It's going through the whole team," he said, too dramatically for my liking. "What is the news of Rhodes? Will he be fit for tomorrow?"

"If the other players go down any quicker he may be the fittest among us as he is the one farthest down the road to recovery," I said. "How about you? No sign of the Delhi Belly yet? I feel all right but who knows where it may strike next."

"I don't expect to be ill," said Jake, cheerful as ever and looking fitter than ever.

I went to my bed feeling that the day would bring worse news and I was right.

Six o'clock in the morning, after a restless night's sleep, is not the best time for bad news; it may even be the worst. But I was awakened at that hour by another call from George Ramsey. He had been running from room to room through the night and he had drawn up a list of those who were fit and those who might struggle on to the pitch.

John Littleboy was seriously ill and it would be a few days before he was fit for action. Tom Abbey seemed to be the least affected and said he would field "even if it means wearing a nappy." Rhodes was getting stronger, Hobbs was fully fit as I was and Jake Johnson was. Ken Hutchinson was saying that he had not had a day's illness on the entire tour; underlying message that none of this would have happened if he had kept his place. Douglas Tidy was insufferably well and constructing new tales about the effect of Delhi Belly and the importing of specially-woven nappies to keep cricketers on the field despite all their troubles.

As for the rest - the all-rounders Jimmy Lane-Wood, George Thompson and Bill Gardener - they all claimed to be well but, as Major Potter pointed out with some force in our meeting at the breakfast table, there are men who want to be part of the team to such an extent that they will catch any illness that is going, become drunkards or womanise if that is the general feeling within their party.

He thought they might develop illness just to fit into the pattern. "It's a form of barrack room hysteria," he said. I knew exactly what he meant. Such mental illnesses sweep dressing rooms just as easily as they sweep an Army camp. Within an hour of this speech Thompson and Gardener had both come to me saying they had the first hint of illness and I feared what I was beginning to call Potter's Hysteria might still turn into what some others call the Rajah's Revenge.

Nonetheless, when I arrived at the ground we had 12 fit men, of whom Tidy was undoubtedly the fittest, running round the ground while jeering at Tom Abbey who was looking greener than a cabbage and clearly not in the mood for jokes about his condition.

"Buck yourself up, man," Tidy shouted each time his circuit of the ground took him past Abbey who was sitting in the shade on the verandah. "A few laps of this ground in the heat and you will be fit to take part in the Olympics, never mind stand at short leg all day." Abbey moved out of sight and sound in the pavilion and, I suspect, within reach of the latrine.

The storm that disrupted the match the day before had passed but there was still no question of play until all the water had run off the surface and the pitch was a good deal drier. In one sense I hoped it was soon fit for play since I wanted to get at the Indians while their morale was still low and in another sense I wanted a delay so that I might have a clearer idea which of my men would be on the field helping me and which might be sitting in the latrine of no help to anyone.

An hour after noon the two umpires walked to the middle and pronounced the pitch fit for play and fifteen minutes later we were underway again. Rhodes was with us and looking a great deal better, but of course there was always the dread of a return of his illness, or that his strength might have gone. I need not have worried.

The openers, threatened by the unpleasant Mahmood Baig as we heard all too well through the flimsy woodwork between the two dressing rooms, presented a solid defence and attempted to score few runs until tea time. Rhodes with all his variations could not shift them, and John Sharp, who was the quickest bowler we had chosen, lacked the power and the sheer speed to take advantage of what little help was in the pitch.

Nor was there any better news after tea. The pitch had dried flat and hard but without pace. It was an open invitation to any batsman to make runs and although we got out the left-hander, a big solid man without imagination and with few strokes, the youngster was still batting and Mahmood Baig was finding life easy. By the close they had 118 for one, a fine contrast with their 118 all out in the first innings.

I had tried everything; used every combination of bowler; tried to nurse Rhodes but at the same time make him a powerful attacking device; Sharp at both ends and even a few balls round the wicket, although that was clearly a new departure for this traditional fast bowler. As they settled in comfortably I kept hearing the sneers of Baig and wondered if he might have been right. As we walked off he made an attempt to catch up with me, no doubt to deliver another strong opinion on my foolishness, but I was not in the mood and I walked faster and disappeared into the dressing room before he could grab me by the sleeve.

Inside there was none of the usual chatter of the contented team. Instead we had a gloomy silence and I felt unable to produce the words to break the spell. I tried another tack. "Come on, Douglas," I shouted to Tidy, who had been twelfth man all afternoon, and seemed as down as the rest by the lack of success. "Give us a few words that will cheer us all up."

I will give that man credit. He is never short of an answer. "Yes, captain, I'll make the lads laugh. If I was out there bowling there would be no crisis. I know just the length, I would stick one up the snout of that wretch Mahmood Baig and I would skittle the rest in no time.

"Now look, lads," and here he pretended to place his thumbs inside his waistcoat in the way of the great orators, "you know the skipper and his mates on the selection panel are far wiser than the rest of us. You know that if they made a judgement they cannot be wrong. They have ordained, despite my own advice I have to say, that I am a lesser bowler than Wilfred Rhodes, a lesser bowler than John Sharp and, for all he is reaching the veteran stage, a far lesser bowler than our new quickie John Littleboy."

By this stage they were all giggling, although one or two were casting a glance at me to see how I was taking this piece of insubordination. I laughed too. We needed the relief, frankly.

"So if that is the case, and I say that I can bowl out these dusky chaps, why can't you lot." Looking back, as I do now while I am writing this in my diary, I realise that Tidy's words are not all that funny, but in the atmosphere of a dressing room full of gloom they set my lads laughing at themselves and that was exactly the tonic we needed.

But Tidy did not know when to stop. "And if at any time tomorrow we are running out of overs in which to get rid of the dusky ones," he said, his face bursting with pleasure at the thought of such illegal tactics "he can sneak me on to the field, pretend I am Tom Abbey and I will do the job for him, see if I don't."

I would not, of course, have taken any notice of this bit of vainglorious boasting if it had not been for what happened in the next few hours.

CHAPTER FIFTEEN
December 30th, 1906.
Karachi

The good piece of news came first with the extraordinary announcement that Miss Jameson was back in her father and mother's care in their flat at the top of the hotel and in perfect health.

The information came from The Captain who had, if you remember, been absent without notice for several days and who did not seem the least concerned about our worries even if he knew or cared. He had, I have to say, given a completely different picture from the interested and helpful man who presented himself to me a couple of weeks ago and who was, according to MCC and the government, my link with authority.

He simply knocked on my door very early on the last day of the match, barely paused as I went to open it, but pushed past me most determinedly and said: "You know, do you not, that Miss Jameson is no longer in danger."

I was not pleased with his pushy behaviour. "I do not, Captain. No-one has told me any such thing. Is it true? If so I am very pleased for I do not like to think of any lady in distress." I was not so pleased to receive the news in a roundabout way and if, as he seemed to be suggesting, it was general knowledge why had I not been told.

"No doubt her father would have informed you in due course. Miss Jameson returned to her family last night. She did not seem able to account for her absence in any great detail but perhaps she has had a shock which has left her with an imperfect memory of the events." The Captain seemed to be telling me to mind my own business to the extent that I wondered he had bothered to tell me at all.

"Are there no details at all? I think I should be told something since I was required to lose a match to save her and, initially thinking that she might be in danger, I was about to lose it to save her skin." I was completely put off by this unexpected turn of events and its presentation.

182

I walked across the room and picked up the letter from Lord Curzon. "Can you settle my curiosity by telling me what is the meaning of this letter, how it came to be sent to me and whether I should obey its instructions?" I asked. He barely troubled to pretend to look at it.

"An obvious forgery," he snapped. "I am surprised you did not detect that immediately."

I looked at him straight in the eyes. "You are not being honest with me, Captain," I said. "I feel there is more in your arrival here, more in the return of Miss Jameson and more in this whole business than you are prepared to let me know. The least you can do, since I have been put in jeopardy and your adopted daughter has been killed over this business, is to tell me what you know or guess."

The Captain stared straight back at me and did not speak for the best part of half a minute.

"All right, Collinson," he said. "I will tell you since I think we are almost at the bottom of this matter.

"Long before you were appointed MCC were concerned that there was a conspiracy by players to change the result of matches at the behest of a gang of bookmakers. There were certain indications that the gang had Indian connections and that they had made the best use of modern methods of communication - that is, the telephone, telegraph and telegram - to obtain their nefarious ends.

"It was Lord Curzon's idea to send a team to India in order to flush the fox from his lair, so to speak. It was thought that the rogues would not be able to resist the chance of making a fortune by exploiting a visit by MCC to this country and plenty of matches were arranged so that there were ample opportunities for betting to take place.

"Frances got wind of their identity which was why she was killed. They quite clearly thought you were her accomplice since they saw her leaving your flat and her body was left in your hallway as a warning to you that you were dealing with ruthless men who would not hesitate to kill to achieve their ends.

"Incidentally, you may be interested - flattered even - to know that you were given the captaincy of this side because no word of dishonesty on your part has ever been whispered and I am glad to say that this view has been fully supported by all those people who have dealt with you on this trip.

"Davenport has given you a vote of approval in his own solid way. Mansfield has, if one can ever interpret what that odd young man says, indicated that you are a straight dealer and I have observed your capacity to deal with your players and approved." The Captain paused and I guess that if he had been a tobacco man he might have filled his pipe at this point.

I said nothing and he picked up his story again.

"Davenport and the police tracked down some of the gang hanging around the docks at Tilbury as I am sure he told you and after that little incident he kept an eye on you, or rather he made sure you were watched all the time by that bizarre couple who made the acquaintance of George Ramsey on the ship coming out here. They have never been far from you all the time the team has been in India.

"They were made aware of your kidnapping by your maid within a few minutes of the gang striking so that the trail was hot although the search was bungled. It was not all luck that Davenport was in the vicinity to pick you up when you were allowed to escape. We knew from the maid's visit that they were somewhere in the vicinity.

"All the way through India you have been under close watch: by the couple, by your room maids who have all been in our employ, by Mansfield, by Davenport, by Dunne Sahib. You have not once been in danger since that kidnapping and by the time you arrived here for the final match we were sure they had realised that your association with my daughter was nothing to do with the search for their illegal trade."

"And Miss Jameson? What is her part in this matter? Is she friend or foe, agent or bystander? Or bookmaker?" I had more reason than one for wanting to know the answer.

"Miss Jameson is, I am afraid, the victim of a plot too. She is an innocent in one sense since she knows nothing of cricket, nor betting, nor the rigging of matches. In a different sense she is no innocent but slipped away, as the gang knew she might, to see a boy friend. He is an Indian and she knew her parents would disapprove.

"The gang seized their opportunity. They saw her leave, tracked her to her lover's abode, rushed in and both drugged and bound the pair, and then delivered their note. They supposed no harm would come to her in the few days of the match but in any case she showed a great deal of initiative in coming round, unfastening her ropes and escaping."

"What of her boyfriend?" Of course, I had several reasons for wanting to know his fate. Jealousy that she already had a lover was high on my agenda. I confess that readily. I was also curious to know what part he played in this little drama.

"He is safely under arrest and will, no doubt, in time come to trial," said The Captain. "She merely left him tied up since something he said made her suspect he may have been behind her abduction. She told the police where to find him and they searched his house before releasing him. There was enough evidence of betting to have him convicted; but other hints of drugs, liquor, luring young girls into an unsavoury life. I think you may find her enthusiasm for him has dwindled, if that is what you have in mind."

I felt I would like to know how far their affair had gone, but it seemed an improper question at this moment and besides there was a match to play and a medical parade, as Major Potter insisted on calling his meetings with my players, to attend.

"I must go," I said. "There is a match to win and now that Miss Jameson is safe no reason not to press the Indians for victory. Can we meet tomorrow during the morning and take a celebratory glass of something or another and have a longer talk about all that has happened here?"

The Captain said he saw no reason why not but he insisted on giving me an explanation that I had not considered. "You do understand, I trust, that two separate forces are at work, both trying to achieve the same ends. There is probably someone within your own camp ready to sell any game to make a profit and there are also Indian men ready to take any action which will achieve the same end.

"Just consider this. Every piece of unpleasantness, every distracting moment since you arrived in this country has been designed to put you off balance, and to create a state of mind in which you will concentrate less on winning matches than on some outside event. The betting men here can make a big enough purse by betting on any result except an MCC victory and if you are distracted they are more likely to achieve that end."

I had hardly time to consider this interpretation of events before I had to dash off to the breakfast room where the reports were, I am sorry to say, grievous.

We could barely get 11 men on to the field and of those it was clear that Tom Abbey was far from fully fit. I accepted his offer to field on because the remarks of Douglas Tidy continued to ring through my brain. "If you wish to go off for a few minutes, you can call Douglas on as substitute," I said. "Leave the field as often as you wish and I am going to thank you in advance for your loyalty to our cause."

Tom grinned. He was one of those players who would give his soul if the captain asked and thanked him afterwards. Salt of the earth, son of a farming family and, although he was never a great player, a cricketer with his heart in the game.

It was boiling hot when we reached the ground an hour before play was due to start and by the time we got out into the middle the temperature had risen above 100 again and there was no relief for any of us. I kept Douglas as twelfth man so that he could run messages, bring on drinks and, most of all, keep us cheerful.

Rhodes bowled beautifully, but he was still not strong and, although he picked up wickets regularly, we had taken only three by lunch - which meant they were four down - and two more by tea. They were creeping towards our score but we needed their last four men out and frankly I was worried about the consequences of keeping Rhodes on the field and doubted if he had more than another few overs in his locker.

He took another wicket after tea but then the gallant chap had to go right off the field. None of the others seemed likely to give me any help and, worst of all, the dreaded figure of Mahmood Baig was still playing with little difficulty.

With half an hour to go I was desperate. Baig and their wicket-keeper, a stout man with agile feet and the appetite for a battle, were holding out and I needed a fresh man.

At the end of an over I walked across to Tom Abbey and told him I was ready to put the Tidy plan into operation. I said in a loud voice: "If you must go off Abbey, so well and good. But you must be back by the start of the next over because I want you to bowl."

I expect Baig barely heard what I was saying. He certainly seemed completely taken in by the subterfuge and raised no objection when Tidy ran out at the end of the next over and made little fuss about bowling.

I whispered to him: "Any mixture you like Douglas. Let 'em have it full bore; no holding back. I will excuse any excesses even if they are spotted by the umpires but just bear in mind that I would be very happy to win this match. I am also holding a small amount of MCC's cash to pay out as a bonus and I am sure we can pick up a bargain or two if we spend it wisely before the boat sails."

It was the most dishonest moment of my sporting career to date. Using a twelfth man to bowl and telling him that if he threw one or two deliveries and was caught was against not only the spirit but the letter of the law. But by this time I was obsessed with the idea of winning and I was prepared to risk anything. Tidy raised no objections. I think he is a practical joker through and through.

Baig said nothing. He took a fresh guard and said something in Urdu to the umpire. "Are you passing the time of day with the umpire or offering him a bribe to turn down our lbw appeals?" I asked with a smile. "Bribery - what else?" he said. He too smiled.

Tidy's first ball was short and Baig rocked back and, instead of giving it a fulsome square cut which the ball deserved, patted it past point for a single. The second ball removed the wicket-keeper's off bail as neatly as if he had never seen the ball.

"That was quick, Douglas," I said as the umpire trudged after the bail. "If only it might have been legal as well," Tidy said. His grin was threatening to split his face.

Three balls later their fast bowler was caught at slip and then came the most curious incident of the entire tour.

Tidy's next ball was another blatant chuck. The only men on the field who did not identify it as such were the umpires. Their batsman - a medium pace bowler I think and the term batsman flatters him - tried to fend it off but it went into the covers and was gathered instantly by Hobbs who threw it straight to Jake Johnson, by now only a few feet from the stumps.

The two batsmen were in mid pitch but instead of taking off the bails at his own end Jake threw the ball to where the bowler might have been. Except the bowler was completing his follow through and the ball sailed for four byes. "For God's sake, Jake," I shouted but I thought no more about it and in another half dozen overs, with five minutes or so left, they were all out for 235, leaving us the winners and mighty pleased with ourselves.

This time Baig, who was the last man out, did catch up with me near the pavilion. "You are a cheat, Collinson," he said. "You have cheated me and my side and you have cheated yourself. The umpires may not have realised that you bowled the twelfth man and they have certainly not observed that he threw almost every ball for three overs. But umpires are not in cricket to detect the deliberate acts of criminality. They are among us to hold the balance, to see there is no doubt, to allow the status quo to be maintained whenever there is a doubt.

"I am sorry to say that what has happened here in the last half an hour has not only spoiled this match and this tour but the memory of your actions will still be with us 100 years from now. Other captains of India and of England will react to what you have done. You have offended against the spirit of cricket and you will never be forgiven for that, Bernard."

Off he went, leaving me to wonder whether I had done very much wrong. I shall not trouble my own conscience about this little episode but I can leave it to the historians, to Wisden and those who have nothing better on their minds than the fine points of cricket.

Back in the dressing room we cheered ourselves noisily, and those who were not still under the strict nursing discipline of Major Potter were given bottles of champagne, the custom since those hairy old professionals toured England and then Australia 50 or more years ago. We made a fine mess of ourselves and asked no leave to celebrate in our own manner and cared not whether the local Moslem authorities were offended by our use of alcohol.

After two months in the dusty parts of India, after all the time away from home, after a tour surrounded by death, by the nastiness caused by gambling, by cheating captains, by dysentery and other noxious bugs, we felt we had the right to cut loose.

Half way through our party, which lasted little more than a couple of hours, there was a knock at the door and when I was summoned I found both the umpires standing there. "Gentlemen," I said, slightly the worse for alcoholic wear, "come and join our little celebration."

The elder said: "No, sir, we have just come to collect the contribution made by every captain towards the services of the umpires." He grinned obsequiously and held out a hand. I had no objection to his request and handed each of them a dozen or so silver rupees. "Is that enough?"

"Yes, sir, most certainly sir but there is one more little matter."

"Yes," I said half suspecting what might be next.

The senior of the two delved into the folds of his shalwar kameez and pulled out my lucky gold guinea. "Baig Sahib told me he did not want this because of the matter of the last half hour and said that he would not find it lucky. He said you might reward me if I returned it."

I paused. I could tell him to go and boil his head; but I wanted my lucky coin back. "Here, wait a minute," I said. I dived into my leather purse and pulled out some more coins including the silver rupee belonging to Mahmood Baig. "This is Baig Sahib's coin," I said.

"He told us you might return that coin and that we should keep it if you did. He says you have soiled it," said the senior man. He spat on it and put it in his pocket. I have not cared to analyse this gesture.

They handed over my old gold coin and accepted their silver ones and thanked me and wandered off. The match was finished and we had won and that was all that mattered to me, whatever some Indians might think.

CHAPTER SIXTEEN
New Year's Eve, 1906.
Karachi

I have just visited Justin Davenport in his room, mainly to watch the sun sink in the west. It's a dramatic sight in this part of the world where one might easily be led to imagine that some great god leant across from his throne in the heavens and turned off a switch, so dramatic is the transition from day to night. One moment the light is fit for play; the next you are plunged into darkness.

I thought the moment symbolic. Our tour had come to a successful end and if we had to bend the laws a little to achieve that end, I find no fault in myself for engineering that manoeuvre. Illness had reduced our side to impotence, Baig had tried every trick in the book to unsettle us and the cat-calling, whooping and whistles from the crowd were deeply upsetting to my men. If India visit England they will not find such a reception even if they win every match. Those who know about the use of the twelfth man to bowl have given me their support which is very satisfying.

Cedric Mansfield was a little difficult. Of course, in his dual role as scorer and reporter he was in a unique position to observe what happened and came to see me soon after the game and inquired, with such an innocent look on his face: "How did Tom Abbey come to bowl - if I may use the term - so quickly?"

I had forgotten Mansfield's presence in the excitement of the match. "You saw what a stroke we pulled?" I asked.

"Yes, and I found it disturbing."

"We were at our last gasp and Douglas Tidy suggested it as a joke last evening. We all entered into the spirit of the thing. Without Rhodes in full flight, with Littleboy ill and with no-one else to fall back on, what other choice lay open to me? Besides, if an umpire had objected I would have immediately sent Tidy away and called one of the regular bowlers into the attack."

A frown crossed his face. "But, what you did is against the Laws" he said and I felt I had to persuade him of the necessity for my actions lest he blurt out the story to his wretched newspapers and so put us all in hot water when we returned.

"Now look, Mansfield," I said, as sternly as I could. "Your entry in the scorebook will be that Abbey bowled those last four overs from the pavilion end. The umpires have been to see me and they have gone away perfectly satisfied that the game was played in the proper spirit. Mahmood Baig is unhappy, but as losing captain you may expect him to be disappointed with the efforts of his men in failing to bat out time.

"What you write in the London Press is, of course, your own business but I would remind you that there is a trade agreement at stake here. I can tell you confidentially - and not to be repeated in the columns of any newspaper - that I have had a note from Lord Curzon, counter-signed by the Prime Minister, giving me to understand that there was great importance attached to the result of this game." Not a bad lie in the circumstances. The circumstances being that I had had quite a few drinks and that my brain still appeared to be working satisfactorily

"In that case I will officially report that Abbey made the vital breakthrough in the last half an hour and amend my scorebooks to tally with that result," he said. "I thought something of this nature must be afoot for you to take such a gigantic risk with your career but I can now tell you that in preparation for such an eventuality I used a light lead pencil for the final overs just in case a change of entry was needed. My fellow scorers, the Indian gentlemen, were very amused."

He smirked in self-satisfaction and to be honest I almost allowed myself a grin of pleasure. Pulling the wool over the eyes of this self-opinionated young prig gave me a lot of enjoyment and I looked forward to seeing his reports when I returned home. My parents were readers of the Daily Mail, a paper to which he had been sending his despatches and I guessed they would save me some cuttings to read on my return.

I gave myself a big task today. I went to each player in the team and thanked him for his effort and made sure I mentioned his best individual performance and presented him with a small envelope filled with enough in English currency to make his homecoming a happy one. I did not use all the money MCC had donated but I felt it was worthwhile to offer some reward to a bunch of fellows who had done their best even though some of them were less than giants of the game.

Men like Hobbs and Rhodes had better contracts than the other professionals but I gave them the same amount as the rest - it would be invidious to say precisely how much - and I also saw that the amateurs had a token of my esteem too. After all it was not only the end of the tour but the beginning of the New Year and I felt I was right to be generous.

I also went to the other men we had come to know well. George Ramsey had plenty of money and was an unstinting giver anyway so a monetary gift would have been inappropriate, but he was pleased with an MCC tie pin and my offer to find a proposer so that he might join MCC. So was The Captain, who was curiously annoyed that he had, in a life devoted to the game, not received so much as a thank you letter for any of his services. Odd how such small but important matters are overlooked. Part of his bitterness stemmed from this omission.

When I came to Mansfield I gave him the balance of his money for his scoring duties and a tie pin and he said he would treasure the pin more than the money. Frankly he seemed to have made a small fortune by his hard work on this trip so his scoring for the team may not have been so important to him, but he had carried it out conscientiously and added to our store of knowledge by the observations he based on his statistical notes.

Justin Davenport was clearly not overwhelmed by my gift but he was a prosperous man when he inherited his father's money - if his own version of his life was correct - and spent with abandon when he felt the need so I did not imagine he was poorly off. He too wanted to join MCC and I said I would help if I could.

Having dispensed gifts to everyone else I determined to go in search of a little present for myself and so wandered into the offices of the hotel in search of Miss Annabelle Jameson. I had only heard the story of her escape at second hand and wondered if it might be true and if, in being asked to tell the story a second time, she might trip herself up.

Our interview was not, I am sorry to say, satisfactory. She was summoned by one of the clerks in her father's office, told me she was having lunch, she was tired after her recent misfortune and had a full diary right until after I had sailed off two days hence. "I should very much have liked to spend some time with you, Mr. Collinson," she said, "but it does not seem to be possible. Perhaps you would be good enough to leave your card at the reception desk marked for my notice and I will see if there is time for a visit when we all visit London sometime in the next two years."

I nodded and left and then the strangest coincidence occurred. As I turned out of her office I almost collided with the gaunt and muscular figure of a man I last saw at my meeting with the Prime Minister and his friends in the house near Lord's. I was so sure it was him I almost spoke but he hurried on and I was left staring after him. He was the sinister and savage looking gentleman who I had assumed was supposed to throw himself between the Prime Minister and any passing assassin's bullet; perhaps catch the bullet in his teeth; a sadist on the side of government and therefore able to carry out his whims without let or hindrance.

What was he doing here and clearly on his way to the offices I had just left? Was he on some mission like The Captain, Davenport and Mansfield? Or merely a friend of the Jameson family? Or simply staying in the hotel like any other innocent guest? I supposed that even a man with such an unpleasant mien might have a wife, a honeymoon, family in India? And I could have been mistaken.

So I had nothing better to do than return to my room and write the final pages of my diary. It is what I am completing at this moment although I have an invitation to join Jake Johnson in his room where he has gathered the rest of the party to celebrate the New Year.

Jake is, by the way, the strongest candidate for conviction as the villain of the tour. I am sure that he tried to change the course of the match which has just ended when he saw that there was a victory in the offing by deliberately throwing the ball to the other end. The whole team ragged him about it and he said that he thought it more important to run out Baig than "some wretched tail-ender". Unhappily for that reading of history, Baig was only a few feet from Jake's wickets when Hobbs' throw came in and besides it was clear that, having detected our little ruse, Baig had washed his hands of the match.

Rhodes was very cross with Jake and said: "Mr. Johnson, if I had done what you did this afternoon I would be thoroughly ashamed of myself. Where I come from we attempt the meanest tricks within the Laws but I have never known any Yorkshireman do what you have just done. There will be those who will criticise Mr. Collinson for his actions today but he was trying to win the match for his side against a dastardly and impertinent foe. I am not convinced that was your intention."

I had to step between the two, particularly when Hobbs lined up behind Rhodes and I thought there was every sign of fisticuffs in the offing.

"I have nothing further to say to you, Rhodes," said Johnson, making it quite clear that Rhodes should back off. I stepped in and said their quarrel was spoiling a great victory and no harm had come from Johnson's error and we should forget it.

Rhodes would not let go. "There are two of you here who might have had fine careers with Yorkshire," he said, "and I regret that Mr. Collinson, foolishly in my opinion, chose to play his cricket elsewhere. Particularly among the brown hatters of Surrey." The enmity between Surrey and Yorkshire is deep-seated and he fairly spat out the words. "But I have no regrets that you did not take up the challenge to play with us for you are not a proper cricketer, Mr. Johnson."

I said: "If you are to continue in this vein, Wilfred, I think you should not stay in the dressing room. Shake hands with Jake and let's continue our party." They shook with great reluctance and for a minute I thought Rhodes was about to begin again but Hobbs took him by the arm and they wandered off to the far side of the dressing room, pulling Littleboy into their clique and marking out their distance from the rest of us.

Whatever anyone says, and notwithstanding our friendship going back to school, I feel Jake deserved the opprobrium he received. His actions when I was unfortunately absent in the first match of the tour barely stand up to close examination and there have been other instances when he seemed to be dancing to a tune no-one else could hear. In Poona he skied a ball on 49 and there was such a shouting and yelling on the far side of the ground that we all wondered if he had planned to get out caught at mid-off. Someone said bets were taken on precise scores too; but I said that surely no man sacrifices a fifty. After the little incident in this most recent game I was beginning to wonder.

Jake's absences from the team hotels when I needed him, his disinclination to be a proper vice-captain and his sneering references to me as "skipper" or "captain" - even though he had appeared delighted with my appointment in the first instance - all added to the mystery. I still felt a great affection for him but it was clearly not returned.

There was another riddle which I have not exposed in this diary before. Twice in recent days I have spotted a Western face that I could have sworn was that of Jake's father. He is not a distinctive man and I might have been in error, but I am usually quick to identify someone I know. But on both occasions the quarry was too far distant for me to see him a second time or get a long look.

Yet I am sure that figure this week-end in the bazaar was his father. How could this be, particularly as the last time I spotted the old boy he was wrapped against the cold on Tilbury Dock, being handed a few pounds by his son to keep him going all winter. At that point he and Mrs. Johnson hurried off because the evening was cold and the weather inclement.

When I mentioned my sighting to Jake he just laughed. "No-one looks like dad in this part of the world," he said. "He'll be at home nursing himself at the side of a blazing fire at this moment, I dare say."

Well, maybe. These tiny matters apart I cannot help feeling that we have had a most successful tour, a fact evidenced in part by a total stranger who has sent me a bottle of whisky, "to celebrate your victory and the New Year, dear sir" it says on the label.

It will go down well at the party tonight and, although I have not tasted the stuff before, I might have a glass to start the night in good form.

CHAPTER SEVENTEEN

REPORT ON THE TOUR OF INDIA 1906-7
CAPTAIN R. H. CROSSLAND TO MCC

Crossland Cottage,
St. John's Wood,
NW8.
21st November 1907.

The Secretary,
MCC,
Lord's.

Sir,

I have allowed some time to pass so that all the loose ends of the notorious tour of India in 1906-7 could be gathered together before submitting a report. This letter is to be read in conjunction with the diary kept by the captain Mr. Bernard Collinson and which is presently lodged with you. Please also note that I wish the diary to be returned to me at the above address as soon as possible.

The inquiry into the poisoning of Mr. Collinson, and the inquest into the death of his vice-captain Mr. Johnson, have now been completed and the police have stated that there will be no further investigation. This right and proper decision marks the end of a most unpleasant matter, one which nearly ruined our great game. The yellow press, in their search for more readers, chose to exaggerate its importance under the headline The Great Cricket Betting Scandal. I sometimes wonder if editors think of the damage they do to cricket when they write such trash.

In contrast, I am sure that whatever I say here will be seen only by men with sufficient good sense to keep quiet about the seamier side of that tour. I propose that, when the appropriate MCC committee has dealt with it, to keep this diary with the papers I found after Mr. Collinson had his unfortunate accident and the note left by Mr. Johnson after he gave himself too large a dose of morphine. They will be placed in the safe at this address and shown only to those who have a special reason for knowing how dangerous it can be to follow in the footsteps of the special category England captains. I propose to allow any captain given the special status to be allowed to read Mr. Collinson's diary, and its attendant papers, and my notes, and then to make up his mind whether he wants to continue in the role. I urge the committee to accept this recommendation since I believe that reading such notes will be the final test of a candidate. Destroying this material, which might seem the most attractive course, would mean that many lessons learnt from the Collinson incident will be lost.

Those who read the newspapers will remember, for all the gory and misunderstood details, that I found Mr. Collinson - only a few seconds after his accident apparently - when my attention was attracted by the screaming of his room maid in the Grand Hotel, Karachi. I dashed down the corridor from my own room and discovered him lying a few feet from his door, doubled up as if he might be in agony and his face contorted in pain. He had clearly suffered in the few seconds after leaving his room and he would have been dead but for two marvellous pieces of luck. By the time a doctor was fetched there would have been nothing that could be done to help him.

An empty glass of whisky stood on the table where he had been completing his diary just before he decided to leave the room; presumably to meet someone within the hotel since he had not taken a hat. There was a conjecture, born out by his diary, that he was on his way to join his team's party to celebrate the New Year, but as Collinson did not always write the truth in his diary we have to wonder whether he might have been about some other mission. It is probably immaterial.

An analysis of the dregs remaining in the glass showed that a poison had been added to the whisky; a poison that acted so quickly that it could have killed the man in the few strides to the door. His maid, coming to tidy his room, saw him as he collapsed. He said nothing to her, or so she told the police and in any case I am sure he would not have been so foolish as to say something important to an Indian maid, even in great agony.

He had been saved, first, by his own lack of a taste for whisky. He had not tried the drink before and when he took his first mouthful he simply spat it out. Hardly the act of a gentleman, of course, but it meant that he was merely seriously ill. If he had swallowed any quantity of the stuff he would not have lived for half a minute.

Mr. Collinson was taken to hospital, the poison that had gone down his throat was drawn off his stomach and he made a full recovery. As we all know he was sufficiently well to play for Surrey on a number of occasions last summer. In the meantime I thought it prudent to suggest to the more gullible Indian newspapers that he had died and reports to that effect became widespread. They reached a number of English papers with consequences that will become obvious. I also managed to influence Mr. Cedric Mansfield, the only reporter with the party, and a man of good commonsense who has worked with me before, that no immediate report should be sent to the papers he represented until Collinson had made a full recovery. MCC should be grateful to Mansfield that more was not read into this difficult incident. I should mention that if their gratitude was shown in the form of a membership it would be well received by Mansfield.

By this time I had had the opportunity to read the diary Collinson kept from the moment he was made England captain and come to the conclusion, as indeed Mr. Collinson had, that Jake Johnson was the man behind the betting scandal. I could not prove that Johnson also poisoned Mr. Collinson but I think it is probable. I discount the maid and there was no-one else near enough to be in a position to feed him anything. Talk in the Indian newspapers of "notorious dacoits" - by which they mean common felons - being in town intent on revenge for the defeat of the Indian team I have also dismissed.

While the team were still in Karachi waiting for their ship to sail home, I sought out Johnson in the dressing room of the ground that had been used for the final match against An Indian XI. (Incidentally, the wide publicity given to this match in the local newspapers, who insisted it was a Test with the same status accorded to matches against Australia or South Africa, was a factor in whipping up feeling and giving rise to a great deal of betting in large amounts, as Collinson indicates in his diary. MCC might be advised to wait a long time before they consider another tour of India and they might wait even longer before they offer their cricketers a Test match either in England or their homeland.)

It was pretty dark inside this dungeon-like room and I could see him crouched over some papers. He looked up as I came through the door and I thought I saw horror spread across his face. He must have known that I ranked high among the men who see cricket is run according to the principles laid down by our forefathers and he must also have guessed that I came as an avenging angel.

His first words proved he knew exactly who I was. "Hello, Captain," he said. "Just putting a few things straight before we sail."

"I'd like a few minutes of your time, Johnson, if I may," I said. "I wish to ask you about the match in Lahore and your behaviour on the final day of the game here against An Indian XI. There are certain rumours going round London and being repeated here that large sums of money were bet on the Indians to win this latter game and I have some evidence that you were at the back of it. Let me have your side of the story. I may tell you that Mr. Collinson has left some details in his room which show you are the guilty party and that I consider we have sufficient evidence for a conviction under British law. But you must be given your chance to explain yourself."

None of this was true. Collinson had left only the vaguest feeling in his papers that Johnson might be the villain. None the less Johnson fell into my trap.

He put down the paper he had been reading and looked away. I was sure that through Mr. Collinson's observations and my own reading of the situation we had the right man. Johnson never attempted to deny what I was saying.

"Yes, I did have a bet on the Indians a couple of days ago and yes, I did make a mess of that run-out on purpose, and yes, it was my father who sought out the bookmaker in Lahore and placed money on us to lose. I am sure you know by now that my father was not ill at all, and that he came to this country on the same ship as the rest of us and made money all across India by his skill at betting."

He seemed determined to make a full confession. Once he began to talk he could not stop.

"My father's fortune, such as it is, came from placing bets at the right moment. He was working in the railway yards at York when I was born but one day during a dispute over pay and conditions he became involved in a game of Crown and Anchor which brought him a good few pounds. He used the money shrewdly but best of all he realised he had a talent for gambling.

"'I'm an investor rather than a gambler,' he used to say. 'Other men bet when they feel an urge. I bet when I know there is a good chance I can win.'

"He went to racecourses everywhere and he kept his eyes and ears attuned and he gambled rarely. My father had a sort of genius for betting and he rarely made a serious mistake. Sometimes he brought home large sums so that, unusually for a family of working class, we had fine things about the house, and father had a bank account at a time when working folk never expected to need such things. His fortune piled up. I went to Cambridge with Collinson, I was able to play as an amateur for Surrey when Yorkshire said they had no vacancy for a wicket-keeper, and I always had money in my pocket.

"When he heard I was coming here he said he would like to try his hand at betting in this country. 'I'm told that it is strictly illegal which makes it easier for a shrewd man to make even more money,' he said. He had never asked me to do anything underhand when I played at the university or for Surrey but he said that, since there was no management of any consequence for this tour save for a bookmaker in George Ramsey, a little jiggery pokery might go unnoticed. We tried our hand with George, suggested he might like to make a few shillings, but he turned out to be as honest as any man who ever lived. 'Beyond corruption, is George, bless him,' my father said.

"Father was only hoping to make the cost of his trip, to see a little of the country and to have some fun but, being my father, he piled bet on bet and by the end of the first week he had done more than enough to live comfortably. All he had to do by way of subterfuge was to keep out of the way of the team since both Bernard and Rhodes knew him. We thought Bernard spotted him in the bazaar and that brought the tricks to an end. We only had a small bet on the final match. By that time my father was off back to the old country." He emphasised this last point so heavily that frankly I did not believe a word of it.

"By the way neither of us had anything to do with the

kidnapping of Bernard, but when we heard what had happened it was an ideal chance to turn the game on its head. So dad wrote that note. Nor did we have any part in his poisoning. Bernard was my pal. I could not harm him. And why should I? Making money, if you do not have a rich sponsor like Bernard, is one thing; murder is quiet a different kettle of fish." He gave me pause to speak. His words had come in such a torrent I had no wish to interrupt him before.

I said: "Your honesty is a credit to you and you have cleared up points which neither Collinson nor I understood. Would you be good enough to continue. Your straightforward account will at the very least clear other men of suspicion and you have nothing to fear."

"I think you will find," Johnson said, as if I had no brain of my own, "that Bernard was far cleverer. He suspected something and so set young Cedric Mansfield on to me. Mansfield has already compiled a dossier of crime, as he calls it, which he wants me to read before he hands it to the police and MCC. He has asked if I can add anything before he sends a third copy to one of the Sunday newspapers at home. I have his word that there is 'not enough evidence to hang you' as he put it so charmingly; but I think there may be." Of course, Johnson had no idea that Mansfield was partly in the employ of the authorities and was on the look-out for suspicious circumstances and any attempt to change the course of these matches. I made no comment on his mixture of good and bad information, although it suited my purpose for him to believe that Mansfield was about to write about him in the newspapers.

Johnson continued with his tale. "I have committed no crime. It is not a crime to bet against one's own team, however damnable that might seem in the eyes of MCC and their cronies. It is certainly not a crime to help one's family make a decent living. Look around among the high and mighty the next time you are at Lord's and see if their fortunes are not based on the same ability to take an opportunity which I have shown in the last three months. Oh, and by the way, the money is far away by now. My father did not wait for the end of the match but caught a liner that is now half way to Suez if I am any judge."

I let his words sink in. No doubt a clever lawyer could find charges on which to arraign Johnson but that would only mean more unsavoury publicity which would not help cricket and besides we have our own methods of dealing with rogues.

(In fact when his father came to Lord's to inquire about the circumstances of his son's death I found him a sad but interesting and intelligent man despite my prejudice against him. He would not, however, admit he had ever been to India. No matter. His son's words were good enough for me and recently I had the pleasure of seeing that his application for membership of MCC was black-balled.)

So I left this wretched man Johnson and sent a cable back to my superiors in London. First, to the Secret Service, for whom I had a suggestion. I had seen evidence of opium in the pupils of Johnson's eyes - you get to know the signs when you spend as long as I have in the foreign service - so I hinted that he might be offered morphine. The Service have men who specialise in such matters and one happened to be in India in a private capacity at the time.

I never inquire if my advice is carried out but there was evidence at the inquest that Johnson had taken an overdose of morphine and a verdict of death due to an overdose of morphine was registered. It was a more pleasant end than he deserved and I have no regrets that actions of mine may have led to his death.

Of course, there is one other rogue; but no matter. As Collinson suggests in his diary, Dunne was probably behind the attempt to disturb Collinson's mind, by the two kidnappings and by a dozen other apparently unconnected events. Knowing Dunne as well as I do, nothing about this depraved man would surprise me; but he is useful to his country and no advantage can be gained by inquiring if he was connected with the poisoning of Collinson and certainly there are many disadvantages to the government if he had to be brought to trial.

As for Mr. Collinson, I have to register disappointment that he was not the captain England needed and particularly not one in the special category able to serve government and MCC in equal measure. His actions in a number of instances are deplorable.

I will mention only his mercenary decision to keep an account of his life as captain of England as if he were a common Grub Street hack or penny novel author; his setting out in detail his brief encounter with my daughter; his failure to attempt to escape from the ruffians who kidnapped him for whatever reason in

Lahore; his over-familiarity with his team; his decision not to avail himself of the captain's room but to change with the rest of the side; and his use of the twelfth man to bowl in Karachi.

Since his illness a number of myths have grown up about his wonderful skill with his men, his captaincy and his heroism, patriotism and affection for his country. Although these diaries will only ever be seen by a limited number of highly trustworthy men it is as well that some of these fables be dispelled.

Mr. Collinson had the support of most of the experienced members of his party and I have had conversations since with both Rhodes and Hobbs who thought his leadership exemplary. (Hobbs is over-inclined to agree with authority and one can discount his views as being an example of telling someone in a high position what he wants to hear; but Rhodes spoke bluntly and at times critically of Collinson so there is no reason to suspect he was gilding the truth).

As for the other apparent achievements we have to judge them harshly. Mr. Collinson was not a good captain, a fact ascertained by Rhodes in the game against Yorkshire during the 1906 season. Collinson made a number of tactical errors. "He was a learner," said Rhodes, "so we must not judge him too severely, but he had some way to go before he led Surrey to a championship." In fact he blamed him for their failure to capitalise on good positions.

Collinson makes much at the beginning of his diary about the way he encouraged his young fast bowler Ernest Caversham. His account is said by some to be fiction. Hobbs says Collinson never spoke to Caversham after the betting story was revealed and the Surrey committee deny any money was paid by way of a bonus to Caversham. I even went so far as to speak to Caversham but he was not helpful. I think he felt I was trying to trap him.

As for Collinson's heroism, his devotion to the Royal Family and his spirited adventures - which are the commonplace of much of the trash written - we can see from his own account of his kidnapping that he made no attempt to escape from the band of outlaws in Lahore. I should have thought that any red-blooded Englishman would have talked his way out of such a situation. Davenport, a reliable man if somewhat lacking in imagination, says such deeds are "the stuff of adventure comics" and adds "we must not hold foreigners in such contempt that we believe they are all half as bright as we are." I am afraid I do not have the words to respond to that analysis.

So it can be seen that Collinson was a flawed man, for all his potential as an England batsman, which was undoubted. The selectors have ignored him since that tour of India and I doubt if he will play for his country in any Test worth the name. I will certainly consider it my duty to place a question mark in the minds of the authorities if the need arises. It is a matter of some sorrow to me that I failed to spot the obvious deficiencies in his make-up and that I recommended that he should be a special category England captain.

Here we had a university graduate, with an MA in history, with, whatever his social status when he obtained his scholarship to Cambridge, a private income provided by a generous if slightly foolish and romantic benefactor; with a great skill for the game, who was very properly made captain of his country. And how does he respond to this honour? By writing every nasty dot and comma down; for the education and uplift of the masses no doubt. His account of his visit to our good friend Dunne in Karachi is disgusting and his inclination to speak of every woman who crosses his path as if she might be a Falklands Road whore is unspeakable.

He has argued eloquently in his report to MCC that many of the decisions he made in India indicated the pressure he was under, that there was an inadequate management structure for the tour, and that the team was forced to make arrangements for their daily lives which indicated a lack of planning ahead. He argues, and he has a point, that the knowledge accumulated by the Army in India over a number of years should have been utilised by MCC and that he hopes they will do so in future. I commend this point to the MCC committee.

However we must not accept that because life is difficult there is an excuse for bad behaviour. Trips to Australia in the second half of the last century were fraught with difficulty yet captains did not use it as a reason to cheat their opponents (although one has heard rumours that cast some doubt on the absolute integrity of the early tourists. The dreadful story of a wicket-keeper duping New Zealanders into bets and being arrested is uppermost in my mind at this moment).

I think we have to conclude that Collinson's background

let him down in the end as it always will. I met his parents, nice enough people if you ignore the father's broad accent, and his mother's twitterings in an English so basic it was difficult to make sense of her thoughts. I suppose she was upset about the continued illness of her son and the prospect that he might never play cricket again, but at one time I had to speak quite sharply to her when she burst into tears for the second or third time in a short conversation.

Her husband, an impertinent man for a former NCO, accused me of lack of compassion. "I have lost my dear adopted daughter in this affair," I told him, "and I'll thank you to show a lot more respect in future." He swore at me and I had them both turned out of my home in quick time. Afterwards a trail of spittle was to be seen running down the front door. I shall say no more than that I was uncertain who had left it, the man or the wife.

I will refer only once to the disgusting way Mr. Collinson made light of - or more probably lied about - an encounter with my daughter. Imagine how I felt when I read this filth and lies. Imagine how I might have felt if she had been my natural daughter and not the young girl who came to us when my wife and I found we could not have more children after the birth of my son. Frances had no idea she was anyone but our own child, of course, and when her mother died I decided that I would never tell her.

How she conducted her life was either a sad reflection on my family, which goes back to the Conquest and beyond, or a set of damnable lies written for his own gratification by Collinson. Still I have left it in these notes - when I could easily have removed it - as a detail that may attract the historians long after I am dead. My son will inherit the book with the other treasures in the safe at this house, and he may gain some insight into life by reading it. I have to say that it has made me very sad.

None of us who read this account of the first MCC tour of India will feel any pleasure. It is a tale of the weakness of men and there is no place in the game for such people, and even if Collinson has atoned in some way by heading off this winter to Rhodesia to spread the game in that fascinating country, we must always wonder about his motives. Personally, I am pleased he no longer plays a major part in this great game of ours although I have to confess that I admired some aspects of his character and certainly enjoyed watching him bat.

I suppose, to take a compassionate view of his actions, we must conclude that men under pressure will take extraordinary decisions and that Collinson was simply a man who could not cope when the heat became intense. But if Grace and Livingstone, Wellington and Nelson and other great men of our country could live clean lives under the pressure they must have felt, there is no reason why Collinson should let the side down quite so badly.

Yours faithfully,

Captain R.H. Crossland.

FINALE
2 August, 2007.

Andrew Goode put the massive leather-bound file back on his desk. "Christ, it's bloody seven in the morning," he muttered. Time to get to bed.

Funny book, written all those years ago, but still full of incidents he could relate to; especially that girl going straight to bed with Collinson only an hour after they met. Must have been hundreds of tales like that around the dressing rooms. Cricket's urban myth, he thought. But the girl murdered, Collinson kidnapped, poisoned, and his pal killed so that it looked like a drug overdose. Never heard anything like that before. Good job the old News of the Screws was not so active between the sheets in those days.

As for the cheating. Shit! "Pressure to win," he murmured. "Everything got to him - government on his tail, the opposing captain baiting him, worried who was betting, who was pulling for him, men ill and then the joker of the team gives him the perfect solution. No doubt a few dodgy decisions went against him. So he pulls a stroke. Well, I wonder. I don't think you'd get away with that now. Fifteen bloody great TV cameras up your nose, twenty replays every ball, five umpires, two match referees and every short leg miked up to the coach. Just think about it!"

And who was The Captain? Was the pleasant guy he met yesterday the same bitter old man whose letter was crammed into the back of the diary in a dirty old envelope, who had spied in India, who ran between government and MCC all those years ago? Surely it could not be. His son perhaps. "That Captain I met was at least 90, but he would have to have been around 130 to have . . .no, it's a stupid idea."

Goode was frightened of the very thought of someone so old. "It's not possible, yet the man Collinson describes him very much like The Captain I met. It must be the son he spoke about in the last chapter. Sad about the way his daughter died. I guess that in those days she must have seemed like a right tart but he did not have to get so twisted. No-one would even notice these days.

"What sort of captain have England got now?" Goode asked himself. He looked in the mirror at the bottom of the stairs. "A dishevelled, scruffy bugger at the moment," he thought. "If The Captain sees me he'll arrange for me to have an overdose too." Better get that alarm going for 9.30; oh, and I must ring Kate. Funny old world. One of the Collinson birds was a Kate too.

"Still," he thought, "I am the first black man to captain England. That will cause some problems. Another laugh. Better make the best of it. Captain of England, required by the government to act as 007 and asked by every newspaper, magazine and broadcasting organisation in the world, or so it seemed, to talk about the pressure of being a black man in a position of power that had been exclusively held by white men for 130 years. And now upset by a story of derring-do that was already 100 years old."

Goode would have been happy enough to discuss the race problem if he had ever considered it before. Ted Leigh and the selectors had thought it through.

"We have considered your colour, and I won't pretend we haven't," Leigh had said. "There's a lot of racism in this game, on the field, in the pavilion and on the terraces. A lot of it is not funny; but I'm sorry to say you already know all this. No need to nod your head. We have heard some of the stories. I gather you usually manage to find an answer to shut up the worst of your tormentors.

"We have picked you because we just happen to think you're the best man for the job. You've got the respect of every player in the country, not just because you can bat and bowl a bit and field a lot; but as a bloke.

"They don't see the colour in your face; they think 'old Goode is a bloody nuisance batting all day, bowling those leggers, fielding at slip, thinking his way out of difficulties, never lets his side down'. They know you're one of the better cricketers in the country, that you treat your own county men properly and even those who have not met you have seen you talking on chat shows, heard you on the radio, taken in the Internet and they know you make sense.

"So we thought 'they react to this guy, they admire the way he plays and they know he's straight' - er, sorry, I mean honest. We have talked to everyone who understands cricket in this country. As you may have guessed we always take soundings before we make a permanent appointment. You came out top of pretty nearly everyone's list. We expect you to last. We think you can shoulder the burden, that you have spare capacity, that the extra pressure of captaincy will not throw you and that in fact you will think about the job and relish it and make something of it and not find it a burden.

"Public school, university, three years in the Army; background of discipline and sophistication and intellectualism; religion in your family; mother and father decent people, teachers. We respect the way you have come up in the world. You may be black but you are part of our world. We think we know how you think. We empathise - isn't that the flip phrase of the moment - with you."

Fair comment, thought Goode, as he mounted the stairs. At the last minute he turned back and went to pick up the morning papers. "Goode Heir Day" one headline screamed. "That'll do me," he thought, happy that he was the hero of the moment.

One more job he thought as he told his best toy the Single Electronic Gadget to wake him. He spoke The Captain's number and heard the old-fashioned answerphone message. He wondered if it might begin "This is Your Captain speaking" so that he could say "And this is Your captain speaking", but instead there was simply another recorded voice ordering him to "Leave your message in the usual manner."

He said: "Captain, it is 7.15am on August the second. I have read the diary and come to two conclusions. Yes, I will take the appointment you and the Prime Minister have offered me. Despite all those nasty details about poison and strange bets in Collinson's diary. And, no, I do not drink whisky and I don't do drugs so if I'm to be bumped off you'll have find another method. Oh, and no orgies please, I'm engaged."

He was still grinning when he fell asleep with one last thought. "I really must make sure the old SEG is taking in all the details. You never knew when you might need evidence you have not sold the fifth Test for a bet."